"A novel like no other you are apt to have encountered recently or perhaps ever."

—*New York Herald Tribune*

Hal Borland's

***When the Legends Die***

"Thrilling and uplifting. . . . You will live with the Ute customs, feel the biting mysteries of the white man against his brother, trace the love of animal and nature which has always been so admirable in the American Indian."

—*Best Sellers*

Bantam Starfire Books of related interest
Ask your bookseller for the books you have missed

*The Incredible Journey*
by Sheila Burnford

*Where the Red Fern Grows*
by Wilson Rawls

*Ishi, Last of His Tribe*
by Theodora Kroeber

*Drums Along the Mohawk*
by Walter Edmonds

*Downriver*
by Will Hobbs

*The Cage*
by Ruth Minsky Sender

*Farewell to Manzanar*
by Jeanne Wakatsuki Houston and James D. Houston

*Echohawk*
by Lynda Durrant

# When the Legends Die

by **Hal Borland**

BANTAM BOOKS
NEW YORK•TORONTO•LONDON•SYDNEY•AUCKLAND

This edition contains the complete text
of the original hardcover edition.
NOT ONE WORD HAS BEEN OMITTED.

RL 4, IL age 11 and up

WHEN THE LEGENDS DIE
A Bantam Book / published by arrangement with
Harper & Row, Publishers, Inc.

PRINTING HISTORY
Lippincott edition published April 1963
Reader's Digest Condensed Book Club edition published
October 1963

Bantam edition / September 1964

Cover illustration by Stanley W. Galli courtesy of the
Reader's Digest Condensed Book Club from
WHEN THE LEGENDS DIE


For information address: HarperCollins Publishers,
10 E. 53rd St., New York, NY 10022.



ISBN 0-553-25738-2

Published simultameously in the United States and Canada

---

Bantam Books are published by Bantam Books, a division of Bantam Doubleday Dell Publishing Group, Inc. Its trademark, consisting of the words "Bantam Books" and the portrayal of a rooster, is Registered in U.S. Patent and Trademark Office and in other countries. Marca Registrada. Bantam Books, 1540 Broadway, New York, New York 10036.

---

PRINTED IN THE UNITED STATES OF AMERICA

OPM 70 69 68 67 66 65

**For Barbara**

Who has gathered piñon nuts
and heard the old songs
in the firelight

# Contents

When the legends die,
the dreams end.

When the dreams end,
there is no more greatness.

# 1. Bessie

# 1

He came home in midafternoon, hurrying through the alley. She was sitting on the back step of the unpainted two-room house, peeling willow twigs with her teeth and watching the boy chase butterflies among the tall horseweeds. She looked up and saw her man come in from the alley, through the horseweeds toward her. His face was bloody, his shirt torn and bloody down the front. She clapped a hand to her mouth to stifle the cry of hurt and surprise, and he stepped past her, into the house. She followed him and he gestured her to silence and whispered, in the Ute tongue, "They will come after me. Bring water to wash. Get the other shirt."

She went outside, filled the tin wash basin from the water pail on the bench beside the door, and brought it to him. She got the other shirt while he washed his face. There was a cut over his left eye and a darkening bruise beside his mouth. He washed his face, then his hands, and gave her the pan of red-stained water. She took it outside and poured it on the ground among the weeds, where it sank into the dry soil and left only a dark, wet spot. When she went inside again he had taken off the torn shirt and wrapped it into a tight bundle with the bloody places hidden. He pulled the clean shirt over his head, tucked the tails inside his brown corduroys and said, still in the Ute tongue, "I shall go to the stream with black-stem ferns on Horse Mountain. Come to me there." He went into the other room and came back with the rifle. He tucked the bundled shirt under his arm and went to the door, looked, waited, then touched her face with his free hand and went outside. He hurried through the weeds and down the alley to the place where the scrub oak brush grew close by. He went into the brush, toward the river. The magpies screamed for a moment, then were silent. He was gone.

She wiped the water from the table where he had spilled it, searched the floor for spots of blood, and wiped the tin basin with the rag. She went outside and put the basin beside the water pail and looked at the place where she had emptied the basin after he washed. The wet spot on the ground was almost gone. She came back and sat on the step again.

The boy, who was five years old and only an inch or so taller than the horseweeds, came and stood at her knee, asking questions with his eyes. She smiled at him. "Nothing happened," she told him. "Nobody came. Nothing happened. Remember, if they ask." He nodded. She handed him a willow twig. He peeled the bark with his teeth, as she had done, chewed the bark for a moment, tasting the green bitterness, and spat it out. "Go catch a grasshopper," she said, and he went back among the weeds.

She waited half an hour. Then they came, up the street and around the house. They came and stood in front of her, the tall man who always came when there was trouble, the short, fat one from the sawmill, and Blue Elk, with his squeaky shoes, his black coat and derby hat, his wool-bound braids, his air of importance. She looked up at them, each in turn, and she clapped her hand to her mouth and began to wail. "You bring trouble!" she cried. Then, to Blue Elk, in the Ute tongue, "My man is hurt?"

The tall man, the sheriff, watched her and said to Blue Elk, "See what she knows."

Blue Elk rubbed his hands together. They were the soft hands of a man who has not worked in a long time. He said, "Bessie! Stop the wailing. The wailing is for another woman. Let her make the mourning."

"My man is not hurt?"

"You know he is not hurt. Where have you hidden him?" They both spoke Ute.

"He is not here. Why do you come here for him?"

"He was here. He came here."

"If you know this, then find him." She gestured toward the house.

"What does she say?" the sheriff asked.

"She says he is not here. She says we should look."

The sheriff and the sawmill man went inside. She sat waiting. She asked Blue Elk, "Why do you want my man? What happened?"

"He killed a man."

"Who?"

"Frank No Deer."

"That one." Scorn was in her eyes.

"I know. Frank was a thief, a no-good. But George killed him. Where did George go?"

She shrugged.

The sheriff and the sawmill man came back. "No sign of him. What does she say now?"

Blue Elk shrugged. "Nothing."

The sheriff and thc sawmill man talked in low tones. Blue Elk turned to her again. "Where is the boy?"

She glanced about the weed patch before her eyes met Blue Elk's. She waved her hand vaguely. "Boys play, go where they will."

"They will watch you," Blue Elk said, still in the tongue.

"If they want me, I am here."

The Sheriff turned to Blue Elk. "Tell her we'll find him if we have to run down every little bunch of Utes in the mountains, every fishing and berry camp. If he was here, he covered his tracks. Or she did. Tell her we'll find him."

Blue Elk said to her, "You heard. For the cost of two horses I could settle this."

"I have not the cost of two horses."

"One horse," Blue Elk offered.

She shook her head. "I have not the cost of one goat."

"What does she say?" the sheriff asked.

"She says he did not come here. She says she has not seen him."

"I think she's lying."

"My people," Blue Elk said in English, "do not lie."

The sheriff grunted. "They just kill each other over a lunch pail. Some day one of them is going to kill you, Blue Elk."

"I am an old man who has done much for my people."

"He's probably hiding in the brush down along the river," the sheriff said. He turned to the sawmill man. "We'd better go find Frank's woman. She's probably heard by now, but you better tell her you'll pay for the funeral."

"For a coffin," the sawmill man said. "Fifty dollars for a coffin. That's all."

Blue Elk's eyes had darted to him when the money was mentioned. The woman on the steps saw, and she said to him in Ute, "The cost of two ponies?" There was scorn in her voice.

"What does she say?" the sheriff asked.

"She says she is glad it was not her man who was killed."

"You know where to find Frank's squaw?"

Blue Elk nodded, and they left.

She sat on the steps another ten minutes. Then she said, "Come now," and there was a movement among the horseweeds near the alley. The boy stood up and came to her and they went indoors. She praised him. She walked about the house, choosing certain things, not taking them from their places, but choosing them. The extra box of ammunition for the rifle. The package of fishhooks and spool of line. Two butcher knives. Spare moccasins for herself and the boy. The boy's blue coat. Two brown blankets.

She sent the boy for kindling, started a fire in the iron stove and put the piece of meat to boil. She neatened up the house, to leave it clean . . . and to occupy the time. It was a company house. The man at the pay desk took money from her man's pay every week to pay for rent of the house and for buying the furniture, the old iron bed, the dresser with the broken leg, the four chairs, the table, the stove. For two years he had taken money to pay for these things and he said there was still more to pay. By now, she told herself, they had paid for the two blankets, and that was all she was taking, the blankets. The butcher knives were hers, from before they came here. She had made the moccasins, and the coat. She was no thief.

Her choosing done, the house neat, she went outside and sat on the step again. The boy sat with her, in no mood for play. When the meat was cooked, they would eat. When it was dark, they would pack the things and go. Two years ago Blue Elk had brought them here, from Horse Mountain. Now, in a way, Blue Elk was sending them back to Horse Mountain.

She thought of the summer two years ago.

## 2

It was hot, that summer of 1910. They lived near Arboles on the Southern Ute reservation in southwestern Colorado, and her man had a cornfield. The drought came and the corn burned up. In July her man said one evening, "We are going fishing."

"Who is going?"

"Our friends, Charley Huckleberry, too, so it is all right." Charley Huckleberry was a member of the council. "Maybe we will smoke fish, so take salt."

The next morning they went, in six wagons. They went up the Piedra to the reservation line and camped. The men caught fish and they ate their fill, and it was like the old days when they were children and all summer they ate fish and picked berries and there were no cornfields to worry about. In the evening the men wrestled and ran races and the children threw stones at the magpies and the women sat and talked. It was a happy time.

The next day someone said they should go in to Piedra Town and buy candy for the children. Charley Huckleberry said it was all right to go. So they broke camp and went in to town and bought candy for the children and the women went to the store and fingered skirt cloth and admired it, but they had no money for skirt cloth. They had spent all the money they had. Then someone said, "Let us go on up the river and camp and catch fish." Charley Huckleberry said he guessed that would be all right, too.

They went on up the river and camped, and there were plenty of fish. Serviceberries were ripe. The men caught fish and the women and children picked berries, as in the old days, and they set up racks and smoked the fish they didn't eat.

They stayed there a week. Then they went up the river another day and found a place where there were more berries, more fish. And the men killed two fat deer that had come down to the river to drink. The venison tasted good after so much fish, and the women told the men to go up on Horse Mountain and get more deer and they would dry it, the old way, for winter. There were many deer on Horse Mountain and they made much meat. Nobody remembered how long they were there because it didn't matter. When they had made meat for the winter, they said, and had smoked fish and dried berries for the winter, they would go back to the reservation.

Then Blue Elk came and found them there, and Blue Elk said they were in bad trouble. He said the police would come after them because they had come to Horse Mountain without a permit.

They all gathered around Blue Elk to hear this news. Charley Huckleberry said there wouldn't be any trouble because he was in charge and he was a member of the council. But Blue Elk said the council had sent him to find them.

"The council sent you?" Charlie asked, and everybody knew that Charley Huckleberry was worried.

"They said when I found you," Blue Elk said, "I should tell you this. That there is trouble."

Then Charley asked, "Who paid you to come? Somebody always pays you to come to tell of trouble. The council didn't pay you. Who did?"

"I worry about my people," Blue Elk said. "That is why I came."

Charley said, "The sawmill man in Pagosa pays you to do these things." But Charley was worried. Everyone knew it. He said, "We came here because our cornfields are burned up. We came to dry fish and berries and make meat for the winter. Nobody can make trouble of this. We did not kill sheep or cows for meat. We killed deer. You are the one who is making trouble."

"I came to warn you," Blue Elk said, "and to tell you that this trouble can be taken care of."

Johnny Sour Water said, "Maybe we should let our women put you on the drying rack, like a fat fish, and smoke you, too."

Everybody laughed at that because Blue Elk looked a little like a big, fat fish. But they didn't laugh much. They didn't know how this would come out.

Bessie's man, George Black Bull, said, "We made meat for the winter, and that is all we did. We will go back now and there will be no trouble." Bessie was proud of him.

"If you go back with me," Blue Elk said, "I can take care of this for you."

"How?" Charley Huckleberry asked.

"I can get permits, and that will make it all right. When you have the permits I can get work for you and you will not have to worry about the winter."

"We do not worry about the winter," Charley said. "We have made meat."

Blue Elk said, "You made meat without permits. Do you think you can keep that meat? You are not so foolish as to think that!" Then he said, "Your cornfields are burned. Your blankets are thin. Your women need new skirts." Which was true. They had torn their clothes and worn them thin picking berries and smoking meat. "And," Blue Elk said, "you already owe money to the trader."

Then Charley Huckleberry asked, "What do the sawmill men pay for you making this talk to us?"

Blue Elk said, "I am an old man. I have nothing but the clothes I wear. I worry for my people. That is why I tell you now that the sawmill man will give you jobs. He has bought many more trees and he needs more men to work. He will pay two dollars a day, silver. And he will pay those dollars to you, not to me."

There was talk, at that. Two dollars, silver, for each day's work! The men talked among themselves, and the women talked to the men.

Charley Huckleberry said, "Don't listen to old Fat Belly! He speaks lies about these things."

Blue Elk didn't answer. He went off to one side and let them talk. And Charley Huckleberry said Blue Elk was right about the permits. It was all right to go on a fishing trip and stay a few days. The council would not make trouble over that. But they had come too far and stayed too long. About that, Blue Elk was right. Probably they would have to pay a fine for that. A fine that the council would write down in the book and they would pay when they had money to pay it. That was not big trouble. And that was all the trouble there would be, Charley Huckleberry said.

But there still was this other matter, this two dollars a day, silver. The women said this might be a good thing, and even some of the men said it might not be too bad a thing. The women said they needed new skirts. They said the beans in tin cans would taste good with the meat they had made. The men said that if all of them went together to Pagosa it would be a happy time, maybe. And they said they did not have to stay very long. In two months, at two dollars a day, they would have more than a hundred dollars. The women said that was many dollars, and all silver.

That was the way it was decided. They broke camp and went back to the reservation with Blue Elk. Charley Huckleberry told the council what they had done and where they had gone, and Blue Elk said everything Charley had told the council was true. Blue Elk said that there should be a fine for this so that they would remember next time, and since they had no money he said it would be right for the council to take the meat they had made and the fish they had smoked. That was done. Then Blue Elk got permits for them to go to Pagosa and work in the sawmill so they would not have to be hungry that winter. The trouble was taken care of.

So they went to Pagosa and Blue Elk helped the men to make their sign on the papers that said so much would be kept out of their pay each week to pay rent for the houses and to buy the furniture. And on the papers it said they could buy what they wanted at the company store and it would be paid for by taking part of their wages. The papers said they could not quit and go away while they owed money for these things. Blue Elk helped them sign the papers.

## 3

That was two years ago. Some of them wanted to quit after they had been there two months and go back to the reservations, but they owed money to the company store and they had no money to pay it. Sometimes when pay day came they had only two or three dollars instead of two dollars a day. So they could not quit because they had signed the paper.

One day Blue Elk came to the house and told Bessie that she and George must get married. Bessie said, "George is my man. That is enough. That is married, as it always was."

Blue Elk said, "There is the boy. You must be married for the boy, and he must be baptized."

"What is this 'baptized'?" Bessie asked.

"The preacher sprinkles him with holy water and gives him a name."

"I wash him with water when he is dirty," Bessie said. "I have given him his name. Can the preacher do more than this?"

"It must be done," Blue Elk said. "It will cost five dollars."

"I do not have five dollars," Bessie told him. "They take my man's money and do not pay it to him."

"I will see that he gets five dollars this week," Blue Elk said. And he did. George got the five dollars from the man at the pay desk and gave it to Blue Elk and he took them to the preacher. The preacher said words and wrote on a paper and they were married. Then he asked what they wanted to name the boy. Bessie said, "He is Little Black Bull. He will choose when he needs another name."

The preacher said he must have another name now, and he said Thomas was a good name. They could call him Tom, he said. And Bessie said it didn't matter because Little Black Bull would pick his own name when the time came. So the preacher sprinkled water on the boy's head and Bessie laughed when it ran into his eyes and down his nose. The preacher said, "I christen this child Thomas Black Bull, in the name of the Father, and the Son, and the Holy Ghost." So Bessie and George were married and the boy was baptized when he was two years old, almost three. George got no pay at all at the desk the next week because he had gotten that five dollars to pay Blue Elk for the marriage and the baptism.

They were in Pagosa all that winter. When the aspens came to leaf the next spring Bessie said she wanted to go back to the reservation. George told the man at the sawmill he was going to quit. The man looked in the book and said George owed forty-two dollars at the company store and he must pay that money before he could quit. George said he did not have that money. The man said it was less than four weeks' pay and if George worked four more weeks and paid that money he could quit. George told Bessie this and she said they would stay four weeks. She could wait that long. But when George went to the pay desk the next week the man gave him only seven dollars because they kept part of his wages for rent and the furniture. And the next week the man gave him only five dollars because the sawmill broke down and didn't run for one day that week.

In four weeks George saved fifteen dollars. But that was not enough to pay the company store, so they could not go back to the reservation. It would take longer, George said. But he would save that money. He hid it in his lunch pail. But someone stole his lunch pail. Nobody saw the thief; but Frank No Deer, who was a mixed-blood from the Jicarilla Apache reservation in New Mexico, bought a new hat and new boots that cost exactly fifteen dollars. George accused Frank No Deer of stealing his money and Frank laughed at him and said he had won that money in a dice game. Nobody knew of a dice game where Frank No Deer or anyone else had won fifteen dollars, but George could not prove this thing. So he started again to save his money to pay the company store.

It was August before he had saved fifteen dollars again. He put the money in a bean can and buried it in the back yard and did not even tell Bessie where he had buried it. One morning he found holes where someone had dug in the back yard in the night and the money in the bean can was gone. He went to Frank No Deer and said he had stolen that money, and Frank No Deer laughed at him again. There was nothing George could do about it. But Frank No Deer had bought a suit of clothes, the coat as well as the pants, and the man at the store said it cost exactly fifteen dollars. George had a fight with Frank No Deer and tore the coat off his back, and Frank said, "You will buy me another coat."

They did not go back to the reservation that summer, and that fall they did not go back either because now they owed fifty dollars at the company store. But all that winter George saved money again. This time he saved it in green paper money because the paper did not make a noise like silver. He kept his green paper money in his pocket where he could feel it with his hand and nobody could steal it from him. He saved forty dollars that way, and two days ago he had told Bessie that in another two weeks, maybe three, he would pay the company store and they would go back to the reservation. They would go back even if they were hungry next winter. Bessie said that would be a happy time.

That money was in his pocket when he had gone to work yesterday. It was there when he quit work to eat his lunch. He went to get his lunch pail and someone had taken it. He went out to where the other men were eating and Frank No Deer had that lunch pail. George went to Frank No Deer and said, "You are a thief. But this time you did not steal my money because it was not in my lunch pail and it was not in a bean can. It is here in my pocket."

Frank No Deer said, "I took your lunch pail because you did not buy me a new coat for the one you tore."

George said, "I did not buy you a new coat because you stole my money to buy that coat," and he took his lunch pail. Frank No Deer tried to take it back and they had a fight. They fought and wrestled on the ground. The other men said George should give Frank No Deer a good beating, but George did not want to make bad trouble. He sat on Frank No Deer and pounded his head on the ground. Then he let him up and Frank No Deer went away. He did not come back to work all afternoon. After Frank No Deer had gone, George felt his pocket and his money was gone. Frank No Deer had taken it from his pocket while they wrestled on the ground.

George had told this to Bessie last night. He said, "I am going to kill Frank No Deer for this. Three times he has stolen my money and tomorrow I am going to kill him."

Bessie remembered all these things. She looked at the boy and thought it would be good to go away from here. The boy should know the old ways.

In her mind was one of the old songs that her mother had sung when Bessie was the age of the boy. It was a song about the roundness of things, of the grass stems and the aspens and the sun and the days and the years. Bessie sang it now, softly, and she added words of her own about the roundness of a little boy's eyes and arms and legs. The boy smiled as he heard it, this old song about the roundness of life. And Bessie sang about the roundness of a bird's nest and a basket, which was coiled and woven and complete, a part of the roundness of the whole.

She thought of the peeled willow twigs and shook her head. There were willows and there were black-stem ferns on Horse Mountain. She would leave the willow twigs here, as though she was coming back.

The meat was cooked. She smelled it. They went inside. She said to the boy, "You will eat well. Then you will sleep before we go." They ate, and it was sunset. She put the boy to bed and he put his head against her and touched her cheek with his hand. Then he went to sleep and she waited for the deep darkness, saying thanks that there would be no moon.

## 4

The star that was a hunter with a pack on his back was halfway down the sky in the northwest when she went out on the step and listened. Everything was quiet. She had made no light in the house, so her eyes could see in this darkness. As she waited, listening, she saw the horseweeds in the starlight and the shadowy trees and brush on the hillside beyond the valley. She went down the path to the alley, and nobody was there. As she came back she saw the ax beside the kindling pile. She had forgotten the ax. She set it on the step, then went around the house. Nobody was in the street. There was a light in the house where Fred Badger and his woman, Sally, lived, and there was another light down the street. But nobody was watching. She knew this.

She went inside and wakened the boy. She smoothed the bed, then whispered to the boy, "Do not talk. Stay close to me. When I let go your hand, hold to my skirt and walk where I walk. We will make a game." She picked up the pack, put it on her shoulders, and they went out and closed the door behind them. She took the ax.

They went to the alley and turned left, not the way her man had gone. After a little way she let go the boy's hand and he held to her skirt and they followed a path up the hillside. They came to a street and crossed where there was no light and followed the path through the brush again. Her feet knew the way. She had gathered wood for the fire from this hillside for almost two years.

They came to the top of the hill and waited to catch their breath. In the starlight she could see the road at the foot of the hill. The road led west, toward Piedra Town. If she followed the road seventeen miles she would come to the road that came up from Arboles, on the reservation. There she would turn north. But tonight she would go only half that far, to the stream for which she had no name. That would be as far as the boy should walk tonight.

They went on, keeping to the hillside above the road, following the paths the goats had made first, then the women used when they went to gather wood. In the starlight her eyes saw an owl, two rabbits, a striped cat from town, a jay sleeping on a branch. She wanted to tell the boy, tell him how to see these things in the starlight. But not tonight. Later, other nights. They were going away tonight, and they were not talking.

They walked for an hour and she felt the boy's tiredness as he walked behind her, holding to her skirt. She put down the pack and held him in her arms while they rested. They went on again. The star that was the hunter with a pack on his back was down near the horizon, making the big circle the stars made every night, the circle, the roundness. It was good to know the roundness, the completeness again, not the sharp squareness of houses and streets.

Twice more they stopped to rest. The boy's legs were weary. She carried him in her arms for a little way but he protested. He was not a baby. She put him down and they walked together again, and they came to the hill at the bottom of which was the stream for which she had no name. They went down to the stream and drank and rested, then went up the stream to a grove of spruces with a deep mat of needles. She pushed the drooping branches aside and they went into that green spruce lodge and she spread the blankets and they slept.

She wakened soon after sunrise and lay listening. The jays were scolding. A squirrel cried at them and she knew it was only jays and squirrels. She tucked the blankets around the boy, who had half wakened, and told him to sleep, and she took a fishhook and the spool of line and went through the dew-heavy bushes to a grassy place beside the stream. She caught four grasshoppers still stiff with the night chill and went to a pool below a rapid in the stream. She put a grasshopper on the hook and tossed it out onto the quiet water. The grasshopper struggled on the water, went this way and that, and there was a rush and a swish of water as a trout grabbed it. She caught four fish and went back past the grassy place and thanked the grasshoppers before she returned to the spruces for the knife to clean the fish. She gathered dry aspen wood and built a fire beside a rock near the stream, where the thin smoke would rise with the morning mist from the water, and she put green sticks inside the fish to hold them open and set them against the rock beside the fire to cook. When they were cooked she took them back to the spruces and wakened the boy and they ate. Then they went down to the pool and washed themselves and they sat naked on a rock, clean and rested and fed, and watched the sun rise over the mountain on the other side of the road, half a mile away. She sang the song to the sun rising, the song for washing yourself in the morning when the sun is rising. She sang it softly, and the boy sang a part of it with her. He did not know all the words. She said he would learn the words another morning, as she had learned them from her own mother, as those words had come down from the mothers and grandmothers since long ago. They put on their clothes and went back to the spruces and packed their things. Then they went on again.

That afternoon they came to the place where the road from Arboles met the road from Pagosa to Piedra Town. They sat in the scrub oak on the hillside and rested and she watched the roads. Nobody came along either road. Then they went north where there was no road but only the game trails and before sunset they came to the east branch of the Piedra River. There she caught fish before she and the boy followed a small stream up a rocky hillside and found a cave in which to spend the night.

The next afternoon they came to the foot of Horse Mountain.

She did not go to the place where the black-stem ferns grow. She turned the other way and went for almost an hour up a valley with a stream so small she could step across it. But there were fish in that water. She caught enough for supper and built a fire of dry wood and cooked them but did not eat them. She wrapped them in leaves and climbed the mountainside, being sure they left no tracks, and went back down the valley half as far as they had come. There she found a place to watch the valley, and they ate the fish and watched the valley until the sun sank behind the mountain. Nobody came. They went to a big spruce whose branches came down to the ground like the walls of a lodge and there they slept that night.

They stayed there two days, eating berries, building no fire to make smoke or smell. And nobody came, neither the sheriff nor Blue Elk nor anyone. Then they went back down the valley and around the foot of the mountain to the place where the black-stem ferns grow. She went to the spring beyond the ferns and found the sign that he had left for her, a leafless willow twig that stood in a mossy place. She pulled it from the moss and found that it had been peeled at the bottom. She put it back and chose two more willow twigs and peeled them at the bottom and thrust them into the moss beside it. Then she and the boy went up the slope to a sheltered place among the rocks and waited. From that place she could see the spring.

He came to the spring that evening. It was dusk, but she saw him. He stepped out of the deep shadows and took the three willow twigs from the moss, and then he was gone. She said her thanks to the earth and sky and the quarters of the earth, and when she had done that she drew the blankets around herself and the boy and they slept. He knew they had come.

It was not until the second day afterward that he came for them. He came where they were and he held her hand and he smiled at the boy. He said, "They have not yet come here." And she knew he had gone back the way she came, all the way to the road from Arboles, and made sure nobody had followed her.

That afternoon they went over the shoulder of Horse Mountain to an old bear den under a down tree. They saw four spruce grouse sitting on a low branch and while she walked in front of them to keep them watching her he went around behind them and killed two with a stick. When it was dark he built a fire inside the old bear den and she cooked the grouse and they ate. They were together. It was a happy time.

The next day they went down to the Piedra River and followed it to the big fork. They followed the big fork till they were at the foot of Bald Mountain. It was three days, and he carried the boy all the third afternoon. There at the foot of Bald Mountain they camped for two more days while he went back to the big fork to be sure neither Blue Elk nor the sheriff was coming after them. Then they went to the far side of the mountain and he chose a spot close beside a spring and built a shelter. It was the first week of August.

## 5

A mountain lion killed the deer. They heard the lion's kill-cry in the night and the next morning he went up the mountain to look for the carcass. He found it in a patch of oak brush, partly covered with leaves, where the lion had dragged it after eating a forequarter and the soft belly meat. He searched the brush for the lion, hoping that if he roused it he would not have to use the rifle. But it had gone back to a den on a high ledge and would sleep, sated, all that day. He butchered out the meat and big sinews and took what was left of the skin, and he packed them down to the shelter. They had meat, and she had skin to make leather and sinew for sewing. She built a drying rack, sliced the meat thin to dry and cure. And that night he kept a fire going and sat watching for the lion, which came and prowled the nearby darkness, growling but fire-wary.

She said that if he would get more deer she could make meat for the winter. He said, "The rifle makes too big a noise."

She said, "In the old days they had no guns."

He said, "When I was a boy no bigger than he is I killed birds with arrows." And the next day he cut a scrub oak and split a strip from it and shaped it with a knife. He cured it by the fire and in the sun and he split straight-grain dead pine and made arrow shafts and feathered them with grouse feathers and hardened their points in the fire. He hid where the deer came to a pool at dusk to drink and he shot all his arrows and did not kill one deer.

She said, "We did not sing the song for hunting deer."

He did not remember that song. He said that a rifle was

better than a song for killing deer, but he didn't dare use the rifle yet. "People did not starve before they had rifles," she said. And that night she taught him the song for hunting deer. The next afternoon when the sun was near setting they sang the song. Then he took his bow and the arrows and went to the pool, and that night he killed a fat doe with the arrows. He said it was good to know that song, and he made a small bow and blunt bird arrows and taught the boy to use them.

She made meat. She made leather. She made bags to store the meat and she made leggings and shirts for the man and the boy. She remembered the things her mother had taught her and it was like the old days.

One morning they saw that Pagosa Peak to the east was white with snow. He said, "Soon the leaves will fall. I am going to make a place where we will be warm this winter." He went over to the south side of the mountain and came back and said, "We are going to go to that place." So they made packs of their things and they moved to the south side of the mountain where the sun would shine when the short days came. He had found where an old slide had taken down a whole grove of lodgepole pines. He said, "I am going to make a house of those poles."

She said, "I do not want a house. I want a lodge that is round like the day and the sun and the path of the stars. I want a lodge that is like the good things that have no end."

He said, "You still think of the old days."

She said, "I still think of Pagosa." Then she chanted the old song of the lodge, which is round like the day and the year and the seasons.

He cut poles and made a lodge of the kind she wanted, and he piled other poles around it, and brush; and when the aspen leaves fell and littered the earth with gold you could not see that lodge even when you knew where to look. It was a part of the earth itself.

He built the lodge, and she and the boy gathered seeds of the wild white peas and dug roots of the elk thistle. They gathered acorns. They went to a grove of nut pines and gathered the small brown nuts. She shaped a grinding stone and ground acorn meal and she wove a basket from willow stems and filled it with the meal and leached it sweet with water from the stream. They caught fish and dried them on a rack set over the lodge fire, where the smoke would cure them on its way to the smoke hole in the roof.

The aspen leaves fell. The scrub oak turned blood-red. The wind sang a song of wide skies and far mountaintops. Ice came to the quiet pools along the stream. First snow came, six inches of it in the night, fluffy as cotton grass in bloom. It melted in one day of sun that was warm as June. Then the days were mild, the night frost sharp, from one full moon to the next. And one evening he looked about the lodge, neat and stocked with food they had gathered, snug and safe; and he said, "This is not like having a cornfield on the reservation or the company store at the sawmill." She smiled at him and did not need to say that this was the way it should be. He was content. She was happy. She sang the song of the lodge safe for the winter. The boy sang most of the words with her. He was learning the old ways.

Then the snow came and stayed.

## 6

Winter is long in the high country and the short white days can bring black hunger. But the Ute people have lived many generations, many grandmothers, in that land. They speak its language.

Before ice locked the valleys, Bessie and the boy gathered willow shoots and black-stem ferns and inner bark and ripe grasses for her winter basketry. She made rawhide, and her man cut ironwood and shaped frames on which she wove the thongs, the webs for snowshoes. He made a new bow and he shaped and feathered arrows. Before the snow had built its depths in the valleys he went to the thickets where the deer were feeding and took fresh meat while the deer still had their fat. He taught the boy to set snares for rabbits. Then, when the drifts lay deep and the cold shriveled the rocks and shrank the days, she kept the stewpot full and simmering. She made winter moccasins and winter leggings and shirts, and when she had done these things she wove baskets. And she told the old tales and sang the old songs.

Winter passed. New leaves came again, to the aspens, then to the oaks, and the surging streams quieted and spring was upon them. They fished. They picked serviceberries, then chokecherries. They made meat and dried it. And the boy was big enough to help with all these things. Then the leaves fell and ice came, and snow whitened Pagosa Peak once more. Another winter passed, with its wailing storms, its roaring snow-slides, its shrunken days. And no one came, neither Blue Elk nor the sheriff nor anyone looking for them.

Again the aspens were in leaf. The Mariposa lilies bloomed and the cotton grass came to blossom in damp, cool meadows on the high benches. They gathered food. They lived as their people had lived in the old days. And a third time the aspens turned to gold and showered leaves on the lodge he had made as she wanted it, round like the year. He looked at the boy, now almost as tall as his mother, and he said, "One more winter and he can go with me and kill deer in the thickets." She said, "He sings the song for taking deer. He helps you now, with the songs. And"—she smiled—"he takes rabbits." She was proud of her son.

The winter was half over. It was a winter of much snow, more snow than usual, even for that country. The snow had driven the deer to still lower valleys, and for some days there had been little meat in the lodge. Then he said, "Tomorrow I must go and find the deer." She said, "Tonight we will sing the song," and they did that.

The next morning he put on his snowshoes and took his heaviest bow and best arrows and set out. He said he was going over the ridge, into the valley beyond, and that he might be gone overnight because it was a long trip and because he would be loaded with meat when he came back. He went up the slope to cross the gully an hour's travel from the lodge, then to cross the next ridge. It was a hot-sun morning after a brittle cold night.

He had been gone the space of an hour when she heard the thunder sound. It was the voice of an avalanche, a big snow-slide. She went outside and saw the plume of fine snow that is like a cloud over a big slide, and she knew that the night's freeze had loosened the ice on the high ledges and the morning's sun had started a trickle somewhere, a trickle that was like wet mud under a moccasin. A slide came lunging down the mountainside.

She saw where it was coming, and she clapped a hand over her mouth. She cried out once in horror, and the boy heard and came and stood beside her, watching, as the snow plume floated all the way down the slope and the thunder of the slide echoed into silence. It had gone down the gully an hour's travel from the lodge.

She moaned with grief known as clearly as though she had been there and seen what happened. She said to the boy, "Now we must make mourning. But first we must go and find him."

They returned to the lodge and dressed for the journey. They put on snowshoes, and they went up the slope, following her man's tracks. They went to the top of the slope, and there was the gully, swept as clean as the floor of the lodge. Not one tree was left standing. It was a giant furrow, plowed by the slide as her man once plowed furrows in the soil for his cornfield on the reservation. Far down in the valley they saw the great heap of snow and rocks and broken trees where the slide had run itself out, piled upon itself.

They had followed his tracks here, to the edge of this great furrow. Now she and the boy went down into that slide-furrow and crossed to the other side, and they looked for his tracks. There were no tracks. They searched, and he had not been there. He had not crossed the gully. He had come into it, but he had not crossed it.

They went down to the place where the slide had run itself out. They went along the jumbled face of it, looking. They found nothing. At last she said, "Come," and they started back toward the ridge to return to the lodge. They were almost at the foot of the ridge when the boy shouted and pointed to something in the snow. He ran and stood beside it till she came up to him. It was an arrow, a handsbreadth of its shaft sticking from the snow as though it had been shot from the air. It was one of his arrows.

They dug in the snow and found another arrow. Finally they found him. He had been caught by the slide, crushed by it, then thrown up by its convulsions until he was near the surface when it came to a halt. They found his body and they stood beside it, crying for him; and the boy sang the wailing song for the dead. She had not taught him that song. He had that song in his heart, and he sang it. Then she got the broken body over her shoulders and they went up out of that great furrow and climbed the slope, step by heavy step, and carried him home to the lodge. And all that night they made mourning.

The next day she dressed him in new leggings and a new shirt. They wrapped him in a blanket and a deerskin. She chose her best baskets and filled them with dried berries and smoked fish and cured meat. She made a drag out of a deerskin, looped long thongs to it, and on that skin drag they hauled him up the mountain to a cave among the rocks. They put him in the cave and set the baskets of food beside him, that he might eat on his long journey.

They gave him burial in the old way. They sang the death songs for him, in the darkness with the stars watching them. Then they went down the mountain and back to the lodge. She said to the boy, "Now you are the man."

## 7

It was a long winter. Some days his snares had no rabbits and they went hungry. Each day she told him the old tales and sang with him the old songs. He watched how she wove baskets, since her hands must be busy, and he learned those things she knew. Each day he strung an old bow of his father's and drew the bowstring as far as he could. Each day he could draw it a little farther. His arms grew strong. When there were leaves on the aspens again he could draw one of his father's arrows almost to the point. Then the deer came back up the valleys and he made his first big meat. He killed a deer with his father's arrows. The meat was tough and stringy, the fat and juice sucked out of it by the winter, but it was food, it was meat.

She said, "Soon you will know a name for yourself." He said, "This morning, before I made meat, I met a she-bear and she was not afraid of me. I was not afraid of her. We talked to each other. Then I killed the deer and I left a part of the meat for that she-bear. I shall call myself Bear's Brother. That is a good name."

And that was his name. They sang the songs for finding a name.

They dried berries. They smoked fish. They made meat. Summer passed like a white cloud drifting over the mountain. One day when she was cutting wood for the cooking fire the ax caught in a knot and she tried to drive it loose, using a stone for a hammer. The axhead broke, through the eye, and there was no way to use it except as a fist-ax. She knew they could not cut firewood for the winter with a fist-ax.

She looked around the lodge, and she said to the boy. "We must go to Pagosa. We must have a new ax." Then she said, "They cannot want him now for killing Frank No Deer."

So she took two of her best baskets and they went down to the road from Piedra Town to Pagosa. But she did not go to Pagosa by the road. She was not sure what she had told the boy was true. Maybe they still did want her man. She was tempted to go back, do without a new ax. They camped there beside the road, on the slope where no one could see them, for two days. Then she knew she had to go on.

They kept to the hills, to the game trails, and they went to Pagosa. But when they came to the last hill and saw Pagosa there in the valley she was tempted to go back again, back to the lodge. They spent the night on that last hill, in the brush, and she knew she had to go on.

The next morning they went down to Pagosa and along the street to Jim Thatcher's store. People turned to look at them, because they wore the clothes she had made from deerskins. But nobody stopped them. Nobody said, "Where is your man? We want your man because he killed Frank No Deer."

They went to the store, and Jim Thatcher was there behind the counter. Jim Thatcher was a tall, thin man who had been in that store many years, and his father there before him. He knew Indians. He traded with Indians, for robes and leatherwork and baskets. He traded salt and sugar and knives and axes and tin cans of beans for those things the Indians had made. He sold those things to people who liked robes and baskets, and sometimes he sold them to other traders.

They went to Jim Thatcher's store and she set the two baskets on the counter. Jim Thatcher looked at the baskets and he looked at her, and then he said, "You want to trade these?"

She said, "How much?"

Jim Thatcher looked at her again, and he looked at the boy. He said, "You used to live here, didn't you?"

She shook her head, made the sign that she did not understand, and asked again, "How much?"

"Do you want cash or trade?" he asked.

She looked around the store, went over to the rack of axes and chose one. She laid it on the counter beside the baskets. She went to the shelf of rifle ammunition, chose a box that would fit the rifle. She put it beside the ax. She beckoned to the boy, and together they looked about the store. His eyes were all eagerness and careful excitement. They looked at the clothing, the work gloves, the shoes. He stopped at a case with hunting knives in it. he stared at a knife in that case. Then he turned away and looked at granite cooking kettles, and at calico for skirts, and at blue denim overalls. She asked what he would like. He said, in the tongue, "There is nothing." But his eyes went back to the case of hunting knives.

Jim Thatcher saw this. He went to the case and took out a knife, laid it on the counter. "How do you like this one?" he asked. They came back and looked at that knife. The boy closed his eyes and turned away. He said to his mother, again in the tongue, "There is nothing."

She turned to Jim Thatcher and said, "Candy," and nodded toward the boy. Jim Thatcher filled a small bag with chocolate drops and red and yellow hard candies and set it on the counter with the ax and the ammunition. He started to put the knife back in the case, but she made a quick gesture. She wanted the knife for the boy. Jim Thatcher mentally added up the prices, two dollars for the ax, a dollar for the ammunition, a dollar and a half for the knife, a nickel for the candy. Four dollars and fifty-five cents. He glanced at the baskets. Good work, some of the best Ute basketwork he had ever seen. If somebody came along who knew baskets he might get four or five dollars apiece for them. Even Mike Lawson would give him three and a half apiece.

He put the knife back on the counter with the other things and she nodded, apparently satisfied. He asked, "Where's your man?"

She looked at him, a flash of fear in her eyes. Then she shook her head, shrugged, made the sign of not understanding.

"I remember you," he said. "Your man is George Black Bull."

She wouldn't admit it. She put the ammunition, the knife, the candy in her pack, picked up the ax, motioned to the boy, and started to leave. Jim Thatcher stopped her before she reached the door. "There's no need to run," he said. "They don't want your man. He doesn't have to hide out. That case is all cleared up. Self-defense, they called it. Do you understand?"

She looked at him, bewildered.

"Your man can come back," Jim Thatcher said. "He doesn't have to hide out. This thing is all over, finished." He made the gesture with his hands for wiping clean, making an end.

She stared at him.

"You understand English, don't you? Of course you do."

She didn't answer. She stared at him, searching his face.

"Tell George he can come back. They're not looking for him any more. Tell him—"

She shook her head.

"Why not?"

She spoke to the boy in Ute and they left the store.

They walked down the street. People stared at them, smiled at their clothes, but nobody spoke to them, nobody tried to stop them. They walked down the street to the end and started along the road to Piedra Town. They went a way down that road, and she stopped and looked back. Nobody was following them. But she was not sure. It could have been a trick, what Jim Thatcher had said about her man. And even if they did not want her man, now that he was dead, maybe they wanted her, or the boy.

She walked down the road until they had passed the bend and Pagosa was out of sight. There she and the boy left the road, walking carefully on stones to leave no track. They went up the hillside, through the brush, and there they sat, hidden, watching, for an hour. Nobody came, following them. She opened the pack and got out the bag of candy. They ate the chocolate drops. Then they went on, following the trails through the brush.

## 8

They spent that winter as before. Spring came again, and one day when he went to catch fish at a pool in the stream he met the she-bear again. He was not afraid of her. He said to her, "You gave me my name. I am Bear Brother and we are friends." She listened as he sang a song that came to him, a song of friendship with that bear. Then she went away and he followed her and saw her uproot an old stump and catch three chipmunks and lick up the swarming ants. Then he went to the stream and caught fish and he left half of his fish for the bear.

He told his mother of this and she said, "It is good to have a friend." She told him how their people had been friends of everything in the mountains in the old days—the bears, the deer, the mountain lions, the jays, the ravens. She told him these things. Then she was silent. He waited for her to say more, but she could not tell him the things that were in her mind. Ever since they had gone to Pagosa those things had been in her mind, the things Jim Thatcher had said about her man. She had been so startled, so afraid, that she hadn't really heard what he said except that she should tell her man that the matter of killing Frank No Deer was all settled, over with. She wanted to hear these things again. This time she would listen. She would not be afraid this time.

Then it was summer. Soon the serviceberries would be ripe for picking and they should smoke fish when the berries were ripe. She said to the boy, "I must go on a journey."

He said, "When you say, we shall go."

She said, "I must go alone. You will stay here until I come back." She still worried a little that they might want the boy.

If they took her, she could manage to get away, somehow. But the boy might not know how to get away. She said, "You must stay here."

That is the way it was. She went to Pagosa again, and the boy stayed there on Bald Mountain.

She went to Pagosa. She took two baskets to trade at Jim Thatcher's store. She did not need an ax or a knife, but she took the baskets to trade so that she would have a reason to listen when Jim Thatcher talked to her, asked questions.

Jim Thatcher liked the baskets, as before. He asked her what she wanted to trade them for, and she chose calico for a skirt, and cloth for a blouse, and a blue coat with brass buttons for the boy. It was more than he would give her for the baskets. She knew this. She wanted him to talk.

He said, "This is too much, Bessie."

She pretended she did not understand. She took one basket from the counter.

He said, "*This* is too much," and he put a hand on what she had chosen.

They haggled. Finally he said, "You are a smart woman, Bessie. But you didn't tell your man what I said to tell him. He hasn't been to town."

"There is this thing about Frank No Deer," she said.

"I told you that was all settled."

She shrugged.

"You didn't believe me?"

She smiled, deprecating.

"Well, it is. All settled." He made the gesture, cut-off, finished. Then he asked, "Where is George?"

She made the gesture he had just made. Cut-off, finished. It also meant dead.

"That's too bad. What happened?"

"The slide, the snow-slide." She unconsciously fell into English. "He was hunting. The slide came. He is dead, two winters gone."

He watched her, knew she was telling the truth. "I'm sorry, Bessie. And the boy?"

She smiled. Then she held out a hand, held it as high as her own head. She put her hand on the blue jacket. "For him," she said.

Jim Thatcher went to a rack and got a denim jacket the same size. Something more practical. But she shook her head. She wanted the serge jacket with the brass buttons. He looked at the baskets again, figured that they would just about cover her purchases, and gave in. He was tempted to throw in a bag candy. But she hadn't asked for it. He let it pass.

She put the purchases in her pack and left the store. She went down the street, and at the corner by the bank, with its big windows and brick front, she met Blue Elk.

Blue Elk saw her, and stopped, his mouth shaped in surprise. He said, "I have waited a long time to see you."

She said, "I am here. You see me." Her voice was cold.

"We must talk," Blue Elk said.

She said, "I will listen."

They went across the street and down toward the bridge where there was a vacant lot. There she sat down and put the pack beside her. Blue Elk sat awkwardly. He was used to sitting on a chair. He took off his derby hat and she saw streaks of gray in his hair though his braids were still black. His cheeks hung down like the cheeks of an old dog and his belly was even fatter than she remembered.

He said, "Where is your man? And the boy?"

She shrugged.

"He can come back," he said. "I settled that thing. I took care of it. He can come back and work in the sawmill again."

"No," she said.

He glanced at her pack, then at her clothes. "You are living in the old way," he said.

She didn't answer.

"Where?" he asked.

Still she didn't answer.

He sat silent a long moment, then said, "I settled this thing for your man."

She said, "It is settled."

"I did it. I said I would do it for the cost of two horses. You owe me the cost of two horses."

"I told you I did not have the cost of one goat. I have no horses. I do not even have one goat." And she made the cut-off sign. She said with the sign that it was finished.

He said, "They did not follow you when you left."

She did not answer.

"They did not follow you to find him," he insisted.

"They did not find him," she said.

"It is as I said. I told them he killed Frank No Deer because Frank tried to kill him. That is the way it was settled."

"Frank No Deer stole his money. Three times he stole it. That was enough."

Blue Elk shook his head. "That was not enough. To be a thief is not enough."

"This is a strange thing you say," she told him angrily. "You say it is not bad to steal my man's money three times, but it is bad to kill Frank No Deer for that."

"I say it is the law. That is the way it is."

"I do not like this law."

"I settled this. You owe to me for settling this."

"My man will pay you."

"Where is your man?"

She looked at him and she made the cut-off sign.

"Dead?" he asked, and he unconsciously put his hand to his mouth for saying it.

She nodded.

He shook his head, sat silent for a time. Then he said, "The boy?"

She did not answer.

"The boy should be in the school at Ignacio."

"No."

"That is where he should be."

"No!"

He stretched his legs, stiff from sitting on the ground. He reached for her pack. She held it from him. He grabbed it, pulled it open. The cloth for the skirt and the cloth for the blouse and the blue coat with brass buttons fell out. He reached for them. She caught up the blue coat and held it away from him. He took the cloth. He said, "You owe me for settling this thing for your man. I will keep this cloth. Give the coat."

"No." She tried to take the empty pack from him.

He was on his knees, holding to the pack, holding the cloth in his other hand. She had the coat. She turned and ran from him, to the street and up the hill away from the bridge. There she ran down the street and out of Pagosa. She went a little way along the road, then left it and went up the hillside, where she knew her way. She started back to Bald Mountain, with no pack, no food. But with the blue coat with brass buttons. And with the knowledge that it was settled, this thing about her man and Frank No Deer. It was three days back to the lodge, but there were berries to eat, and there were roots.

## 9

It was another summer before she went to Pagosa again. She went alone, as before. This time she took four baskets to trade.

She was no longer afraid of the sheriff or the sawmill man, but when she came to two Indian women gathering firewood on the hill near Pagosa she stopped to talk to them. She did not know these women. They seemed not to know her, for they looked at her with curious eyes and smiled at her clothes and looked at her pack. She made the sign of greeting and she asked if Blue Elk was in Pagosa. The one with a purple blouse pointed with her chin toward Bessie's pack and said to the other, "This one has a gift for Blue Elk." The other one laughed. She said, "No. This one thinks Blue Elk has a gift for her. That is why she brings the big pack, to carry it in." They both laughed.

Bessie said, "I have come to trade with Jim Thatcher. Blue Elk stole skirt cloth and blouse cloth from me last summer."

They said, "Oh-oh." Then the one with a purple blouse said, "Fat Belly is not here. He is at the reservation."

Bessie said, "This is true?"

They both said, "This is true. He is not here to steal from you. We know that one."

She helped them gather wood for a little time, to pay them for this. Then she went on to Pagosa.

She went to Jim Thatcher's store and she traded the four baskets for a red blanket. Not the Navaho kind, which were black and white and gray as well as red, but the white man's kind, which was all red. When she had finished trading and put the red blanket in her pack Jim Thatcher said, "Watch out for Blue Elk this time, Bessie."

"That one!" She said it like a curse.

"He tried to sell that skirt cloth back to me last summer. I wouldn't take it and he made quite a fuss. What happened?"

"He stole that cloth from me."

"Where?"

"Here. In Pagosa."

"Why didn't *you* make a fuss?"

She shrugged. "He said I owed him the cost of two horses."

"What for?"

"For settling that thing about my man."

"Why, the old scoundrel! He wasn't even a witness at the inquest. Well, he's out of town today."

So she went back to Bald Mountain. She gave the red blanket to the boy for his bed. She said she wanted him to sleep warm in the winter. She did not say, even to herself, that red is the rainbow color for protection. The boy knew this. She had told him this when she told him the old tales.

The boy had begun to fill out, to have the stocky frame typical of the Utes. He could drive an arrow all the way through a deer and he could carry the hindquarters of a buck on his shoulders. He had braids almost as long as those of his mother and he kept them wrapped with red wool at their ends. He wore a breechclout and moccasins in the summer and in the winter he wore the winter leggings and the winter shirt. Now he had the red blanket.

That was a bad winter. There was much snow and the deer moved to the lower valleys. Even the rabbits were scarce that winter. Their dried fish and cured meat were gone before the daylight began to lengthen, even though she ate little, saving the meat for the boy. "You must be strong," she said. "When these storms end you must be strong to go to the lower valleys and get meat."

At last the storms eased. He prepared to get meat. She said she would go with him and he said she should not do that.

She remembered what had happened to her man at such a time. She did not say this thing, but she went with the boy to the lower valleys.

She was weak and could not travel fast. The cold made her cough. But they went all the way to the place where the deer were in the thickets and he took a deer. They ate deer liver and those parts that make strength for a weak body. They made packs of the meat and they went back to the lodge. It was a long journey and she was tired when they returned. She was so weak she could scarcely stand on her feet. He made her lie on her bed and he cooked soup from the tough winter meat for her. She drank some of the soup, but she was too weak to eat the meat. She had a pain in her chest and she coughed and would not let him see what came out of her throat.

She said, "Help me to sit up," and he helped her. She tried to work at a basket, but her hands would not do what she told them to do. He helped her. He sat beside her and he made the basket for her. She said his hands were better than her hands at this. He said, "My hands have watched your hands many times. My hands are your hands now."

The pain became worse. She was so hot she could not have even one robe around her shoulders. Then she was cold, so cold that he put his red blanket around her and still she shivered. She said, "I am sick." He said, "I am singing the songs for making you well." She said, "I do not hear these songs." He said, "I am singing them inside." She said, "Sing them outside. I am very sick."

He sang the songs all that night. He made soup, but she could not swallow it. She said, "I am not going to get over this sickness, my son." He said, "I will not sing the song for going away yet." She said, "No. Not yet."

All that day he sang the songs for making her well. Late that afternoon she could not hear those songs. She talked about things he did not know. About Pagosa, and the sawmill, and Blue Elk, and Frank No Deer. He heard these things for the first time. Then she did not talk. It was dark, it was night. Then she said, "Sing the song for going away, my son." She tried to reach up and touch his face. Her arm was too weak. He took her hand and held it to his face. Then she died.

He made mourning all that night. When it was daylight he put her new deerskin dress on her and wrapped her in the red blanket, then in a deerskin robe, so she would be warm on the long journey. He put dried berries and dried meat, the last there was in the lodge, in two baskets. Then he made a drag of a deerskin and he took her up the mountain to the cave in the rocks where they had buried his father. His father was no longer there; only a few bones and a part of a robe and a broken basket. The boy buried his mother there, in the old way, and he sang the old songs. Then he went back down the mountain to the lodge, and he was alone.

## 10

Spring came again. The snow melted, the streams flooded, the aspens were in catkin, then in leaf. The deer came back to the upper benches and dropped their fawns. Strawberries made the grass white with blossom and red anemones were in bloom. The boy caught trout in the pools, and he watched for his friend, the she-bear.

He saw his friend one morning in a wild meadow, eating grass and strawberries. She had two cubs with her. He watched her and he talked to her, but she did not listen. A she-bear with cubs is not friendly. He talked to her and walked toward her, and she shook her head and growled and told him she did not want to talk. She did not even want to listen. Her cubs listened, curious about this boy, but she cuffed them and hurried them away and into the brush.

For days he watched them. He found where the she-bear ate grass and strawberries, where she caught fish, where she dug for mice and ground squirrels. He found where she slept with her cubs. But she would not listen to him. They were no longer friends. One day he said to the cubs, "I am Bear Brother. You are my brother, and you are my sister." But the she-bear growled and came toward him and told him to go away.

He went back to the lodge and made friends of the squirrels that lived in a hollow pine tree. He talked to them and they listened to him. They came and sat in his hand and talked to him. Then the chipmunks that lived in the rocks came to him and asked to be friends. They came into the lodge and lived with him. A jay came and said it wanted to be his friend. It ate from his hand and rode on his shoulder and pecked at the lobe of his ear.

Serviceberries ripened and he went to gather them to dry, as he had learned from his mother. Among the berry bushes he met the she-bear again, and her two cubs. He told her he was gathering berries to dry for the winter and she let him gather berries, but she would not listen when he talked to her. When he talked to the cubs she took them with her to another berry patch.

He gathered berries and dried them, and he made meat and smoked it, as he had learned from his mother. Then the man came.

The boy was fishing and his friend the jay was perched in an aspen near by, watching. The jay called an alarm. It said a stranger was coming. The boy drew in his line, took the fish he had caught, covered his tracks and left the pool. He went up the hillside and sat in the brush and watched. The jay flew down the valley, screaming, and it came back, tree by tree, telling the boy about this stranger. Then the man appeared, with his mouse-colored burro. He came up the creek and stopped at the pool where the boy had been fishing. He drank and his burro drank, and the man picked up a handful of sand from the shallow water and looked at it.

He was a tall man. He had gray whiskers and he wore a black hat and a blue shirt and brown pants and boots. He carried a rifle. His burro wore a packsaddle and a pack covered with gray canvas.

The man looked at the sand in his hand and let the water trickle between his fingers. He shook his head and threw the sand back into the water. Then he spoke to the burro and went on up the creek, the burro following him. The jay flew back to the boy and sat on his shoulder and was silent.

The boy followed the man and watched him all afternoon. The man went slowly, scooping a handful of sand from every pool and looking at it. Toward evening he found a handful of sand that seemed to please him. He took a pan and shovel from the pack on the burro and scooped sand into the pan and put water in it and slowly swished the water and sand out. He rubbed his fingers on the bottom of the pan and put sand in the pan and swished it out again. He did this several times. Then he unpacked the burro and made camp beside the stream. He had found something there that he wanted.

The boy watched until the sun sat on the mountains and the man built a fire and set food to cook. Then the boy started back to his own lodge. On the way he met the she-bear and her cubs. He tried to tell her about this strange man, but she did not want to listen. She told him not to talk to her. The cubs wanted to listen, but she cuffed them and told them not to listen. The jay sat in a scrub oak and told her these things, but she would not listen to the jay either. She took her cubs and went away, and the boy went to his lodge and ate and slept.

The next morning the boy was halfway to his watching place above the man's camp when he heard the thunder of a gun. He knew that sound because after his mother died he had got out his father's rifle and fired it by mistake. It made a sound that seemed to lift the roof from the lodge. He put the rifle away and never touched it again. But after that he knew the voice of a gun. He heard it three more times, all from the man's camp. Then there was silence.

He did not hurry. What had happened had happened and could not be changed. But soon he heard the man shouting anger-words. Then the boy reached his watching place and saw the man at the creek, his left arm red with blood from his neck to his fingers. He was trying to wash the blood away and he was still shouting. The boy knew some of the words. His father had spoken those words when he was angry.

The man washed his arm, but could not stop the blood.

He came back to his camp, and then the boy saw the she-bear. She was a grizzled-brown heap beside the man's fire, which was still burning. She was dead. The man walked around her, afraid even though she was dead. He tore a shirt into strips and wrapped them around his arm, but they were red with blood before he finished the wrapping. The man's talk became fear-talk. He tied a strip of cloth around his arm and put a stick in it and twisted the stick, but the blood still ran from his fingers.

The man kicked the coffeepot, which sat steaming in the fire, and it rolled on the she-bear, spilling a wet brown stain on her fur. Then he went to his burro, grazing a little way upstream, and tried to lead the burro back to his camp. The burro was afraid of the bear and braced its legs. He went back to the camp and picked up his folded blanket and his rifle. He put the blanket on the burro's back and he was so weak he almost fell before he got on the burro. His feet were close to the ground, the burro was so small, but he kicked the burro's ribs and shouted and beat the burro's ribs with his gun. The burro went around the bear and went down the valley at a slow trot.

The boy waited, listening to the man's voice thin away in the distance. He wondered if the man was singing his song for going on the long journey. He knew it was a fear-song. The man had killed the she-bear. Now he was afraid the she-bear was going to kill him.

When the distance had swallowed the man's voice the boy went down to the camp. He looked at the dead she-bear, and he saw the dead cub beside her. It was the smaller of the two cubs, the female. He said the song for a dead bear. Then he looked at the tracks, the signs, and knew what had happened. The she-bear and her cubs had been on the hillside, near his watching place. They had smelled the food the man was cooking. The cubs had gone down to the camp and the man had tried to drive them away. He had shot one cub. The she-bear had charged him, and he had shot her three times. Before she died she reached him with one angry paw that slashed down his arm. That was what had happened.

He looked for the other cub. It was nowhere in sight. He looked at the gear the man had left. It was of no use to him, the shovel, the battered coffeepot, the frying pan. Then he heard the other bear cub crying in the brush beyond the creek. He went there and found it, and he talked to it until it was not afraid of him. It went with him down to the man's camp and cried when it nosed at the dead she-bear. He talked to it again, and he fed it the food the man had been cooking. Then he started back to his lodge. He told the bear cub to come with him, and it came.

That is how the boy and the bear cub became brothers and friends. That is how it happened.

After that the boy was not alone.

## 11

It was the noon hour on a warm July day and Jim Thatcher was alone in the store, both his clerks having gone home for dinner. Jim always ate early and used this slack time to check invoices. He was at his desk when he heard the yelps and howls of a dogfight in the street. He glanced up but paid no more attention until some shouted, “Get a gun! It’s a bear!” Then he jumped to his feet, picked up a .30-30 from the rack, broke open a box of cartridges and jammed three of them into the magazine. He levered one into the chamber as he hurried to the door to the street. Deer and even bobcats, but few bears, had wandered into Pagosa on occasion.

He stepped out onto the sidewalk and couldn’t believe his eyes. There in the street was a grizzly cub, hunkered back in the dust, with three dogs yelping and dancing around it. One dog darted in, the bear whipped a paw, and the dog went end over end, howling in pain. Then Jim heard the boy shouting, in Ute. The boy was standing at the curb, and he was as incredible as the bear cub. He was just a youngster, ten or eleven years old, and he was dressed in the old way, moccasins, leggings, clout, no shirt, and braids. He was shouting at the cub, and the cub looked at him, started to go to him, only to be attacked by the dogs again. It snarled, slapped another dog and knocked it sprawling with a gash along its ribs.

Men were running up from all directions. Someone shouted, “Kill it! Jim, kill that damned bear before it kills all the dogs in town!”

The cub, having momentarily disposed of the dogs, went

to the boy and licked his hand, then faced the crowd, frightening by the uproar, growling, ready to fight.

Jim said to the excited men, "Take it easy! Can't you see it's a pet cub? For God's sake, don't start anything!" He turned to the boy. "Tell your friend to behave himself, son."

The boy looked at him, as bewildered as the bear cub. He said something in Ute, then caught the bear's scruff in one hand, picked up a pack that was on the street beside him, and walked away. The crowd fell back, stumbling over one another's feet. The boy and the cub went to Jim Thatcher's store and walked in, both of them.

Two men came running up the street, rifles in their hands. "Where's the bear?" one shouted.

"In Thatcher's store!" someone answered.

The two armed men started to the store, but Jim Thatcher stepped in front of them. "Keep your shirts on, both of you," he said firmly. "The bear's just a cub and a pet. I'll handle this. If anybody starts shooting, I'll finish it! Understand?" Then he turned and went into the store, closing the door behind him. The crowd stayed outside in the street, watching through the windows.

The boy was at the counter, the cub sitting like a big shaggy dog beside him. Jim went back of the counter and the boy opened his pack, took out three baskets, and set them on the counter. Then he turned and looked around the store.

Jim said, "You want to trade?"

The boy looked at him, still not understanding a word he said. He went over to the knife case, glanced into it, moved to the case of fishing tackle, then to the shelves of canned goods. He paused at the bolts of cloth and the piles of overalls. Finally he found what he was looking for, the blankets. He went down through the pile until he found a red one exactly like the one Bessie had traded for the last time she was here. He pulled it from the pile and brought it back to the counter. The cub had been at his side everywhere he went.

Now it stood beside him, watching the crowd outside the windows and lifting its forefeet nervously.

Jim asked again, "You want to trade?" and still the boy did not answer. Jim picked up one of the baskets and examined it. It was identical with the last ones Bessie had brought in, though of slightly better workmanship. He looked at the boy and asked, "Where is your mother? What are you doing here alone?"

There was no answer. The boy pushed the three baskets toward Jim and drew the red blanket toward himself.

"Your mother brought four baskets for a blanket the last time," Jim said, then shook his head at himself. No use talking English to this boy. He was a throwback, right out of the old, old days. Either that or Bessie was trying a trick so clever Jim couldn't believe it. She could be hiding in the brush. She could have sent the boy in with these three baskets and have told him to act dumb but to get another blanket. It could happen, but—well, it just didn't make sense. The boy wasn't dickering. He *couldn't* dicker, not without at least a few words of English.

Jim looked at the other baskets. All of them were of superior workmanship, the best Bessie ever made. Actually, they more than covered the price of the blanket. But if he let the boy have the blanket for three baskets this time, next time he would come in and try to get a blanket for two baskets.

He asked, "Don't you know any English at all?"

The blank look in the boy's eyes said, truthfully, that he didn't.

Jim glanced toward the street and saw Blue Elk, who had just arrived. Blue Elk seemed to be asking what had happened. Someone told him. Blue Elk approached the door, hesitated, looked in through the glass. Jim motioned to him, beckoned him in. Blue Elk opened the door and several others started to come in with him. "Just Blue Elk!" Jim ordered. "The rest of you stay outside."

Blue Elk came in and closed the door behind him, beaming with importance at being so singled out. Then he saw the boy and the bear cub, which looked at him and raised its hackles. Blue Elk hesitated, his hand still on the knob. He was puffing as though he had hurried. Now he caught his breath in fear and surprise.

"Come on in," Jim said, "but don't come too close. And for God's sake don't touch the boy or the cub or there'll be all hell to pay."

Blue Elk came a few steps toward the counter. His shoes squeaked and the cub's ears stiffened. Blue Elk stopped, took off his derby hat and wiped his forehead.

"This is Bessie Black Bull's boy," Jim said. "He came in here alone and he doesn't savvy English. Find out why he came alone."

Blue Elk spoke to the boy in the tongue. "We are of the people, we two. I am your friend. The man wants to know where is your mother."

The boy said, "My mother is where I left her." He lifted his chin in pride.

"Why did you come here alone?"

"I came to trade the baskets for the blanket."

"What does he say?" Jim asked.

"He says his mother is at home. He says he came to trade for a blanket."

"Why did he come alone? Why didn't Bessie come?"

Blue Elk put the question. The boy shrugged and did not answer.

"Why did not your mother come to trade for the blanket?" Blue Elk asked again, his voice sharp this time.

The cub bristled at his tone. The boy put his hand on the cub's head and it turned and licked his hand, then lifted its lip at Blue Elk. The boy said, "My mother—" He made the cut-off sign. It could have meant that he was through with talk. He folded the blanket and put it in his pack.

Blue Elk said, "I speak of your mother, not your father. I know your father is dead. Where is your mother?"

The boy impatiently made the cut-off sign again.

"She is dead?"

The boy scowled and nodded his head.

"Where do you live, if she is dead?"

"I live in my lodge."

"Where is your lodge?"

The boy shrugged off the question.

"What does he say?" Jim asked.

"He says his mother is dead."

"Dead? I don't believe it!"

"My people do not lie. He says she is dead."

"But she made these baskets he just brought in! They are the best baskets she ever made. When did she die, anyway?"

Blue Elk turned to the boy again. "The man does not believe your mother is dead. Who do you live with?"

The boy said, "I will not talk of this thing," and he made the cut-off sign, sharply, incisively.

"Boys do not speak to the old men of their people in this way!" Blue Elk said impatiently. And he asked again, "Who do you live with?"

The boy said, "I live with my brother." He shouldered his pack, then put his hand on the cub's scruff. They started toward the door.

Blue Elk stepped aside to let them pass. The crowd at the doorway pushed back, making room. The boy opened the door, went out into the street and turned toward the hills and the road to Piedra Town, the cub trotting beside him.

Nobody tried to stop them, but before they reached the end of the street someone shouted, "I'm going to get that bear! Who's coming with me?" Several shouted, "I'll go!"

Jim Thatcher came out of the store into the street. "Let that boy alone," he ordered. "And leave his bear alone. Understand?"

Then the sheriff appeared. He wanted to know what had happened, what the crowd was doing. Jim said, "They want to go kill an Indian kid's pet bear. Put a stop to it, George. Right now!"

The sheriff said, "I don't know what this is all about, but I'll go along with Jim Thatcher. If anybody starts a posse, the whole posse will land in jail!"

The crowd began to break up. Jim started to tell the sheriff what had happened, and Blue Elk went down the street, puzzling over this matter. He had gone only a little way when the preacher caught up with him. "Who was that boy, Blue Elk?" he asked.

Blue Elk glanced at him. "Bessie Black Bull's boy."

"Bessie Black Bull? George Black Bull's woman? He was the one who killed Frank No Deer, wasn't he?"

"Yes."

"Then that's the boy you brought to me to have baptized."

Blue Elk nodded.

"What's he doing, running around in a clout like a savage? He should be in school."

Blue Elk glanced at him again. "Yes," he said.

"Where is he living?"

"Back in the mountains."

"Have his parents got a permit to live off the reservation and keep him out of school?"

"His parents are dead."

"Who is he living with, then?"

Blue Elk looked around. Several men were watching, listening. He motioned to the preacher and they crossed the street and walked down toward the river bridge where they could be alone.

"That boy," the preacher said again, "should be in school. If he is left running around like this, with that bear, somebody is going to get hurt. Where did you say he lives?"

"Back in the mountains."

"Who with?"

"His brother, he said."

"I didn't know he had a brother. Or does he mean an uncle?"

Blue Elk looked at him shrewdly. "I could find out these things," he said.

"I wish you would. I baptized that boy and I feel responsible for him."

"I worry for my people," Blue Elk said. "I could find out these things, but it is a hard trip and I am an old man. I have no money for this trip."

The preacher felt in his pocket. Blue Elk heard the clink of silver dollars. The preacher drew out one dollar and offered it to him.

Blue Elk shook his head. "This will be a very hard trip."

"How much?"

"Ten dollars."

"I haven't got ten dollars. All I have is the mission money." Then the preacher said, "I might make it five. And if you bring the boy in to the school the agent might give you five more."

"I am a poor old man," Blue Elk said, holding out his hand. "I do this for my people."

The preacher gave him the dollar, produced two more, then drew out a handful of change and counted out two dollars in dimes and quarters. Blue Elk put the money in his pocket and walked away.

He went along the back streets to his house. There he made a packet of food, then went to the open shed behind the house and saddled his pony. He rode down the alleys and side streets until he was out of town, then cut through the brush to the road to Piedra Town. He stopped there and looked for tracks in the dust, and found none. The boy had taken the paths through the brush on the hillside. But Blue Elk knew that a traveler must drink. He rode down the road toward Piedra until he came to the first creek, then left the road and went up the creek. His eyes were not as good as they had been twenty years before, but they still knew a boy's moccasin track and a cub bear's paw print when he saw them, half a mile from the road, in the creekbank mud. After that he followed those tracks along the game trails. The boy, knowing those trails, could travel faster than Blue Elk. But Blue Elk knew that eventually the boy would lead him to his hideout.

# 12

It was midmorning of the third day when Blue Elk came to the hollow and the small stream below the lodge. He sensed that he was near the place, but it took him half an hour to unravel the maze of trails from the stream and come to the tangle of down trees that hid the lodge itself. There he smelled a trace of smoke from a cooking fire, smoke with the faint odor of drying meat. Then a jay screamed at him, and continued screaming as he went on. A squirrel chattered at him.

Blue Elk found the path, found the boy's moccasin prints. But, remembering the bear cub, he did not follow it among the trees. He waited, letting the jay and the squirrel say he was there.

Soon the boy appeared. He stopped a little away from Blue Elk and said, "Why did you come here?"

"I came here to talk with you."

"We have talked."

"I have come to help you. I have come a long way. I am tired and I am hungry."

"I did not ask you to come."

"I am here."

The boy looked at him a long time. The jay perched on his shoulder and talked in his ear. The squirrel came and leaped into his hand and sat there, staring at Blue Elk. The boy said, "You may rest and you may eat. Then you must go away. Come." He led the way among the trees to the door of the hidden lodge. Blue Elk followed.

It was cool and dark inside the lodge. As his eyes accustomed themselves to the dimness, Blue Elk remembered his own boyhood and his grandmother's lodge. The boy set fresh berries and dried meat in front of him, and when he tasted the meat Blue Elk remembered again. It had the taste of meat he had eaten in the lodge of his grandmother.

His eyes searched the lodge as he ate. He saw the bed, the peeled rods with the robes, and the new red blanket. He saw the tanned robes hung along the walls, the new buckskin folded carefully, the sewing basket with its coil of dry sinew and its bone awls. He saw the white smoulder of the fire on the floor beneath the smoke hole in the roof and the drying rack above the fire. Long, thin slices of venison hung on the rack, drying and curing in the smoke and slow heat. He saw Bessie's basket materials, the bundle of willow twigs, the black-stem ferns, the strips thin as a fingernail. There was a coil of strips in a bowl of water, pliant for weaving, and there was a partly finished blanket, its coiled twigs white as though freshly peeled. He saw two ironwood bows, sinew backed, and a quiver of arrows feathered with grouse feathers. He saw a lodge such as only the old people remembered.

He ate, and then he asked, "Where is your brother?"

"My brother," the boy said, "will return when it is time to return."

Blue Elk looked at the unfinished basket. "How long is it since your mother went away?"

The boy did not answer.

"Your mother was here a few days past." He nodded toward the fresh coils of the basket.

"She is gone a long time," the boy said.

"It is not right to tell lies to the old men of your people."

"I tell the truth."

Blue Elk said, "When I was young I knew a lodge such as this. My mother and my grandmother dried fish and cured meat, but when the short white days came we were hungry."

"That is the way it is."

"That is the way it was. The grandmothers said this thing.

Now the grandmothers are gone on the long journey and now it is different. The old days are gone."

The boy did not answer.

"Your father is gone."

The boy nodded.

"When your father had trouble, I settled that trouble for him. Your father was my friend. I knew when I settled that trouble for him that I would be a grandfather to you when you needed a grandfather. I knew I must tell you what to do."

"My mother told me what to do."

"Your mother is gone. And your father is gone."

The boy stared at the white ashes of the fire. He whispered the beginning of the mourning song. He stopped and looked at Blue Elk. "If you are a grandfather," he said, "you will sing the mourning song." He sang the mourning song aloud. Blue Elk tried to sing that song, but the words were dim. He sang a few phrases and was silent. The boy stopped and said, "How can you tell me what to do when you do not know the songs?"

"I sing the song inside."

"My mother will not know if you sing the song inside. My father will not know." He sang the song again, and Blue Elk closed his eyes and sang with him. His memory did not know the words, but his tongue remembered.

They sang the mourning song, and tears came to Blue Elk's eyes. It was a song not only for Bessie Black Bull and George Black Bull, but for Blue Elk's own mother, and his own grandmother, and all the grandmothers. It was a song for the old people and the old days.

They sang that song, and they sat in silence. Blue Elk opened his eyes, and he saw the boy and forgot the old people. He knew why he had come here. He said to the boy, "When did your mother go away?"

The boy said, "She went away in the short white days."

"In the winter that is past," Blue Elk said.

"In the winter before the winter that is past," the boy said. He made the sign that it was a year and a half ago.

Blue Elk stared at him, unbelieving. He saw that the boy was telling the truth. He said, "I did not know. I should have come before this. You have been alone too many days."

The boy made no answer.

"I am here," Blue Elk said. "My ears are listening. It is good to talk of what happened."

The boy stared at the ashes, struggling with himself. It was a long time since he had talked to anyone except the bear cub and the jay and the squirrels. He was a boy, with things to tell, not a man who can contain all the things that happen. At last he said, "I will tell of these things." He began to tell of the winter when his mother died. He was telling of their trip to the low valleys to take fresh meat when there was a whine at the doorway. He stopped his talk. He said, "Come in, Brother. We have one of the grandfathers with us. Come in and sit with us."

The bear cub came inside, sniffing warily. It came to where they sat. It nosed Blue Elk, who sat quietly and let it know his smell. It bristled and turned to the boy. The boy said, "Now you know. Come, lie beside me. I shall tell this grandfather about you." The cub went to him and lay down between the boy and Blue Elk.

The boy told about the she-bear and her cubs, about the man who came with the burro, about how this man killed the she-bear and one cub. He told how the man went away, afraid the she-bear he had killed was killing him. He sang the song for a dead bear, and Blue Elk remembered a part of that song and sang with him.

They sat in silence after that. Then the boy told about his mother again, how they went on the hunt, how she sickened and died. He told about his father, how he died in the snow-slide and they found him and gave him burial.

He told these things, and Blue Elk heard them. Blue Elk was a boy again as he heard. This was the story of his own people.

By then the boy had told what he had to tell. He got up and moved about the lodge, touching the bow that had been his father's, touching the knife his mother had used. He walked about the lodge, and Blue Elk stretched his legs. He was cramped from sitting so long. His joints were old. He watched the boy, and his eyes were full of years. He moved his toes in the boots he wore, and his toes tingled with thorns in them. His legs were asleep.

The light in the sky above the smoke hole was dimming. The day had passed while the boy talked.

The boy left the lodge, and the bear cub followed him. Blue Elk got to his feet. He could scarcely walk, his legs were so cramped. He made his way to the door and stood there until his feet would move again. Then he went outside.

The boy stood in the open, his face lifted to the sun, which was down near the peaks. He was singing a song softly to himself. Blue Elk knew it was the song to the setting sun, to the coming night. He had not sung that song for so long that not even his tongue remembered the words, but he stood silently until the boy had finished. Then he went to the boy, and together they went down to the stream. They drank, and they washed themselves, and Blue Elk went to where his pony was grazing and took off the saddle and the bridle and hobbled the pony for the night. Then they returned to the lodge and they ate.

The boy built up the fire, so there was light in the lodge. He turned the meat on the rack, so that it would cure another side in the warm smoke. Blue Elk said, "The winter is coming."

The boy said, "That is the way it is."

Blue Elk said, "The old days are gone."

"The short white days come," the boy said firmly.

"That is true. I have seen many short white days. Our people have known the white days—" and he made the sign for no end, forever— "Your mother told you this. I tell you the old days are gone. There is an end to the old days."

The boy shook his head. "How can there be an end?" he asked. "There is the roundness." He made the gesture for the circle, the no-end.

Blue Elk said, "There is the roundness. But today is gone. The day before today is gone."

The boy made the no-end sign again. "It is like the sun, and the darkness. It is like the trunk of the aspen. It is like the basket," and his finger made the circle, the coil of the basket.

Blue Elk stared at the fire. Finally he said, "We know these things. You know. I know." He glanced at the boy, whose face was intent. "Some of our people do not know. They have forgotten."

The boy made no answer.

Blue Elk said, "There is a song for remembering. Do you know that song?"

"I know that song." The boy began to sing it. His voice was young, but the song was old, old as his people. He sang it, and it was a part of him.

He finished that song, and Blue Elk said, after a moment, "You are going with me to sing that song for remembering to those who have forgotten. We will go tomorrow, to our people down at Ignacio. You will tell them these things, and they will tell you what they know."

The boy sat silent for a time. Then he said, "You will go and tell them. I will stay here."

"I said I would be a grandfather to you. We will go together."

"I will stay here."

"They should hear these songs." Blue Elk believed this as he said it. *It is good for a people to change but it is not good for them to forget.* He said this to himself, believing it, but he did not say this aloud. Then he remembered the agent, who might give him five dollars if he brought the boy to Ignacio. It had been a long journey here to the lodge. It was worth more than the five dollars the preacher had given him. Then he remembered that the preacher had said he felt responsible for the boy because he had baptized him. He told himself he must do this thing. He said, "Tomorrow we will go to Ignacio."

The boy put a robe on the floor of the lodge. He made the sign that Blue Elk should have the bed. He said, "Tomorrow I will talk of this. Now I shall sleep." He lay down on the robe and drew it around him, and the bear cub lay down close beside him.

Blue Elk went to the bed and lay down and drew the red blanket over him. Sleep was not long in coming. He was weary from the journey and from the long talk with the boy. He had dreams of his grandmother's lodge. He went back to the old days in his sleep, and he sang those songs the boy had sung.

The boy wakened him the next morning and they went together down to the pool at the stream. The boy took off his moccasins and his clout and bathed himself in the pool, and when he asked why Blue Elk did not bathe, Blue Elk said, "I am an old man."

The boy said, "If you are a grandfather and truly one of the people, you will bathe and sing the song to the sun and the morning."

Blue Elk stripped and went into the pool. It was so cold it numbed his legs and took all the breath out of him. Then he bathed in that water and he was warm inside as he had not been warm in a long time. He gasped for breath and every part of him shrank at the icy coldness, but the warmth inside was good to know. He remembered this from the time when he was a boy.

When they had bathed, they sat on the big rock at the

head of the pool and faced the sun rising over the far mountain. The boy sang the song to the sun and the morning, and Blue Elk's tongue remembered. He, too, sang that song.

When they had finished, Blue Elk said, "It is good to sing this song."' Then, remembering why he had come, he added, "Our people should not forget this song."

"It is a good song," the boy said, and he sang another song, to the mountains when they are cool with morning and wet with dew.

"That song," Blue Elk asked; "it is your song?"

"That is my song. I made that song."

"You are a good singer. You make good songs," Blue Elk said. And he urged, "You should not keep these songs to yourself. Our people should hear them."

The boy did not answer. He put on his clout and Blue Elk put on his clothes and they returned to the lodge. They ate, Blue Elk silent, the boy thinking. He put away the food. He put away the robe on which he had slept. He asked, "How long is it to Ignacio?" and Blue Elk said, "Less than three days' journey. It is not long."

Still thinking, considering, the boy put away the robes and folded the blanket on the bed where Blue Elk had slept. Then he went to the door and called the jay. When it came and sat on his shoulder he whispered a question and it pecked his ear. He called the squirrels and they came and one sat in his hand. He held it close to his face and asked the question, and it seemed to answer.

Blue Elk was looking around the lodge with appraising eyes, at the robes, the blanket, the food baskets, all the things worth silver dollars. Now that he had found the lodge, he could return. Even if the agent did not pay him five dollars, as the preacher had said he might, Blue Elk could be well paid for the journey. Then he put that thought away and told himself that winter is long and cold and hungry. This boy should not be here alone in the winter. That was why he had come, he told himself, to see that the boy was not cold and hungry and alone. *I came for the boy's good,* he told himself, *for the good of my people.*

The boy turned from the doorway, his decision made. "I will sing the songs and tell the stories," he said, and he put on leggings to protect his legs in the brush. The bear cub came and licked his hand and whined, and he said, "The jay and the squirrels will stay here and watch for strangers till I return, but you will go with me, Brother." Then he turned to Blue Elk and said, "Come. We will go with you to Ignacio."

That is how it happened.

# 11. The School

## 13

Like all horses, Blue Elk's pony was afraid of bears. He had to send the boy and the cub ahead and walk and lead the pony that first morning. The next day was easier until they approached Piedra Town and Blue Elk realized that the bear would create an uproar and possibly shooting in the town. So he went around the town, through the rugged hills, and reached the road to Bayfield. They traveled that road until they met a horseman who fired several shots at the bear from his revolver. But his horse was dancing all over the road and the shots were wild, and before the man could hit the bear the horse bolted with him.

Blue Elk led the way into the hills again, and on the third day they came to the road south from Bayfield to the agency on the reservation. Few people were on that road, so they followed it. The Utes, even reservation Utes, respected bears. They would shrug off such unexpected things as the sight of a boy in a clout with a bear cub at his heels.

But when they came in sight of the agency Blue Elk wondered why he had done things this way. He wished he could do things over again and be rid of the bear, which made everything hard to manage. But things were as they were. They could not be changed now.

He said, "The bear must stay with you until I tell these people about him. Our people will not make trouble, but the others do not understand these things."

The boy did not understand either, but he nodded.

There were many buildings at the agency, the headquarters and the school and the dormitory and the barns and stables and the pens and corrals. A flagpole stood in front of the headquarters, with a red, white and blue flag at the top. The boy watched the flag, wondering what it meant. Then he looked at the people hurrying from one building to another. Besides the men, who were all dressed in white man's clothes, there were boys and girls, Indians but also wearing white man's clothing. There were more boys and girls than he had ever seen. Only the girls wore their hair in braids, which was a strange thing to see.

Blue Elk said, "We are going to talk to the agent, the head man. He will ask questions and you must not make lies to him. He will want to hear what you have to say, but first you must do as he says. Do you understand what I say?"

The boy understood Blue Elk's words, but he did not know what Blue Elk meant by those words. He said to the bear, "We will talk to the head man in this big lodge."

Blue Elk said, "If the bear makes trouble, the head man will not listen to what you have to say."

The boy nodded and they went on.

Outside the headquarters were half a dozen Indians in blue pants and blue shirts and black shoes. They all had short hair. When they saw the boy and the bear with Blue Elk they talked among themselves, and when Blue Elk and the boy and the bear went up the sidewalk to the doorway the men there moved back and made plenty of room. They did not talk and they did not try to stop the bear.

They went inside and Blue Elk led the way to a white man seated behind a desk. The man looked up and said, "Hello, Blue Elk." Then he saw the boy and the bear. 'What's that bear doing here?" he demanded sharply.

"The bear belongs to the boy," Blue Elk said uneasily. "I have brought the boy to talk to the agent. He should be in school."

"Get that damned bear out of here!" the man ordered.

"Yes," Blue Elk said. "The bear should be put in a strong

pen. But you will have to do this." Then he added, "The boy does not understand your talk. He speaks only Ute."

The man said, "Tell him to stay right there with his bear," and he hurried away. He came back with a strong collar and a chain. He handed them to Blue Elk. "Put the collar on the bear." The bear was watching him, wrinkling its nose as though it did not like his smell. But it stood quietly, the boy's hand on its neck.

Blue Elk turned to the boy. "The man wants you to put this collar on the bear."

"My brother does not need this collar," the boy said.

"Put it on him. It is so he will not be hurt. These people do not understand bears. They are afraid of bears, and they cannot listen to you when they are afraid. Put it on him."

Reluctantly, the boy fastened the collar on the bear cub.

"Come on," the man from the desk said. "Bring the bear."

They followed the man outside. He led the way to the log pen where they kept wild horses while they were being broken. In the middle of the pen a strong post was set in the ground. Watching the bear and staying carefully away from him, the man took the end of the chain and fastened it to the post. "Now," he said, "I'll see if the agent wants to talk to you. Come on."

"Come," Blue Elk said to the boy. "The bear must stay here."

"I do not like this thing."

"Come. The head man cannot hear what you have to say unless the bear stays here."

"My brother will not like this thing."

"That is the way it must be. Come!"

The boy spoke into the bear's ear, then reluctantly went with Blue Elk. The man from the desk locked the gate and they went back into the headquarters building. "You were a fool to bring that bear here, Blue Elk," the man said sharply. "A cub that size can be dangerous. Don't you know that?"

"The boy would not come without him," Blue Elk said. "The preacher told me to bring him in. I did this the only way I could do it."

The man left them at the desk and went to a door down the hallway. After a few minutes he came out and motioned to them. Blue Elk led the way. They went into the office and the man at the desk there said, "Well, Blue Elk, what have you got up your sleeve this time?"

The agent was a red-faced man with patches of freckles on his face and hands. He had thin sand-colored hair and eyebrows and his eyes were so light blue they looked milky. He wore a dark gray suit with a closely buttoned vest, a white shirt and a blue necktie. His neck was fat; it bulged over his collar.

"I brought this boy," Blue Elk said. "The preacher in Pagosa said he should be in school."

The agent looked at the boy. He smiled, then frowned and said to Blue Elk, "Who is he? What is he doing running around in a clout? I understand you were stupid enough to bring a bear cub, too. But that's taken care of. Who is this boy?"

"His name is Thomas Black Bull. He was baptized with that name. He has been living by himself, off the reservation."

The agent looked at the boy again. "Is this true?" he asked. "Is Blue Elk telling the truth?"

The boy stared at him, bewildered, then looked at Blue Elk.

"He speaks only Ute," Blue Elk said.

"How does that happen? These kids pick up at least a smattering of English, no matter where they live."

"He has no English," Blue Elk said. "He has no father,no mother. They are dead. He has been living alone, in the old way."

"That doesn't make sense." The agent frowned again.

"Do you mean to tell me—" He broke off, then asked, "How old is he?"

Blue Elk shrugged. "Eleven years, maybe. I do not know."

"Go tell Fred to send Benny Grayback in. You wait outside, Blue Elk. I want to talk to this boy alone."

Blue Elk said to the boy, "This man wants to hear what you have to say. He says I should bring another person who speaks the tongue." And he left the office.

A few minutes later Benny Grayback came in. He was stocky like most of the Utes, perhaps thirty years old. He wore blue work pants and black shoes, like the Indians the boy had seen outside the building, but he had a white shirt and a blue necktie like the agent. His hair was short and parted on one side. Benny Grayback was a vocational instructor in charge of the carpenter shop.

The agent said, "Benny, I want to talk to this boy. Blue Elk says he speaks no English. Is that true?"

Benny asked the question. The boy answered, and Benny said, "That is true. He knows only Ute."

The agent asked questions, then, and the boy gave answers, and Benny Grayback translated.

"What is your name?"

"My name is Bear's Brother."

"Blue Elk says your name is Thomas Black Bull."

"I do not know that name."

"Who is your father?"

"My father is dead."

"Who is your mother?"

"My mother is dead."

"Where do you live?"

"I live in my lodge."

"Who lives with you in your lodge?"

The boy answered at some length. When he had finished, Benny Grayback said, "He says he lives with his brother. He says his brother is a bear. He says his friends, a jay and the squirrels and chipmunks, also live with him." Benny smiled. "No other person lives with him, he says."

"How long has he lived alone?"

"He says he has lived alone since his mother died. He says she died the winter before last. I think he must be wrong, but that is what he says."

"Tell him he will live here now, with the other boys and girls. He will go to school here and learn the things he should know."

"He says he did not come here to live. He does not understand school. He says he came to tell us of the old ways." Benny smiled at the agent again. "Blue Elk told him we would want to know these things and he should come and tell us. That is what he says."

The agent nodded. "Sounds like Blue Elk. Tell him we will want to hear what he has to say about the old ways at a proper time. First he must learn the new ways."

"He says he will go back to his own lodge until you want to listen to him."

The agent sighed, shook his head. "He must stay here for a while. Put it that way, Benny. Tell him I say he must live here for now. He cannot go back to his lodge."

George said this. The boy did not answer.

The agent asked, "Do you remember a George Black Bull, Benny? Some years back. He got a permit to go to Pagosa and work in the sawmill. I think that was the name. He got into a scrape, killed another man. Self-defense, if I remember right, but he got scared and ran away and hid back in the hills. Remember?"

Benny shook his head. "It must have been while I was in school at Fort Lewis. I do not remember."

"He had a woman and, as I remember, he had a small son. When he ran away he took them with him. Blue Elk says this boy's baptismal name is Thomas Black Bull, so he is probably

George Black Bull's son. Tell him his name from now on is Thomas Black Bull."

Benny told the boy, who shook his head. "He says he already has his name, Bear's Brother."

"He will be Thomas Black Bull here. Go get him some clothes, Benny, then check with Fred. I'll have him assigned to a room. And look after him a few days, get him started. He looks like a bright boy who can learn if he wants to. And Benny, don't let him turn that bear cub loose, no matter what happens. I'll hold you responsible." The agent turned back to the papers on his desk, then said, "Send Blue Elk in again."

Benny Grayback spoke to the boy and they left. A moment later Blue Elk came in, all smiles and expectancy.

"This boy," the agent said, "is George Black Bull's son. Is that right?"

"That is right."

"Who told you to bring him in?"

"The preacher in Pagosa. He said you would want him to be in school. He said you would pay me for the trip. It was a hard trip and I am an old man."

"I haven't any funds for that kind of thing. If you had come and told me, I would have sent my own men after him." He looked at Blue Elk and shook his head. "You would sell your own grandmother, wouldn't you, Blue Elk?"

"My grandmother," Blue Elk said, "is dead."

"I'll tell you what I'll do." There was an ironic smile in the agent's eyes. "I'll give you the bear for bringing the boy in."

Blue Elk shifted uneasily from one foot to the other. "It is the boy's bear. I do not want this bear."

"You could take it to the Bear Dance next spring."

"No," Blue Elk said. "I did not ask for this bear. I did not ask—"

"Very well." The agent cut him off. He turned back to his

desk. Blue Elk waited. "If I need you," the agent dismissed him, "I'll send for you."

Blue Elk went out, hurt and angry. The boy had caused all this trouble by bringing the bear with him. But as he left the building and went to his pony at the hitch rack he knew what he would do. He would go to Johnny No Good's house down near Tiffany. It was almost eleven miles, but he had got Johnny No Good off when he was charged with stealing a goat last spring. Johnny No Good would feed him and give him a bed, and tomorrow he would borrow Johnny No Good's pack horse and go back to the hidden lodge on Bald Mountain. If the agent would not pay him for his journey, there were other ways.

He rode past the horse-breaking pen. The bear cub was pacing back and forth, still chained to the snubbing post, grumbling to itself and biting at the chain. Maybe, Blue Elk said to himself, it was better that the bear was here, chained up here, not loose on Bald Mountain, guarding the lodge.

## 14

They put him in a room with Luther Spotted Dog. Luther was fourteen, had been at the school several years and tried to walk and talk and look like Benny Grayback. He helped Thomas Black Bull put on the stiff new agency pants and shirt and told him to put on the heavy black shoes. Thomas put one on his foot, then threw them both aside and put on his moccasins again. Luther urged him to lie down on the cot, see how soft it was. Thomas felt of it, then tore the bed apart and arranged the blankets in a pallet on the floor. Luther shrugged, said, "I will tell you about the things you must learn," and began to praise the school, the teachers, the classes. Thomas went over and stood at the window, ignoring him.

When the supper bell rang, Luther said, "Now we go and eat." They went downstairs to the dining room. Thomas made a face at the cooking smells, looked at the boys and girls marching in and taking their places at the tables, and sat down beside Luther, not liking any of this. A plate of food was brought to him. He smelled of it, picked up a piece of meat in his fingers and tasted it, then spat it out. Luther asked what was wrong, and he said, "It stinks," and got up and left the table and went out of the room.

Benny Grayback had been watching him. He followed Thomas outside and across the grounds to the horse-breaking pen. He caught up with him at the gate and asked, "Where are you going?"

Thomas didn't answer. He opened the gate and the bear cub ran toward him, was snubbed by the chain and jerked from its feet. Benny caught the boy by the shoulder before he could run to the bear, which was bawling and snapping at the chain.

The boy struggled to get away. "I am going back to my lodge!" he shouted.

"No," Benny said. "You are staying here." He pinioned the boy's arms.

"I shall take my brother and go!" The boy bit Benny's hand. Benny slapped him, shook him, then closed the gate and tried to haul him back toward the dormitories.

"You are an evil person!" the boy cried, and tried again to wrench free. "I hate you! My brother hates you!"

But Benny twisted his arms behind him and forced him into submission. They went back to the dormitory and up to the room. Benny made him sit down and he talked to him, told him he must stay here, go to classes, learn to live the new way. He talked, and the boy sat in defiant silence, and finally Luther Spotted Dog came upstairs from supper. Benny said, "Thomas is to stay here, in this room, until breakfast time tomorrow. Do you understand? I will hold you responsible for him."

Luther looked at Thomas, dubious, but he said, "Yes."

Then Benny left the room and went to find Neil Swanson, the square-faced Dane who was in charge of the stables and the livestock. "I want to secure the bear," Benny told Neil, "so nobody can let it loose unless I say so."

"We will lock him up," Neil said, and he found two padlocks. Then he took a rope and they went to the breaking pen. Neil lassoed the bear, choked it into submission, and they padlocked the chain around its neck and to the snubbing post. Benny pocketed the keys to the padlocks.

The next morning when they came down to breakfast Luther Spotted Dog had three long scratches down his face and a bruise that almost closed his right eye. Thomas walked with a limp and his wrists were raw. Benny went to the table where they sat and said to Luther, in English, "You had a hard time last night."

"It was a bad night," Luther said. "He would have killed me. I had to tie him up. I did not sleep."

"Bring him to my class after breakfast," Benny ordered.

The food came. Thomas smelled the sausage and pancakes and pushed the plate aside. He started to leave the table, but Luther caught him by the arm and forced him back into his chair, and he sat in angry silence till the meal was over. Then Luther took him to the carpenter shop.

There were fifteen boys in the class. Benny introduced Thomas Black Bull to them and Thomas stared at them coldly. The class began and Thomas went to a window and stood with his back to the room. Two boys whispered, in Ute, about his braids. One of them took two long shavings and hung them behind his ears. All the boys laughed except Luther Spotted Dog. Benny told them to be quiet. Then someone whined like a bear, and they laughed again. A boy near Thomas said, in falsetto, "My name is Bear Meat," and without a word Thomas turned on him, picked up a wooden mallet from the nearest bench and flung it. The boy dodged and the mallet clattered the length of the room.

"Stop it!" Benny ordered. "All of you! Get back to work." He took Thomas by the arm and led him back to his desk in the corner of the room. "Why did you do that?" he demanded in Ute.

Thomas did not answer.

"These boys want to be your friends. Don't you know that? Don't you want to have friends?"

"I have no friends here."

"That is no way to make friends, by trying to hurt them."

But it was no use. Benny kept him beside his desk until the class ended. Then he took him to Rowena Ellis.

Rowena Ellis taught English and was in charge of the

girls' dormitory. Unmarried, in her forties, a slightly plump woman who wore her graying hair in braids around her head, she was unofficial mother to every shy, homesick boy and girl in the school. She had taught in reservation schools almost twenty years and spoke several Indian tongues, including Ute.

She told Benny the agent had spoken to her about this boy, then dismissed him with a gesture. To the boy she said, in the tongue, "We should know each other. There are many new things here. This place is full of strangeness. I will tell you about it."

Her Ute was not precise, but he understood what she said. "I came here," he told her, "to tell of the old ways of my people."

"I want to hear of the old ways,"" she said. "But first I will tell you of the new ways." She started to tell him why he must go to school, but he cut her off.

"I do not need these things," he said.

She smiled. She was a patient woman. Then her next class filed into the room. It was a mixed class of boys and girls. Two of the boys had been in the carpentry class. When all had taken their seats Miss Ellis said, "We have a new boy, Thomas Black Bull. He has had a very interesting life and soon he will tell us about it. But first we are going to teach him more English. We will start today, with a review lesson, an oral drill."

Two of the boys groaned and several girls giggled. Miss Ellis turned to a simple lesson, saying first a Ute word, then calling on someone in the class for the English word. The class was restless. They had been through this long before. The boys began to whisper. Miss Ellis silenced them, and the girls giggled again. But she kept them at the vocabulary drill for half the period before she told them to open their readers and called on them, in turn, to read aloud.

Thomas Black Bull, bored by it all, went to a window and

stood with his back to the room until the class was over. Then Miss Ellis went to him and said, "You see, it is not so hard to learn new things. You learned something today. I know this."

"I do not need these things," Thomas said.

"Your mother would tell you to learn these things."

"My mother—" and he made the cut-off sign.

"Tell me about your mother, Thomas."

"You would not understand."

"Who else do you have?"

"I have my brother."

"Tell me about your brother."

He turned away from her and left the classroom.

Benny Grayback was waiting outside the door. The boy pushed past him and hurried down the hallway and outside. Benny followed. He went to the breaking pen, opened the gate and ran to the bear. He talked and the bear whined, and he tried to loosen the chain. He found the padlocks, examined them, then tore at them angrily with his fingers. At last he gave up and stood silent while the bear licked his hands. Then he went slowly, deliberately, to Benny Grayback, who was waiting at the gate. He stopped in front of Benny and said, "I will do these things you tell me to do if you will let my brother loose."

"I am glad to hear this," Benny said. "But we cannot have this bear running loose and hurting people."

"He will not hurt people. He will live with me, where I live."

"Luther Spotted Dog would not be happy with a bear living in his room."

"Luther Spotted Dog can live in another place."

"Come. It is time to eat. We will talk of this later."

So Thomas Black Bull went with Benny to the dining room and Benny put Thomas beside him at his own table. Hungry, Thomas ate two portions of meat, nothing else.

When the meal was over, he said to Benny, "Now we will talk about my brother."

"Tomorrow we will talk," Benny said. "I am busy this afternoon."

"I will go to the place where I live," Thomas said, "until you will talk."

"To your room?"

"Yes. Then we will talk about this thing."

"If you will go to your room and stay there until I come, we will talk."

So Thomas went to the room he shared with Luther Spotted Dog.

Luther did not return to the room until late afternoon, after his last class. He opened the door and saw all his belongings piled in one corner. Thomas was standing at the window. He turned and said to Luther, "Take your things and get out of here."

"No," Luther said. "This is my room."

Without another word, Thomas attacked him, drove him from the room and threw his belongings into the hall. Then he closed the door. Luther hurried away and found Benny Grayback.

They came back and together they forced open the door. "What does this mean?" Benny demanded of Thomas.

"He does not live here any more," Thomas said, pointing at Luther. "Now there is room here for my brother."

"But you can't do this!" Benny exclaimed.

"It is done."

Benny took him by the arm. "Come with me. There is another room where you are going to live."

"First we will talk."

"We will go to this other room. Then we will talk."

He took Thomas downstairs and along the hall to a room so small there was space for only a cot and a washstand. It had one small window, with bars on the outside, and it had a heavy door with a lock. They went in, and Thomas said, "My brother will not like this place."

"We will not talk about the bear today," Benny said firmly.

"Then I will not stay here."

Benny went out and closed the door and locked it. The boy beat on the door with his fists, then began to chant. It was a sorrow song, a song that Benny had never heard because it was the boy's own song. Benny did not want to listen but he heard, and although he wanted to go away he stayed there. Without knowing, he began to hum the chant, then to say its words softly, and to sway with its rhythms. It was a song from far back, not only in the boy but in Benny's own people. Its rhythm was his own heartbeat.

Then he heard his own humming, his own words, and he forced himself to stop. This, he told himself, was nonsense. It was of the old ways, and the old ways were gone. He hurried away.

Benny was still troubled after supper. He went to see the agent. The agent was annoyed. He had enough problems to settle during the day. His evenings should be his own. But he listened as Benny told him what had happened.

Finally the agent said, "Just as I was afraid, this whole thing came about because of that bear cub. We'll have to get rid of it."

"That is not easy," Benny said. "Nobody can touch the bear except the boy."

The agent smiled. "Nobody has to touch it to shoot it."

Benny Grayback gasped. "No!" he exclaimed. "You cannot kill the bear!" Then he clapped his hand over his mouth.

The agent frowned. He had worked with these people, lived with them, tried to understand them, for twenty-five years, and there still were things in them that he could not fathom. Emotions and superstitions that he couldn't reach, somehow, even in one like Benny Grayback, who was civilized and educated.

"I know the feeling about bears," he said, weighing his words. "But when one is a troublemaker you kill it, don't you?"

Benny nodded. "When ones makes trouble."

"This one is making plenty of trouble, isn't it?"

Benny hesitated. "There is trouble, yes."

"Because of the bear."

"I do not know this," Benny said, falling into the old speech pattern even though he spoke English.

"What don't you know?"

Benny did not answer the question. "If you kill the bear," he said, "then you will kill the boy."

"What makes you think that, Benny?"

"My grandmother—" Benny glanced at the agent and broke off. The boy's sorrow chant had beaten at him again. He shrugged it away, shrugged away his grandmother and all the old people, the old ways. "I know it," he said. "That is all."

The agent sighed. "Very well, Benny. Do the best you can with the boy for another day or two. I've got an idea that old Blue Elk can help us solve this. I'll get in touch with him tomorrow."

## 15

Blue Elk did not arrive until the third day later. He came in late afternoon and hitched his pony at the rack and went into the agency headquarters and said to Fred, at the desk, "The agent sent for me. I am here." Fred went and told the agent, who said to send him right in.

"Where have you been?" the agent asked. "I sent for you three days ago."

Blue Elk shrugged. He looked more smug than the agent had seen him in weeks. "I have been busy," he said.

"We have to get rid of this bear you brought in with the boy, Thomas Black Bull."

Blue Elk's eyes narrowed. He made no answer.

"I want you to take the bear back to the mountains."

Blue Elk shook his head. "I cannot do this."

"Why not?"

Blue Elk smiled. "It is not my bear. It does not know me."

The agent smiled grimly. "The boy will take the bear. You will go along and bring the boy back. The bear is to stay in the mountains."

Blue Elk pondered, worrying something in his mind. "This is not an easy thing to do. No, I cannot do this."

"Why not? I know it will not be easy, but that is why I sent for you."

"I am an old man. It will take time."

The agent knew Blue Elk was not giving the real reason. He never did. "You are always glad to give your time for your people. You will do this for the boy."

"I cannot take the bear back to Bald Mountain."

"You don't have to take it that far. Horse Mountain will be far enough. The other side of Horse Mountain."

Blue Elk seemed to relax somewhat. "That is a long journey."

"Five days, no more than that. All you have to do is take them out in the mountains, get rid of the bear, and bring the boy back here. I'll pay you ten dollars, silver. That's two dollars a day."

Blue Elk shook his head. "Fifteen dollars."

"Ten."

"Twelve dollars."

"Ten."

Blue Elk sighed. "I have no money. I need this money now."

"When the job is done. When you bring the boy back."

"I do not like this job," Blue Elk said. Then, "You will give me food for the journey."

"I will give you supper tonight and enough food for the trip."

The deal was made. Blue Elk ate supper in the dining room, a double portion, and, when he had finished, Benny Grayback gave him the keys to the padlocks on the bear's chain and took him to the little room to talk to the boy.

Blue Elk sat down on the cot and said to the boy, "I have come to take you back to the mountains where you came from."

"I will not go without my brother," the boy said.

"Your brother will go with us. He is going to stay in the mountains."

"I do not need you to take us back. I can find the way."

"The agent said I should go with you."

"Why?"

"Because I brought you here." Blue Elk knew that was a mistake as soon as he said it, but it was said.

"Your mouth," the boy said bitterly, "is like Benny Grayback's mouth. It is full of lies."

"I talk straight, Thomas Black Bull."

"I am Bear's Brother. I do not know this other name you speak." And the boy began to chant his sorrow song.

"Be quiet," Blue Elk ordered. But the boy went on chanting. Then he chanted the old songs, and before long Blue Elk was swaying to the rhythm of the chants. The boy chanted for an hour, and Blue Elk was humming and saying words that he remembered.

Dusk came, and darkness. The boy became hoarse from the chanting, and Blue Elk forced the old memories away from him.

"Stop this," he ordered. And after a little time the boy's hoarse voice died away. Blue Elk tried to talk to him about the school, and the boy began chanting again. And again he was so hoarse he had to stop. And Blue Elk talked about the new ways. Then the boy was chanting again.

They talked and chanted through most of the night. Then, at last, Blue Elk fell asleep, there on the cot. When the boy heard him snoring he tried to take the keys to the door and the padlocks out of Blue Elk's pockets. But Blue Elk roused, and the boy did not get the keys. Then the dawn began to come, and the boy chanted a sorrow song again because he could not find his song for this new day. When he had finished, Blue Elk yawned and said, "Now we will go." He unlocked the door and they went down the long, deserted hallway and outside into the coolness of morning.

They went to the horse-breaking pen and Blue Elk gave the boy the key to the padlock on the post. He kept the other key, the one to the padlock on the bear's neck. He would need that key later. The boy unfastened the chain from the post, and he and the bear came from the pen, the bear dragging the chain still locked around its neck, and they started up the road toward Bayfield. Blue Elk got on his pony and followed close behind them.

They traveled all that day, going back the way they had come when Blue Elk brought them to the agency. That night they made camp and ate from the food the agent had provided for the journey. When they had eaten, Blue Elk took the end of the bear's chain and padlocked it around a tree. Then he said, "Now we will sleep." The boy, he knew, would not go away without the bear.

They traveled all the next day, and again they slept with the bear chained to a tree. The third morning they came to the foot of Horse Mountain. Blue Elk said, "We will stop here and rest." He chained the bear to a tree. Then he said, "We are going to leave the bear here."

"I do not like this," the boy said. "My brother wants to go home, back to my lodge."

"The bear can go home," Blue Elk said. "Tell the bear he must go home."

"I will go home with him."

"No. You will come back with me."

Then the boy knew what they had done to him. Without a word, he came at Blue Elk, kicking, clawing, trying to knock him down and take the key to the padlock from him. But Blue Elk, old though he was, was still able to defend himself. The boy struck him in the face and made him grunt with blows in the belly, and he knocked off Blue Elk's derby hat and punched a hole in it. But in the end Blue Elk had him by the arms and dragged him over to his pony. He took a rope from the saddle and tied the boy's arms to his sides, then tied his ankles together. After that Blue Elk sat down to rest. When he had caught his breath he said, "Let us have no more trouble about this. The bear must go away. You must go back with me."

"No."

Blue Elk sat and waited. The bear—which had lunged at the chain, trying to get loose, while Blue Elk and the boy were struggling—quieted down. Finally Blue Elk said, "Tell the bear he must go away. Then I will let him loose."

"No."

Blue Elk waited again. Then he said, "If you do not tell

the bear to go away, we will go back and leave him chained to that tree. If that is the way you want it to be—" He shrugged.

The boy did not answer. And finally Blue Elk got to his feet. He went to the boy and loosened the rope around his ankles. "Come," he said. "We will go back now." He lifted the boy to his feet, took the end of the rope that still bound his arms, and led him to the pony. He tied the end of the rope to the saddle horn and got into the saddle. "Are you ready to go?" he asked.

The boy looked at the bear, and he looked at Blue Elk, and he said, "I will tell my brother to go home."

Blue Elk got off his pony and freed one of the boy's hands. He gave him the keys to both padlocks and they went back to where the bear was chained. Blue Elk still held the end of the rope.

The boy went to the bear. He said, "They have made me do this, brother. They have made me tell you to go away." And he unlocked the chain from the bear's neck. Suddenly he hugged the bear's head to him and buried his face in its neck fur. Then he stepped back away from it. "Go home," he ordered. "Go! Go!" And he turned away.

The bear stood for a moment, then took a step toward him. He turned and cried, "Go! Go before they put the chain on you again!" And the bear turned, uncertain, and walked away from him. The boy went to Blue Elk and said, "I wish you were dead for this thing you have done."

"Unlock the chain from the tree," Blue Elk ordered. And when the chain had been loosened from the tree Blue Elk and the boy went back to the pony. Blue Elk took the keys and put them in his pocket, and he looped the chain and fastened it on his saddle. He freed the boy's arms but kept the rope around his waist, and he got on his pony and they started back the way they had come.

That night he chained the boy to a tree, and late the next afternoon they returned to the agency. Blue Elk took the boy to Benny Grayback, who took him to the little room with bars at the window. The boy did not talk, and he walked as though he was in a daze.

Blue Elk was grim. He had a dark bruise under one eye and his hands were scarred and scratched. He walked with a limp. He didn't stop at Fred's desk. He went directly into the agent's office.

The agent looked up, annoyed, then said, "Well, Blue Elk! Back already? A little battered, but all in one piece. You got the job done?"

"It is done."

"You brought the boy back?"

"The boy is here."

"Fine. And the bear?"

"The bear is the other side of Horse Mountain."

"I can count on that, depend on it?"

"I do not tell lies."

"Not unless there's a dollar in it." The agent opened a drawer and counted out ten silver dollars.

"It was a hard trip." Blue Elk felt of the bruise under his eye.

The agent made no comment. He stacked the dollars on the desk in front of him. Blue Elk looked at the money, then took off his derby hat and pointed to the hole in it.

The agent smiled and slowly shook his head. "A new hat wasn't in the bargain, Blue Elk. But I'll tell you what I'll do. If you really took that bear all the way to Horse Mountain, it won't come back here, not for a while anyway. And maybe it will meet a ranchman or a hunter meanwhile. If that bear doesn't come back here in the next two weeks, I'll see you get a new hat. How's that?"

Blue Elk sighed. "Two weeks is a long time."

The agent pushed the silver dollars across the desk and Blue Elk picked them up, one at a time, and put them in his pocket. He put on his battered hat. Then he turned and left, a tired and bruised old man who somehow, the agent couldn't figure quite how, represented the pride and dignity of a whole race.

## 16

After the trip to Horse Mountain with Blue Elk, Thomas Black Bull seemed to accept the school and its routine. He ate the food served in the dining room, wore the clothes he had been issued, went to the classes to which he was assigned. After a few days he was moved out of the little room with bars. Benny Grayback wanted to put him in a double dormitory room, with another boy, but Rowena Ellis said, "He is an unusual boy, exceptionally reserved and self-sufficient. He doesn't need companionship. I think he will be happier and less of a problem if allowed to have a room to himself." The agent agreed with Miss Ellis, so Thomas was given a single room in the dormitory.

Two weeks later the agent asked for a report on him. His general conduct, it was agreed, was satisfactory. At least he wasn't starting trouble. But Benny Grayback said he thought it was time Thomas went to the barber. "His braids should be cut off," Benny said firmly.

The agent shook his head. "He will have them cut off eventually. The other kids will shame him into it. All boys want to be like the others. What is his attitude in class? That is much more important than his braids. Is he learning the things he should?"

Benny said, "No. Thomas has little interest in manual work. He is the slowest pupil in my classes."

The agent turned to Neil Swanson. Neil said, "He is worse than useless in the stables. Yesterday I set him to work cleaning the cow barn and, when I went back to see how he was doing, he threw a forkful of manure at me. He said that cows stink."

The agent smiled. "I wonder what he would have said if you had put him to work at the pigpens. Try him in the horse barns, Neil." He turned to Rowena Ellis. "How is he doing with you?"

"He is doing very well," Miss Ellis said. "I am sure he has learned far more than he lets on. From all of us," she added. "He never speaks unless spoken to, but he can make himself understood when he wants to. Thomas is an unhappy boy and hard to reach, but he learns fast."

So Thomas was taken out of Benny's carpentry class and assigned to the cobbler's shop. He did better there, not only because he had some knowledge of leather but because Ed Porter was in charge. Ed, a half-blood, was an easygoing man with none of Benny's zeal to cancel Thomas Black Bull's background and inheritance overnight. It was Ed Porter who noted the boy's unusual skill with his fingers and suggested that he might be a basketmaker. So Thomas was sent to the basketry class, where Ed's wife, Dolly Beaverfoot, a Paiute originally from Utah, was the instructor.

Dolly gave Thomas the conventional basket materials and started to show him how to make a simple meal basket. But he pushed the coarse reeds aside and said, "These are no good." He left the room, was gone half an hour, and came back with an armful of willow stems. Dolly smiled with pleasure and watched as he chose among the stems and began stripping the bark from them with his teeth, in the old way. When he had the material to suit him he began to weave a basket in a way that not even Dolly could match. It was, Dolly said, one of the best baskets she had ever seen, as good as those the old ones among her own people made.

Word spread about Thomas Black Bull's basket. The girls in the basketry class—Thomas was the only boy in the class—had whispered among themselves about how handsome he was in a rather sullen way, but now they came to his bench to admire his work and speak open words of praise. And the school's boys, of course, heard about this.

The boys had laughed at his braids, but never openly. Now the began talking about "the new girl" and saying, "She makes better baskets than the teacher," and "She is really Bear's Sister. That is her real name." Thomas heard these things, but he ignored them until one afternoon at the horse barn. He and Luther Spotted Dog and two other boys were cleaning the stalls, and one of the boys said to Luther, "She is the teacher's pet, you know."

Luther grinned. "But she still has to clean the barn."

Thomas tightened his lips and said nothing.

The boy who had spoken first said, "Was she nice to you, Luther, when she lived in your room?"

Luther grinned even more broadly. "No. She was a very poor squaw." And he pretended to trip on his pitchfork and threw a forkful of dirty straw at Thomas.

Thomas said, "Don't do that again."

One of the boys behind him threw another forkful at him, and Luther laughed and said, "Bear's Sister is getting mad at us!"

Thomas hit Luther in the face with his fist, and the fight was on. He knocked Luther down, and another boy leaped on his back. He caught the boy by the hair and threw him to the floor. Luther came at him again and he bloodied Luther's nose before the other boy got to his feet.

The fourth boy ran to find Neil Swanson. But before Neil got there Thomas had bloodied the noses of both his tormentors and backed them into a corner, where he was pounding their faces in turn.

Neil caught him by the arm, dragged him away, and ordered the other boys to their rooms. Then he demanded, "Why did you start this fight?"

Thomas faced him, silent and defiant.

"I won't have such goings-on in my barn! Why did you do it?"

Thomas still refused to answer.

"All right," Neil said, "I'll have to teach you a lesson." He took Thomas Black Bull to the harness room, got a strap and flogged him. Thomas took it tight-lipped and without a sound. When he had finished, Neil said, "Let this be a lesson to you. Do it again and you'll get another licking. Now go to your room."

Thomas went to the school building instead of the dormitory. He went to the basketry room, and before Dolly Beaverfoot could even ask what was the matter he took his partly finished basket and tore it to shreds. Then he went to the dormitory and to his room and locked the door.

Twenty minutes later Benny Grayback was at the door. "Thomas," he ordered, "unlock the door. I want to talk to you."

There was no answer.

Benny pounded on the door. He ordered, he pleaded. He got no answer at all.

A little later Rowena Ellis came to the door. She knocked and said, "Thomas, this is Miss Ellis. I want to talk to you, Thomas."

No answer.

"I want to know what happened. You have done something very bad, Thomas, but I am sure it was not all your fault. You can talk to me and tell me about it, can't you, Thomas?"

Still no answer.

She pounded on the door. "Thomas!" she shouted. "Open this door at once!"

But the door did not open and there was no sound from inside. She waited ten minutes, then said, "Thomas Black Bull, if you do not open this door at once I will not try to keep them from punishing you severely! Do you hear me, Thomas?"

Silence.

And finally she went away.

He stayed in his room all that night and all the next day. Benny Grayback came to the door again the next evening and ordered, then threatened. Rowena Ellis came again and pleaded, then threatened. He answered neither of them. And the agent said, "Leave him alone. He'll starve out in another day or two."

## 17

He didn't starve out. The next night he took off his shirt and pants, put on his clout, his leggings and his moccasins, took a blanket from his cot, and climbed out the window. He slid down a drain spout to the ground, forced his way into the kitchen and took a butcher knife, a ball of strong cord and the two-pound remnant of a pot roast. Then he started north, eating the meat as he traveled in the darkness.

It was October. The valley cottonwoods had shed their leather leaves and the aspens were in full gold. It was mild autumn on the lowlands of the reservation. But the nights were already frosty in the mountains and there were snow caps on the higher peaks.

He had no trouble finding the way. He had been over it before. And he lived in the old way, striking fire from a piece of flint with the butcher knife, killing spruce grouse with a club, snaring rabbits with the strong cord. He avoided the roads and the traveled trails, and the second day he went around Piedra Town and on up the valley.

He went to Horse Mountain, to the place where Blue Elk had forced him to send the bear away. He looked for bear sign and he sang the bear song. There was no sign, and there was no answer to his song. Then he went on, hurrying because the season was late. But he went to the foot of Granite Peak on the way, and again he searched for bear sign. The only sign he found was of one big grizzly, and he knew the cub would not be there. Not with Grandfather Bear marking the whole area as his territory. He saw the claw marks high on a dozen big pines.

He went on to Bald Mountain. He was going home, back

to his own lodge. Perhaps his brother, the cub, would be there. If not, it would return next spring, after hibernation. If he did not find his brother now, he would find him later. Now he must go to his lodge, get things in order, make ready for winter. It was late, but he must do what he could.

He went to Bald Mountain. He drank at the stream where he had drunk many times, washed in the pool where so many mornings he had sung the song to a new day. He started up the path his own moccasins had helped to make. It was no longer a clear path. The bushes already were beginning to overgrow it.

He watched for the jay, thought he saw it. He called to it, but it sat silent in a tall aspen, watching him, them screamed and flew away. He watched for the squirrels and the chipmunks, called to them. The chipmunks chattered at him and ran and hid among the rocks. The squirrels scurried up the pines, peered at him from the high branches, scolded at his intrusion.

He came to the last turn in the path, the place where he could see the lodge. He stopped and put a hand to his mouth to stop the cry of pain. There was no lodge. Where the lodge had been was a charred place, a circle of ashes. Not a post or a beam remained. Nothing.

He went to the charred circle and poked among the ashes. He found nothing there, not even a knife blade. And then he knew. It was no accident, no hidden coal that flared into hungry flame soon after he went away with Blue Elk that morning. Someone had come and taken everything, even the worn-down knife, even the battered cooking pot, and burned the lodge.

He stood among the ashes and whispered his sorrow chant, not even saying it aloud. For small griefs you shout, but for big griefs you whisper or say nothing. The big griefs must be borne alone, inside.

When he had finished he looked up the mountainside,

thinking of his father and his mother. He did not climb to the cave among the rocks, for his father and his mother were not there. They had gone on the long journey many days, many moons ago. He looked up the mountainside for a long time. Then he went back down the overgrown path to the stream and made his camp there. He killed a spruce grouse and made a fire and ate. And that afternoon he sang his bear song. He sang it as loudly as he could sing. There was no answer. At dusk he sang it again. There was no answer.

That night he thought of his footsteps in the path, which would be completely wiped out soon, when the snow came. He thought of the lodge, now a circle of leaching ashes. He thought of the jay that had sat silent when he called to it. He thought of the chipmunks that hid among the rocks and of the squirrels that fled and scolded. He thought of his brother, the bear.

It was as though he had never been here.

He was very tired. He put out his fire and slept.

The next morning the clouds hung low over the mountain and the valley was filled with mist as cold as sleet. He bathed at the pool, but he sang no song for a new day. He did not even whisper the sorrow song. There was no song in him. Only a numbness, a nothing.

He ate the rest of the grouse from the night before and he put out his fire and scattered the ashes, removed all trace of his presence there. Then he folded the blanket and drew it around his shoulders and started back down the valley. There were spits of snow in the mist and the dead leaves in the oak brush whispered of winter.

# 18

He met them at the foot of Horse Mountain. There were only two of them, Benny Grayback and an old man called Fish. Fish was known as a tracker because he sometimes found lost horses by following their footprints, especially after a rain when the ground was muddy. The agent had said the boy probably would go to Horse Mountain, so that is where they went to look for him.

They were just starting to circle Horse Mountain when the boy came down the valley and saw them. He stopped and waited, and they saw him, and Benny said, "There he is!" Fish said, "I have found him, as I said I would."

The boy came up to them and Benny said, "We came after you, Thomas Black Bull, to take you back to the reservation."

Thomas shrugged. "I will go back," he said, in English.

They had a pack horse. Benny told Fish to divide the pack, put part of it on their saddle horses, so the boy could ride on the pack horse. "I should make you walk," he said to Thomas, "but you would walk slow and I am in a hurry to get back. Shall I tie you on the horse, or will you promise not to try to run away?"

"I will go back," the boy said again.

Fish helped him up onto the pack horse and they went back down the valley. To Piedra Town, and the agency, and the school. They were two days going back, and the boy did not try once to run away.

The next day after he returned to the school, Thomas Black Bull went to the barber and had his braids cut off. The next morning he put on his shoes instead of his moccasins. And not once after he returned did he speak Ute. He spoke to no one except when he was spoken to, but when he did speak it was in English. Within a month Miss Ellis told him that if he kept on as well as he was doing he would speak English as well as any boy in the school by next spring.

Because of the trouble over the basket, they did not send him back to Dolly Beaverfoot's class. Instead, Ed Porter took him back into the cobbler's shop, but now that he knew about the boy's skill with his fingers he gave him rawhide and horsehair and started him plaiting quirts and fancy bridles. As he had expected, the boy was almost as skillful at this as he had been at basketry. He even made up his own designs for the horsehair work.

He still made no friends, however. Several of the girls admired him and would have liked to be friends, but he was, as they said, "always somewhere else." He seemed unaware of their existence. The boys who had taunted him now left him alone. They knew what a beating he had given Luther Spotted Dog and that other boy in the horse barn. Besides, he often carried one of the rawhide quirts he made in the leather shop.

So the winter passed, and when he got the periodic reports about Thomas the agent said, "That boy has settled down. We'll make a farmer out of him yet. Or something."

The winter passed and late March came. There were catkins on the willows and tassels on the aspens. Spring was coming to the lowlands and the snow was beginning to melt in the mountain valleys. Bears would soon be coming out of hibernation. It was the time for the Bear Dance, the traditional ceremony at which the Utes used to gather and dance and visit after the winter's isolation. In the old days it was a time for courtship among the young folk as well as for singing the old songs to the bears. But now only the old people remembered the Bear Dance in late March. It interrupted spring work on the farms, so the agency people had persuaded the young folk to change the old ways and wait for May, after the corn was planted, to hold the Bear Dance.

Thomas Black Bull, seeing the tassels on the aspens and the spears of new grass and the change in the days, sunrise to sunset, knew what time it was in the year. He knew the bears would soon be leaving their winter dens, to travel, to claim their old ranges, to challenge intruders and fight their fearful battles among themselves. He felt these things in his blood.

Then a moonlit night came and he sat in his room and knew what was going to happen. He hoped it would happen, and he wished it would not happen. He waited, and the cattle bawled in their pens. The horses snorted and raced about their corrals. He opened his window, and in the moonlight he saw the bear beside the horse-breaking pen. It stood there nosing the air, then shuffled its feet like a great shaggy dog and nosed the air again. It whined softly.

Other windows opened. Someone shouted an alarm.

Thomas picked up a heavy quirt and hurried from his room. He went down the hallway, down the stairs and out into the moonlight. He ran toward the corral, and he began singing the bear song.

The bear came to meet him.

He stopped singing and shouted warning words, then angry words. The bear stopped and growled, then came on, whining again. The boy screamed at the bear in Ute. It stopped again and the boy went up to it, swished the quirt in its face and shouted, "Go away! Go back home, to the mountains!"

The bear rose on its hind legs and spread its forepaws as though to tear the boy to pieces. Its teeth were white in the moonlight. It was a two-year-old now and stood taller than the boy. The boy lashed it across the face with the quirt, again and again, screaming, "Go! Go! Go!"

The bear dropped to all fours, whimpering. It nosed the boy's hands, and it cried like a child. And the boy dropped the quirt, put an arm around its neck, buried his face in its fur and wept. He wept until the bear drew away and licked his face and whimpered and licked his face again.

The boy backed away. "I do not know you!" he cried. "You are no longer my brother. I have no brother! I have no friends!" Then he said, "I had a brother. But when I went to find him and sang my song to my brother he would not listen. Now there is nobody."

He stood silent in the moonlight, his head bowed, and the bear swayed from side to side, from foot to foot, moaning.

"Go away," the boy said. "Go, or they will kill you. They do not need guns to kill. They kill without guns. Listen! I speak truth. They will kill you. Go away!"

The bear still stood swaying, moaning.

He put a hand in the fur on the bear's neck and he said, "Come. I will go a little way with you." And they slowly walked away from the horse-breaking pen, the boy and the bear in the moonlight. They walked across the grounds toward the aspens with catkins like chipmunk tails. They walked among the trees and into the shadows, and after a little while there was the sound of the sorrow song. It was a song so desolate that the coyotes answered it from the gullies beyond. But the coyote cries were not so full of wailing as that song. The coyotes have brothers.

After another little while the boy came back out of the shadows of the trees, walking alone. He walked with the weariness of one who sings the going-away song for the only other person in the world. But he sang no song.

Men and boys were standing beside the doorway, but he seemed not to see them. They stepped aside, made way for him, and later they said it was like seeing a strange man, a remote and terrible man, not a boy.

He walked past them and along the hallway and upstairs to his room.

The next day he went to his classes as though nothing had happened, but those who looked into his eyes saw something there that made them afraid to talk to him. Nobody spoke of what had happened in the moonlight.

## 19

The agent said they would make a farmer out of him yet, and that spring they tried. He learned, readily enough, to harness a team of work horses, and he learned how to hitch the team to a plow. They showed him how to hold the plow handles and turn a furrow. Then they took him to a field that was soon to be planted with corn and set him to work. They hoped to make a plowboy of him.

But plowing seemed stupid to him. Why should anyone rip up the grass, even if it was sparse grass, and make the earth grow something else? If left to itself, the earth would grow grass and many other good things. When you plowed up the grass you were making the earth into something it did not want to be.

And plowing one furrow after another, side by side, was like walking in a room if you walked only on one board, then on the next, and the next, and the next. You went nowhere. The world was a big place. Why should you stay in one little field and make all your footsteps side by side?

The horses knew what to do. They followed each furrow to the end, then turned and followed the next furrow back again, and all he had to do was to hold the plow handles and keep the plowshare in the ground at an even depth. But he kept thinking of how senseless it all was and he let the plowshare drift up and down and make a deep furrow here, a shallow furrow there, no furrow at all in many places.

Neil Swanson came and looked. "Maybe you could do a worse job if you tried," he said, "but I doubt it." He took the team and showed Thomas Black Bull how to hold the plow handles steady and turn a clean, uniform furrow. He plowed to the end of the field and back, Thomas walking beside him. "Nothing to it," Neil said. "Now you do it." And while Neil watched, Thomas turned a perfect furrow. Neil said, "That's it. All you have to do is keep a steady hand and pay attention." He went back to the barns, and Thomas plowed just as he had before, deep and shallow and no furrow at all.

After two weeks Neil said, "We can't plant corn in a field like that." He brought another boy and set him to plowing the field all over again, and he took Thomas back to the cow barn. "Since you won't learn to plow," he said, "you'll have to clean the cow barn and learn to milk."

Thomas knew this was punishment for not becoming a good plowboy. But punishment no longer mattered. The smell of the cow barn nauseated him, but he cleaned it. The smell of warm milk made him feel sick, but he learned to milk a cow. He had to work in the cow barn only a few hours a day, morning and evening. And in a few more weeks most of his classes ended for the summer and he became a herd boy. After the morning milking and the barn cleaning he took the cows to pasture on the grass two miles from the barns. He stayed with the cows, seeing that they did not wander too far, until late afternoon. Then he brought them back and helped with the evening milking.

For a herd horse he had a stringhalted old nag with a saw-toothed backbone. He hated the horse and its limping gait, which kept his bottom raw, but he learned to ride after a fashion. And the long hours in the open, even though it was a land of sagebrush, cactus and scattered grass, were a relief from the cow barn. The open country smelled clean, even when the wind blew and the dust rose with its acrid alkaline smell. There was sunshine, there was sky, there was distance and a degree of freedom. He didn't mind being a herd boy.

Then it was June and the cornfields were green. The cows, with only sparse grass to eat, smelled the corn, and one afternoon when Thomas was watching a meadow lark's nest the whole herd broke through a fence and got into a field of corn. It was an hour before he could get them out again, and that night three of the cows were sick from eating green corn. Neil Swanson found out what had happened, and as punishment he kept Thomas at the barns all day and put another boy out as cowherd.

When he had been punished in this way for two weeks, Neil Swanson said, "You should have learned your lesson by now. We'll see if you can herd the horses." So, though he still had to help clean the cow barns and milk the cows morning and night, he was sent out for the day with the horse herd. The horses were pastured five miles from the barns and well away from the cornfields.

Half the horses in the herd were still unbroken and, after the first week or so, Thomas wondered what it would be like to ride an unbroken horse. So he took a rope with him when he took the horses out to their pastureland, and that afternoon he roped a two-year-old colt and got on its back and tried to ride it. He was thrown after the first two jumps. He caught the colt and tried again. He was thrown, as before, and that time he landed in a bed of cactus. He spent the rest of the afternoon pulling out cactus thorns. But the next day he caught another colt and tried to ride again. It was a tamer colt. He rode it for several minutes before it bucked him off.

For two weeks he tried to ride the colts in the herd, and he found that he could stay on three of the tamer ones. He began to learn how to ride. Then one afternoon, trying to get the rope on a particularly wild buckskin, he drove it into a dry creek bed and there in loose sand hock deep on the horse he looped the rope around its nose, got on its back and rode it to a standstill. He had discovered something—no horse can be a vicious bucker in deep sand. After that, when he wanted to ride a horse that was too wild to ride on hard ground he drove it into the creek bed and rode it there in the sand.

He learned that each horse has its own rhythm, not only in its walk and trot and lope, but in the way it bucks and pitches. He found that if he rode the horse with its own rhythm, and if he gripped with his knees and thighs and kept his sense of balance, he could ride every horse in the herd in the sand.

When he had ridden them all, he looped a rope around a horse's belly and made a kind of surcingle to which he could hold and help keep his balance. With the rope, he found that he could ride some of the unbroken horses out on the hard flats. He still was thrown from time to time, but he began to know a sense of mastery, something he hadn't known since the day he stood in front of the burned lodge on Bald Mountain and knew that everything that had ever mattered to him was gone.

One afternoon toward the end of August he was riding a particularly mean two-year-old pinto when Benny Grayback rode out to the grazing ground. He was so intent on riding the pinto that he rode it to a standstill before he knew that Benny was there, watching. He slid off the exhausted horse, removed the surcingle and nose rein, and waited for Benny to speak.

Benny glared at him and asked, "How long has this been going on?"

Thomas didn't know what to answer. He said, "I rode till he stopped bucking. I don't know how long."

"How long have you been riding the colts?"

Thomas shrugged.

"You are supposed to let them graze, not ride them and make them thin. Neil Swanson says the horses are all too thin. I came to find out why."

"The grass is poor," Thomas said.

"You give them no time to eat what grass there is," Benny said sharply.

"I was taming them to ride."

"When they are needed, they will be tamed," Benny said. "By those who know how to break horses."

Which was true. Each year the horses were broken to harness or the saddle, usually in the spring. They were driven into the breaking pen, roped, choked and water-starved until they could be saddled or harnessed. If they still had the strength to fight, they were beaten and choked again, until there was no fight in them. In the old days the people had respected their horses, tamed them. But the old days were gone. Now they broke the horses, broke their spirit.

"Come," Benny Grayback ordered. "Bring the horses."

Thomas Black Bull caught his listless herd horse and gathered the herd, and he and Benny took them back to the agency. Thomas penned them and Benny went to the barn and talked to Neil Swanson. Then Thomas went to the barn, and Neil shook his head and said, "You never learn, do you? If there are a hundred ways to do a thing right and one way to do it wrong, you always find that one wrong way." He shook his head. "Lickings do no good. Nothing does any good. Well, classes start next week. Then you'll be out of my hair till it's time to pick corn. Go on over to the cow barn and get to work."

And that was the end of Thomas Black Bull's horse herding.

Classes started again, and because he seemed useless at any other craft they sent him back to Ed Porter to plait rawhide and horsehair into quirts and riatas and bridles and reins. He still worked morning and evening in the cow barn, and when the corn was ripe he helped shuck corn.

Then it was winter, and when the winter began to thin away Neil Swanson said, "It's almost lambing season," and Benny Grayback said, "Albert Left Hand needs a helper." Neil said, "Why not? That boy isn't good for anything else. He might make a sheepherder." The agent said, "It's worth a try."

## 20

They took him to Albert Left Hand, who ran a little band of sheep on the sage flats at the northern edge of the reservation.

Albert Left Hand was a short, fat man who smelled of rancid mutton tallow. He had a rib-thin team of horses, a rickety wagon, a tent, and range rights. He seemed to eat nothing but prairie dog stew. His range was pock-marked with prairie dog towns and when he was not napping or sitting in sullen silence beside his tent he hunted prairie dogs with a single-shot .22 rifle. He had been without a helper for more than a month, so for the first few days he was grudgingly grateful to have a boy to tend the sheep.

He was a surly old man of few words, and those words usually were abusive. But for those first few days, hungry for company, he complained to Thomas Black Bull about his wife's death two years ago and about the way all eight of his children had grown up and left him. Then he relapsed into his usual silence except when he was berating Thomas for being lazy.

Despite Albert Left Hand, Thomas found a degree of peace and contentment. Spring was at hand, and even the arid sage flats soon came to life. Only a few of the flowers were old friends, from his life at Bald Mountain, but the desert plants were soon familiar. Ground plum came to purple flower, then bore fleshy, grapelike pods. Prairie onions sent up green shoots from their pungent bulbs and bloomed in white and rosy heads. Bird's-next cactus, prickly balls the size of his fist, put forth intricate starry purple blossoms. The white stars of sand lilies, the white spikes of larkspur, the snowy balls of sand verbena delighted his eye. In the evening there was the gold of pucker-petaled sundrops and the fragrant moon glow of golden primroses.

Meadow larks greeted the sunrise and cheered the evening. Horned larks spilled song all day in their spiraling flight. In the prairie dog towns grotesque burrowing owls tilted on their long, slim legs and hissed and screeched. Prairie falcons with wings like curved knives coursed the flats, hunting ground squirrels and young prairie dogs. Long-tailed magpies jeered among the cottonwoods in dry watercourses, and bull-bats boomed in the dusk and peeped plaintively as they winged the sky.

For a little time he sensed a kinship with all these. Then the ewes began to drop their lambs. Albert Left Hand stirred himself away from his tent and showed Thomas how to help a ewe struggling in the throes of birth, how to get a lamb on its feet and sucking at its mother's teats. For two weeks they worked together. They saved almost sixty of the seventy-odd lambs dropped. When a lamb failed to survive, Albert Left Hand skinned it, pegged out the pelt to dry. "Worth a quarter," he said.

Then the lambs were born and Albert Left Hand went back to hunting prairie dogs and sitting beside his tent. Thomas was busier than ever, for the lambs had even less sense than their foolish mothers. They strayed, they fell off cutbanks and into canyons, they thrust stupid noses at buzzing rattlesnakes. And, especially at dusk, the coyotes got one now and then.

June came, and they had saved forty-five lambs, which were growing swiftly. The ewes, recovered from their lambing, had begun to put on fat and show prime fleeces. Albert Left Hand had a pile of dry, stinking pelts, not only of the dead lambs but also of those ewes that had died in lambing or in the difficult weeks soon after.

Then it was July, and one morning Albert Left Hand said, "Come. Now we will take them to the shear pens."

He caught up his horses, patched his makeshift harness and hitched them to his paintless lumber wagon. He and Thomas loaded in the pelts, the tent, the dirty blankets from their beds, and Albert Left Hand got in and led the way across the flats. Thomas gathered the flock and herded them behind the wagon.

They went to the shearing pens near the agency. While Thomas penned the sheep, Albert Left Hand talked to the man in charge. Then he called Thomas. "Now we will go to Bayfield. I will sell the skins. I will buy you a bottle of pop."

Thomas got into the wagon and Albert Left Hand drove up the road to Bayfield.

## 21

Drowsy Bayfield had its Saturday afternoon crowd. A dozen saddle horses were hitched at the long rack in front of the general store, and wagon teams and a few saddle horses were in the cottonwood grove at the end of the street. The two saloons spilled loud talk and laughter onto the board sidewalk. Cowhands loafed in doorways and at the edge of the walk. They glanced up as Albert Left Hand drove up the dusty street and stopped his team in front of the big store. Thomas sat in the wagon, holding the reins, while Albert went in and talked with the trader. He made his deal, then came out and ordered, "Go around back and unload."

Thomas drove the team up to the corner and around and back down the alley to an open shed where Albert Left Hand was waiting. Thomas unloaded the stinking pelts and piled them as Albert Left Hand directed. Then Albert Left Hand gave him a nickel. "For the pop," he said. He took charge of the team and Thomas went back the way he had come, to the main street.

He didn't know where to get the pop. Looking, he came to the saddlery shop. In the window was the most beautiful saddle he had ever seen, ornately tooled and polished till it shone. He stared at it, admiring with all his heart. Then he saw the bridle hanging from the saddle horn. It was a black and white horsehair bridle with long round-braided reins. He recognized that bridle. It was a bridle he had made, with a pattern he had thought up. It had a price tag. Five dollars. He gasped. Five dollars! He hadn't got anything for it because it was work he was assigned to do, schoolwork, and when it was sold to a trader the money went to pay for his keep.

He stared at the bridle and the price tag, and his eyes returned to the saddle. There was no price tag on the saddle. It cost too much to say, he decided. But if the bridle was worth five dollars, and if he could make bridles and sell them, then some day he could buy that saddle. He didn't have a pony for the saddle, but some day he could buy a pony, too.

He was still there in front of the window, staring at the saddle, when two cowhands came out of the nearest saloon. They talked loud and laughed. They saw the boy and the tall, slim one jabbed a thumb into Thomas's ribs and demanded, "What's your name?"

Thomas stepped back and tried to hurry away, but the cowhand caught his arm. "I asked what's your name?"

"Thomas."

"All right, Tom. Want to earn a quarter?" He winked at his dark-haired companion.

Thomas didn't answer.

"Know how to ride a horse?" the cowhand asked. "Sure you do. All Indian kids do." He drew a quarter from his pocket. "Look, Tom. You go get my horse and ride it back here and I'll give you this quarter."

Tom stared at the quarter. He had never owned a quarter. This man was offering him a quarter just to ride a horse. He looked at the cowhand again, wide-eyed, and started to leave.

The cowhand caught his arm again. "Just a minute! Get the right horse or you don't get the quarter. The black gelding with a one-ear bridle and a red and white saddle blanket. He's hitched right down there in the cottonwoods."

Again Thomas started to leave, and again the cowhand caught his arm. "Ride him. Don't try to lead him. Understand? He don't lead very well." His companion laughed.

Free at last, Thomas hurried down the street. He found the horse, hitched by a neck rope. It was so skittish he had to drive it around the tree until the rope was wound tight. Then he snubbed the reins to the saddle horn, untied the rope, got his foot in the stirrup. The horse danced away, but he swung into the saddle as it began buck-jumping. With the reins snubbed it couldn't get its head down, but it buck-jumped in a circle among the trees before he knew he could ride it, knew he had its rhythm and his own balance. Then he gave it a little slack in the reins and it bucked viciously a time or two before he got it headed up the street. Still holding its head high with the snubbed reins, he rode it to the waiting cowhands. He got off and handed the reins to the one who had sent him on the errand.

The cowhand growled, "You snubbed the reins. You didn't let him buck."

His companion laughed. "He brought the horse, didn't he? He rode him. Pay up, Slim. And let's see *you* ride him."

Slim gave the quarter to Tom. A little knot of men had gathered and someone asked what was going on. The short, dark-haired cowhand grinned. "Slim sent the kid to bring his horse. Now Slim's going to ride him. Unless he's afraid to."

Slim laughed. "I can ride anything with hair and four legs."

"Well, prove it, man. Get in that saddle and prove it."

Slim shortened the reins in his left hand, caught the saddle horn and reached for the near stirrup. The horse shied, tossed its head, got slack in the reins. Slim swung into the saddle, but before he hit the seat the horse ducked its head and began to buck. Slim couldn't find the other stirrup. He didn't have a chance. Three jumps and he was loose. The fourth jump sent him sprawling.

Someone caught the horse and brought it back. Slim got to his feet, cursing, dusted himself and picked up his hat. He limped back to the sidewalk. His companion, laughing, asked, "Want another try, or shall I put the boy on again?"

"Go to hell!"

The dark-haired one turned to Thomas. "I'll give you a dollar if you ride that horse again. Without snubbing the reins."

Thomas hesitated. But he had ridden the horse once, knew its rhythm. And it had worked off some of its meanness. And a dollar, a whole dollar!

He took the reins, gave them one turn around his left hand and reached for the saddle horn. He got his left foot in the stirrup and swung up as the horse shied around. He found the other stirrup and held the horse's head up for one jump while he settled himself. Then he tightened his knees beneath the pommel, let the horse have slack in the reins and rode with the buck. The horse came down stiff-legged and went into a twisting, jolting series of bucks. He rode as he had ridden the unbroken ponies on the sagebrush flats. The horse eased for a moment, then bucked and side-lunged halfway up the block. He kept his seat and it began to subside. Then he put it to a stiff-legged trot. It tossed its head and wanted to run, but he held it in and rode to the end of the block, then turned and came back in a series of short, jolting jumps.

Thomas got off and handed the reins to the dark-haired cowhand, who gave him a silver dollar. Then, both proud of himself and embarrassed, he squirmed through the crowd to get away.

At the edge of the crowd a wiry red-haired man in Levi's and worn fancy-stitched boots stopped him. "You're quite a rider, son," he said. He had a crooked nose and a week's growth of rusty beard. "What's your name?"

"Thomas."

The man sized him up. "How old are you?"

"Fourteen, I guess."

"From the reservation?"

"Yes." Thomas wanted to get away from the crowd. The red-haired man did too. They edged down the street together.

"How would you like to learn to be a real bronc twister?"

Thomas hesitated.

"I'll teach you. How about working for me?"

"I haven't got a permit."

"Your pa in town?"

"My father is dead. I am with Albert Left Hand. I help him with the sheep."

"That fat old man that stinks of sheep? The one in the cafe?" The man grinned. "A boy like you herding sheep! It's time you and me got together. I've got a place down in New Mexico, the other side of the reservation. I've got a whole string of bad horses that you can ride." He laughed. "You just throw in with Red Dillon and we'll both go places."

"I haven't got a permit," Thomas said again.

The man winked. "I'll tend to the permit. The agency's right on our way. You got a pony?"

"No."

"I've got a spare. How'd you get to town? Walk?"

"I came in the wagon with Albert Left Hand. I have to tell him."

"Come on, I'll tell him."

They went to the cafe. Albert Left Hand was alone at the far end of the counter. Nobody wanted to sit near him because of the way he smelled. Red Dillon went to Albert and said he had hired the boy and was taking Thomas home with him. Albert Left Hand didn't even look up. He took another big bite of raisin pie, chewed for a moment, then growled, "Boys come, boys go. That one's no good."

Red Dillon grinned and they turned away. "We ought to eat before we go," he said to Thomas. "Me giving you a job, you ought to treat. Money's no good in your pocket."

So they found stools at the near end of the counter, well away from Albert Left Hand, and Red Dillon ordered chili and coffee for both of them. Then they had doughnuts and more coffee, making an even dollar's worth. Thomas gave Red his dollar and Red paid the man at the end of the counter.

Red's horses were on the far side of the cottonwood grove at the end of the street. Both were saddled, but the saddle on the black had no horn and a tarp-covered bedroll was lashed across it. Red tightened the cinches and tied the bedroll back of the saddle. He saw Thomas puzzling. "Never see a saddle like this?" he asked. "This here's a bronc saddle, for rodeoing. If a bronc comes over backwards onto you, there's no horn to punch a hole in your guts. If you get throwed frontwards by a mean bucker there's no horn to hang you up by your chap strings. That's why the horn's sawed off. You're going to see a lot of this saddle, Tom." He swung into the saddle on the sorrel, a conventional saddle with a horn. "Let's go. Let's get that permit and head for my place."

Tom mounted the black and settled himself in the bronc saddle, and they headed down the road south, toward the agency.

# III. *The Arena*

## 22

Red got the permit without any trouble. It was a formality that the agent was glad to have done with in a hurry. For his records, it solved the whole problem of Thomas Black Bull.

Then Tom and Red Dillon got on the horses again and rode on south, pushing to get off the reservation that evening. The sun had set before they crossed into New Mexico, but they rode for another hour before they stopped, hobbled the horses, divided the bedroll and made a supperless camp. The next morning they rode on, across rolling flats which were much like the land on the reservation except that there was more grass.

Early afternoon and Red said, "Now we're on my range. Another couple of hours and we'll be home. Some folks might not think it's much to look at, but it's a roof and a bed, and old Meo keeps the cook pot going. I will say this," he laughed, "it don't stink of sheep!"

Mirages shimmered and vanished ahead of them and shimmered again on the next rise. "Grass enough here," Red said, with a sweeping gesture, "for a real layout, if I ever figure it's worth while. I could put a thousand head of horses out here and still have grass to spare. But if I did, then I'd have to hay them in the winter. Start haying and you've got to have help. Help eats up all the profits, so I keep my layout small, so me and Meo can handle it."

And a little later he said, "You'll like Meo. He's an old chili-eater and he don't have much to say, but he's all right. Used to be quite a rider himself, till a bronc fell on him eight, ten years ago. Broke something in his back and he's got a hump on his shoulders now. You ever ride in a rodeo, Tom?"

"No."

"Ever seen one?"

"No."

"Well, you will. Things go right, we may go to the show in Aztec next month. We'll go a lot of places, Tom, and we'll get paid for it. We'll make them pay." He laughed. "I got euchered in Mancos last week, but I've got a feeling my luck's turned. Yes sir, I think my luck has turned."

Midafternoon and what looked from a distance like just another wide gully began to spread out ahead of them. It was still two miles away, but Tom could see the dark green of trees. They were coming to the sharp-walled canyon of the San Juan which, picking up the water from half a dozen big creeks after it passed Pagosa, became a river that swept in a great arc down through the corner of New Mexico before it swung north again and plowed its way into Utah and the incredible canyons of the Colorado. Here it looped about like a silvery snake, hiding from the arid flatlands in a bluff-walled shallow canyon of its own.

They came to the rim of the bluff and looked down on huge old cottonwoods and lush grass where the river oxbowed between the canyon walls. A shelving trail led down the bluff. As they rode down Tom saw a weathered cabin among the trees and an unchinked log barn and a set of old pole corrals. Beyond the cabin was a garden patch, green with rows of beans and pepper plants. A bent man was hoeing in the garden.

They rode to the barn, unsaddled and turned the horses into the corral, and Red led the way to the cabin. The gnomish, leather-faced old Mexican with a hump on his shoulders put down his hoe and came to meet them.

"This is Tom, Meo," Red said. "We're going to teach Tom to be a bronc twister."

Meo looked at Tom, then asked Red, "You win at Mancos?"

Red shook his head. "But my luck's changed. Me and Tom are going to Aztec and take their shirts."

"Maybe," Meo said, and he turned and went back to the garden.

The cabin was one long room with a fireplace across the far end. In front of the fireplace was a plank table with two benches. Several bunks were built against one wall, and on pegs on the other wall were rawhide lariats, bridles, spare cinches, two pairs of sleek-leather chaps, assorted riding gear. There was a pile of firewood beside the fireplace, a string of red chilis hung from a beam, and on the white ashes stood a black coffeepot and a slowly simmering iron kettle.

Red tossed the bedroll on a bunk, picked up a mug and a bowl from the table and poured coffee. "Help yourself," he said as he spooned beans and chili from the kettle. Tom got himself a bowl of chili and a cup of coffee while Red found the tortillas in the Dutch oven.

They ate in silence until Red had finished his chili and beans. He filled his bowl again and sat back to let it cool.

"Well, Tom," he said, "the agent asked would I see to it that you had a home and learned a trade. I don't know what he'd say about this place, but it's a roof over your head when it rains. A cut better than a sheepherder's tent, isn't it?"

Tom nodded agreement and went on eating.

"And if you never have less to eat," Red said, "I guess you won't starve. So you've got a home. As for a trade, he must have meant being able to turn your hand to something that would keep you out of the poorhouse. Well, I never been in the poorhouse, and I don't plan to be. You stick with me and I guess you'll make out." His eyes went to the chaps and bridles and cinches hanging on the wall. "We'll both make out." He smiled to himself, then saw that Tom had finished his chili. "Help yourself to some more. Eat up. Put some gristle in your gut. You'll need it, because you're going to start learning that trade tomorrow."

* * *

The next morning Tom got his first lesson as a bronc rider.

Besides the two saddle horses, Red had nine others, all buckers. "Anybody's got an outlaw he'll sell for five dollars, I take him. You get so you can ride my rough string and you can ride any horse you'll likely draw in a rodeo. The kind of shows we'll work, anyway."

So they brought in the rough string, roped one horse, blindfolded it, cinched on the bronc saddle. Red handed Tom a pair of slick-leather chaps he had soaked in the horse trough, told him to put them on. Then he led the saddled horse from the corral out onto the open grass. Meo twisted its ears and held its head while Tom mounted, adjusted the rein in his left hand and settled himself in the saddle. Meo turned the horse loose and Tom rode only four jumps before he was thrown.

Red caught the horse, said, "Too much rein. Try again," and Tom mounted once more. He rode a few jumps longer that time but was thrown again. "Not enough rein," Red announced. "Now do it right this time." And Tom got into the saddle again, bruised and angry. By then the horse was tiring and Tom had begun to know its rhythm. He was loosened in the saddle twice, but the wet chaps clung to the saddle and he recovered both times. He rode the horse to a standstill. "That's better," Red said grudgingly, while Meo brought a fresh horse from the corral. Tom caught his breath while they saddled it. Then he rode again, and was thrown again.

He was thrown five times the first day. But he began to learn how to fall as well as how to ride. The second day the lessons he had learned riding the agency ponies began to come back. He found his sense of timing and rhythm, began to gauge a horse in its first few jumps. These horses were bigger and stronger than the Indian ponies, and each had its own pattern of bucking. He learned the patterns, and he learned to anticipate the horse's next move, be set for it. By the end of the week he rode two horses in succession to a standstill.

Then they moved into the corral and he began riding out of the chute. They built a chute in the corral like a rodeo arena chute, a plank pen with walls just wide enough apart to take a horse and with gates at each end that crowded a horse so it could neither lunge nor buck. There was a narrow runway on each side where he stood to saddle the horse and from which he mounted.

The first horse Tom rode out of the chute was a big roan as mean as a tomcat with its tail on fire. It made such a fuss that Meo had not only to ear its head down but bite the tip of one ear while Red saddled it. Then Tom straddled the chute, let himself down easy into the saddle, got set, and Meo opened the gate. The horse lunged out, bucking, side-jumping, fighting like a fiend. Tom, riding in dry chaps, felt the rein slip in his sweaty hands, tried to recover the slack, lost a stirrup and went head over heels.

As he slowly picked himself up from the hard-packed corral, Red shouted, "Come on back and ride him right this time!" He caught the roan and put him in the chute again. Tom recovered his breath, dried his hands on his shirt, got into the saddle again, adjusted the rein, and Meo opened the gate. The roan went out bucking just as viciously as before. But Tom rode him, for ages it seemed. Twice he was loose in the saddle, and each time he recovered. Once he had to grab the saddle with his free right hand and he heard Red yell something, but he wasn't listening. The roan fought the rein. It reared and came down with a jolt that made Tom's teeth hurt. But he rode it until it was gasping for breath, until it slowed to a crow-hop. Then it stopped, and he eased out of the saddle. His legs were quivering, his belly was drum-tight, his head was ringing, but he led it back to the chute.

"You pulled leather," Red accused.

"I rode him."

"You didn't ride him clean."

"I rode him."

Then Tom knew he was going to be sick. He started for the corral fence but couldn't make it before he threw up. Then he went to the fence and leaned on it till his head began to clear.

"Come on," Red ordered. "You've done your puking. Now you're going to ride like I tell you to." He had a fresh horse in the chute.

Two more weeks and Tom had ridden every horse in Red's rough string to a standstill. He ached from head to foot every night, but he had learned to ride. Red admitted he was doing pretty well. "We're almost ready for Aztec," he said. "But there's still a thing or two you've got to learn."

"What?" Tom asked.

"I'll show you, maybe tomorrow."

The next morning they put a gray mare in the chute. She was a ducker and a dodger. Give her two inches of slack and she would jump right out from under you. But Tom knew her tricks.

He was buckling on his chaps when Red asked, "How does the saddle suit you? Cinches tight enough?"

He didn't usually ask. Tom shook the saddle. It seemed right, front cinch tight, back cinch just snug enough to keep the saddle from rocking. "It'll do," he said, and straddled the chute, let himself down and found the stirrups. He took the rein, threaded it between his fingers, adjusted it for length. He braced his stirrups, set his spurs at the base of the horse's neck.

"Sure you're all set?" Red asked.

Tom looked at him, thought he saw a trace of a smile. "I'm ready," he said, and Meo swung the gate open.

The gray lunged out. She bucked twice and started her ducking and dodging. Tom kept the rein taut, rode without trouble for several seconds. Then she side-jumped and he felt something give under him. The saddle began to turn. He saw a loose cinch dangling and kicked free of the stirrups just in time to be thrown clear.

He landed hard, and as he slowly got up he saw Red laughing. Red didn't catch the mare, as he usually did. Tom caught her, led her back to the saddle, which she had kicked free. He looked at the saddle and saw that both latigos, the straps that held the cinches, were broken. Both were old latigos instead of the good new ones that had been on the saddle the day before, and both had been cut halfway through with a knife.

Tom picked up the saddle, carried it back to the chute and dropped it to the ground in front of Red. "You did that!" he said.

"Sure I did," Red said, still laughing.

Tom was two inches shorter and thirty pounds lighter than Red Dillon, but he lunged at him with both fists. Red dodged back and hit him one quick blow, knocked him down. Tom got to his knees, but Red pushed his shoulder, held him down. "Stay down there and cool off. I've been in a lot more brawls than you have. I'll knock you down as fast as you get up."

Tom crouched there, furious. "You cut those latigos!"

"I said I did. I told you yesterday you still had to learn a thing or two. First one is, don't trust anybody when it comes to your saddle and your gear. Not even me. Check everything yourself before you say you're ready. I asked you twice if you was all set, and you didn't even look at the cinches or latigos."

Tom slowly got to feet, still glowering.

"Second thing you just learned," Red said, "is not to jump somebody bigger than you unless you've got an evener, knucks or a club or a gun. And when you get mad like that, don't try to take it out on me. Take it out on a horse, where you've got a chance to win." He turned and walked away.

Tom watched him go, then caught the gray mare, tied a

rope around her for a surcingle, and mounted her and rode her to a standstill as he had ridden the ponies on the reservation. When she finally came to a stop, snorting bloody foam, he got off and went to the house.

Red was at the table, drinking coffee. "Get it out of your system?" he asked.

"I rode her," Tom said.

"Sure. I knew you could." Red stirred his coffee and watched him for a moment. "You can ride the horses they'll have at Aztec, too. But you're going to lose, just the same."

"No, I'm not."

"I say you are."

"Why?"

"Because I say so. You're just another Indian kid that thinks he can ride. That's what they'll think, and that's what I'll tell them. So you enter the bronc riding, and if you draw good horses you'll score high, may even win the number-two go-round. But you lose the final. Understand?"

"No."

"You damn well better understand, because that's what you're going to do. You lose the final go-round. After that you ride again. Never mind how come. You ride again, and you ride that horse right into the ground."

"But—"

"Don't but me! I say that's what you're going to do! You didn't think I just wanted to make a goddam hero out of you, did you? Not with that Aztec bunch just faunching to bet! I'm setting up the deadfall, and you're riding the way I tell you to. *Now* do you understand?"

Tom hesitated.

Red rubbed his knuckles. "You've got one beauty of a shiner. No need getting another one like it, but you sure as hell will if you get stubborn. You're going to do what I say. Aren't you?"

Tom nodded. "Yes," he said.

# 23

Aztec, as Red put it, was just a wide place in the road, but its rodeo drew ranch folk from the whole area, people eager after a long, hot summer to meet old friends, roister a bit and have fun. The contestants were mostly ranch hands who had learned to ride and rope on the range and in Sunday afternoon show-offs in some ranch corral. The spectators came to see an exciting show, to bet on friends and neighbors, and to cheer any special event that might be offered. Purses were small but betting was freehanded.

Red Dillon had ridden at Aztec the year before and knew enough local people to rouse mild interest by saying he wasn't a contestant this time around. "I just came to see the show," he said, then added, "And to see if the boy, here, can ride. He thinks he can, and I guess this is as good a time as any to find out." His listeners looked at Tom, who was just another Indian boy in faded Levi's, work shirt and scuffed boots and whose hair looked as though it had been cut with dull sheep shears. Several men grinned and asked Red if he'd like to lay a few bets on the kid. Red laughed. "I said he *thinks* he can ride. Let's wait for the first go-round and see if he's good, or just lucky."

It was a two-day show with a parade the first morning, a barbecue at noon, and the first round—go-round, in rodeo parlance—in all events that afternoon. The second day there would be two programs, the semifinals in the morning, the final go-round in the afternoon. The arena was the local baseball field, where pens and chutes had been built of bright new planks in the infield and corrals had been thrown up in the outfield for the bucking horses, the wild steers and the calves. Like most small rodeos, the program consisted of calf roping, steer riding, bareback bronc riding and saddle bronc riding, with a wild-horse race and a wild-cow milking contest thrown in for laughs. Bigger rodeos added steer wrestling to the program and brightened it up with pretty girls doing trick riding; and big circuit rodeo, especially when playing in major cities, was beginning to add horse-show events for glitter and style. But little Aztec's minor show was built around the heart and core of rodeo, men riding unbroken broncs and men roping untamed calves. And the classic event was the historic reason for rodeo itself, the saddle bronc riding.

Fundamentally, it was man against horse, cowboy trying to master an unbroken bronco. It was the same thing Tom had done when he rode a drunken cowboy's fractious horse in the dusty street of Bayfield to win a dollar. But here he would ride out of a chute, just as he had at Red's place on the San Juan, and he would ride according to standard rodeo rules. He must hold the rein in one hand, not touch saddle or horse with the other hand, must rake with his spurs, keep his feet moving, and he must ride ten seconds. Then a horn would blow, a mounted pickup man would come alongside, take the rein from the rider and let the rider pivot out of the saddle, off the bucking bronc, and swing down to the ground. The ride was scored on points based on skill in the saddle and the worse the horse, the more difficult to ride, the higher the successful rider's score. If a rider was thrown or committed a foul he lost the go-round. If the horse refused to buck, the rider got another chance on the same horse or, if he chose, a different horse. In bigger rodeos all the riders rode in all three go-rounds, their points were totaled and prizes were awarded on each man's totals, but at Aztec, as in most small rodeos, each go-round was an elimination contest, leaving only the five top riders for the finals. As Red put it, this was a sudden-death show. You had to place well up in every go-round to stay in competition. "So start right out riding rough and tough," he told Tom. "Take the first two go-rounds."

The first day Tom drew a snaky, wide-winding black that bucked in a tight circle. Tom had no special trouble with him and was surprised when the ten-second horn blew. The pick-up man rode alongside, Tom handed him the rein, grabbed his shoulder and swung out of the saddle as Red had taught him. He was almost back to the chutes before he realized that the crowd was applauding him. Red said he had made a good ride and when the score was announced, Tom placed second.

That evening there was a good deal of talk about this new kid, the Indian who didn't look more than twelve or thirteen but rode like a man. Red had put down a few small bets on him at the last minute, and he made a few more bets on him for the second go-round. But when pressed to bet on the finals Red shook his head. "Let's take it round by round. Tom's luck may run out tomorrow."

To Tom he said, "Now they've weeded out the Sunday riders. Tomorrow morning you'll just have the good ones and the lucky ones to beat. Give them hell. Ride your draw high, wide and handsome."

And that's what Tom did. He drew a big roan that tried to tear down the chute while they were saddling him. When the gate swung open the roan went out with a series of spectacular lunges that brought an instant roar from the crowd. They recognized Tom and they knew a vicious bucker when they saw one. After two jumps Tom knew he could ride the roan, so he raked and gouged with his spurs, the roan bellowed and fought, and Tom punished him every legal way he knew. He rode all-out and, when the horn blew, the crowd was in an uproar. They cheered him all the way back to the chutes.

Red praised him extravagantly, and when Tom was announced as winner of the round Red collected his bets. He offered to bet on the finals, jeered at those who refused to wager, but he kept his bets small.

When the morning program was over and they went to eat dinner, Red had several drinks and began to talk as though he'd had one too many. The betting crowd listened to his brag and winked at each other. A few of them placed bets with him on the finals, but again Red kept the bets low. And when he and Tom started back to the rodeo grounds Red sobered up the minute they were alone.

"Well, Tom," he said, "you've been a hero. Like it?"

"Yes," Tom said.

"I thought so. Well, that's all over now. You're going to be a bum in the finals. You're going to lose, and lose big."

"No I'm not. I can—"

"Shut up! I say you're going to lose the finals! I'm giving the orders! I've got the deadfall all set up. You'll lose the finals and they'll think they've got me on the hip. Then I'll really take them. In the finals you're going to give your horse slack in the rein after the first few jumps and look for a soft place to land. Hear me?"

"I hear," Tom said reluctantly.

"You do like I say, or I'll break your goddam neck! You get thrown. Then, after the final go-round is over, you're going to ride again. A special event. And then you'd *better* be a hero or start running. Now do you understand?"

"I guess so."

"You know so, you damn well know so!"

Then they were back in the arena and Red acted the part of a drunken braggart again.

Tom had drawn the number-three ride in the finals, and his horse was a big black. Red, still playing his drunken role, let Tom do the saddling, but before he mounted Red said, "You know what I told you," and there was both threat and warning in his eyes. Tom said, "I know," and settled himself in the saddle, adjusted the rein, jerked his hat tight, set his spurs. The announcer bellowed, "Coming out of Chute Number Three, on Tar Baby, Tom Black Bull!" and the crowd began to roar. Tom signaled the gateman, the gate swung open and the black lunged out bucking. It ducked, side-jumped and Tom raked with his spurs. He could ride this horse, he knew he could. But after the first few bucks he let the rein slip as the black ducked its head. It got six inches of slack, came up in another buck and Tom had lost his leverage. As he went back in the saddle the next lunge drove the cantle into his kidneys. Then the pommel jabbed his lower gut and he was loose in the saddle, the pain seeming to cut him in two. Another side-jump and he knew it was all over. As the black bucked again he instinctively kicked his feet free and went sprawling, thrown clean and hard.

The crowd groaned. Tom lay for a moment, gasping for breath, aching with pain. And hurting inside, because he knew he could have ridden that horse to a standstill. He rolled over, hunched to his knees till the pain eased and he had his breath again, then got slowly to his feet. He unbuckled his chaps and limped back to the chutes, head bowed in shame as much as in physical pain.

Red came to meet him. He put an arm around Tom's shoulders and said loudly, "Tough luck, kid! Goddam tough luck. What happened?"

Tom looked at him, hating him, and didn't answer. Red's fingers pressed into his arm, warning him, and they went back to the chutes. Tom sat down in the shade of the chutes, head in his hands. He heard a chute gate swing open, heard the grunt and pound of hoofs, the cheers of the crowd, the slap of chaps on saddle skirts, as the next rider made his bid for the purse. It didn't matter. Then the horn blew, the crowd cheered. And a few minutes later the chute opened again and the last rider's horse was squealing, pounding the ground with that punishing, man-killing dance of desperation. The crowd cheered, gasped, then groaned, and Tom heard the thud of the rider striking the ground. He didn't even look up. Somebody else had been thrown. Somebody who had tried, who hadn't been thrown because he was ordered to.

Then the bronc riding was all over. The judges tallied their score cards. The announcer was bellowing the final results. Tom Black Bull, because of his spectacular rides in the first two go-rounds, was placed fourth, just ahead of the last rider, who was also thrown.

Red came and helped him to his feet. "Guess that's it, Tom," he said. "Your luck just ran out." He began stuffing the bronc saddle into the gunny sack. The men who had bets with him came to collect, and Red paid them off, one by one. "You took me," he said. "But I still say the boy is the best rider here. He just had bad luck with that big black."

A stocky black-haired ranchman laughed. Two others who had just collected bets from Red joined in the laughter. "So you still think the boy is top man?" the black-haired man asked, winking at the others.

"Damn right he is!" Red looked around. "I say Tom can ride any horse here, any one of them."

"That's big talk, Dillon."

"I still say it."

"Maybe we could set up a special event for him," the black-haired man suggested. "If you care to make it worth while. What odds will you give on him?"

"Odds?" Red laughed derisively. "The boy just got thrown and you want me to give odds! No, I think we'll go home." Then Red turned to Tom. "Think you could ride that black if you had another chance, Tom?"

"Wait a minute!" the black-haired man said. "You wanted to back him on any horse here. The black's had a go-round. He's tired."

"Tom's tired too. He's ridden two go-rounds today."

The announcer had come over to see what was happening. He turned and bellowed to the crowd, "Don't hurry off, folks! We seem to have a special event in the making. Stick around!"

Red turned to Tom. "Want to make another ride, Tom?"

Tom knew the answer he had to make. Anyway, he wanted to ride again, prove himself. "Yes," he said.

Red turned to the men around him. "You heard him. He'll ride. So let's make it worth while, give me a chance to get back a little of my hard-earned money. I'll tell you what we'll do. Give me two-to-one odds and the boy'll try to ride any horse you pick. Not just to the ten-second horn, but all the way. He'll ride him to a standstill. Maybe he won't rake with his spurs after the horn, but I say he'll ride him clean. Now what do you say?"

"That," the black-haired man said, "I want to see."

A stakeholder was named. Red covered the first few bets, then said, "You boys just about cleaned me out, but I've still got a hundred-dollar saddle and a couple of good cutting horses."

"I can use another saddle," the black-haired man said, and handed the stakeholder money enough to cover the bet. Two other men covered the horses.

Red turned to Tom, "Well, Tom, you either ride now or walk home." He took the bronc saddle from the gunny sack and handed Tom his chaps.

The black-haired man and several other bettors went to the corral and picked out the horse. The announcer bellowed to the crowd, "Well, folks, we've got it! Tom Black Bull, the boy who made two sensational rides before he was thrown in the finals, is going to ride again in a special event. He's going to ride that big bay they're bringing to the chutes right now. And listen to this, folks! Tom is going to try to ride this horse to a standstill! No time limits! This ride will be a showdown, to the finish!"

There was a roar of approval from the crowd.

Red and Tom checked the saddle, cinches, latigos, stirrups, while the bay was put in the chute. They checked halter and rein. Then they saddled the bay. It hadn't been ridden that day, but Red had watched it in action in the first go-round when it threw a rider in six seconds. "He tries to buck right," he told Tom, "in a tight circle. He'll duck from the first jump. Don't, for God's sake, let him get any slack. Remember the big black at home? This one bucks just like him, same pattern."

Tom put on his chaps, tightened his spurs, dried his hands. He straddled the chute, let himself down into the saddle. He adjusted the rein carefully, jammed his hat tight, set his spurs.

"All set?" Red asked.

Tom nodded. The gate swung open.

The bay took two steps and went into the air as the crowd yelled. Tom raked with his spurs and the horse came down, tried to jerk its head. Tom was braced for it. He rode with two twisting jumps, two stiff-legged, spine-jarring bucks. The horse was big and full of fight. It kept trying to get its head around to the right. Unable to, it made zigzag lunges, right, left, right again. It kicked and reared and spun. Tom rode with its rhythm, but at every pounding jump he felt as though his head was being driven right down between his shoulders. His left arm seemed about to be torn from its socket. But he rode, and he rode clean.

The ten-second horn blew. The crowd was in an uproar. But Tom heard neither horn nor crowd. He wasn't riding for time or for the crowd. He was riding for himself. And he wasn't riding the bay. He was riding a hurt and a hate, deep inside. The blood drummed in his ears, his teeth ached with the pounding, but he held his rhythm. Then he began to gouge and punish with his spurs. Dull as the rowels were, they drew blood. He shifted his weight, brought it down with every jump, punishing the horse. He jerked viciously at the rein, giving an inch of slack, then snapping it back as though trying to break the horse's neck.

The bay was grunting with every leap. It seemed to ease off for a moment, then bucked in another pattern of fury. It bellowed and came up in a pawing, dancing leap. Tom jerked off his hat and slapped it over the ears, and it came down with a jolt that jarred the earth. Its snorts became gasps of pain and it slacked again. Tom gave it more rein, and it got its head around to the right and bucked in the tight circle Red had warned about. But Tom was still in the saddle, still gouging with his spurs.

Then the rhythm slowed. The bay stumbled once, caught itself, bucked again. Now it began to come down spraddle-legged, bracing itself. It staggered. He gave it all the rein it wanted, but it merely drooped its head. It began to cough, took a few steps and stood trembling. It tried to buck once more and failed.

The crowd was clamoring. A pickup man was alongside, shouting to Tom. "Get clear! He's going down!" And Tom felt the horse sagging under him. He saw the bloody foam for the first time, gobs of it welling from the horse's mouth. He grabbed the pickup man's shoulder, kicked free of the stirrups just as the horse fell from under him.

Tom's feet struck the ground. He ran a few steps, then his knees buckled. He went down, and looked around and saw the fallen horse thrash, its legs jerking convulsively. It lifted its head and there was a gush of blood from its mouth. Then its head fell back with a thud.

Tom turned away, half sick, and heard the crowd gasp. He got to his feet and walked to the chutes, not looking back. His head was light. He was sweating. He reached the chute, clung to the planks and began to retch.

Men crowded around. Red was there, pushing at them, ordering, "Leave him alone! Give him air!" The crowd eased back a little and Red asked, "All right?" Tom, so weak he could barely stand, nodded and clung to the chute.

A man brought the bronc saddle, tossed it on the ground, and someone asked, "How's the bay?"

"Dead." The man stared at Tom in awe. "Dead as a doornail. Ruptured its lungs, or something."

Tom began to recover. He stuffed the saddle into the gunny sack. Red had found the stakeholder, was stuffing handfuls of money into his pockets. He came back to Tom. "Come on," he ordered. "Let's get out of here." He pushed his way through the crowd around the chutes and started toward the corrals and their own saddle horses.

The crowd of men at the chutes followed them as far as the place where the dead horse lay. Tom glanced at it and turned away. Most of the crowd stayed to look, but the black-haired ranchman followed and caught up with them near the corrals. "Just a minute, Dillon," he said, and Red stopped and faced him.

"That was a setup, Dillon!" The man was flushed with anger.

"What do you mean?"

"You know what I mean!"

"You picked the horse, and the boy rode him, didn't he?"

"Yes, he rode him, and we paid off. But he could have ridden the black in the final go-round, too. Only he had orders not to. Didn't you, son?"

"Leave him alone!" Red snapped. "He made his ride! Go get the horses, Tom."

The man turned to Tom. "You had your orders to throw the final go-round, didn't you?"

Red stepped between them and cocked his fist. "I said leave him alone!"

The man stepped back. "All right, Dillon. You took us.

But don't you ever try it again! Don't you ever show up at another rodeo in Aztec! Understand?"

"Aztec!" Red laughed derisively. "Why, you two-bit tinhorn! We're going where there's *real* money!" He backed away. "Come on, Tom."

And they went to the corral, saddled their horses and headed for home.

## 24

It was fourteen miles to Blanco, the trading post and post office halfway home. They rode at a lope the first five miles and Red kept watching the road behind them. Then, since nobody was following them, they slowed to a trot and Red began gloating over the way he had outsmarted the Aztec betting crowd. He boasted, and he laughed, and he boasted again.

Tom paid little attention. He was still living the afternoon. He could have ridden the black in the finals. He knew that. He could have ridden it, clear and clean, and been champion, taken top purse money. But Red ordered him to lose and he made that one mistake, made it deliberately, and got thrown. Then he rode the bay, which was a meaner horse than the black, a worse bucker. He rode it to a finish. Rode it to death. He still saw the bloody foam, heard the cough and the final spurt of blood, the thud of its head on the ground, and he felt queasy.

He looked at Red, heard his braggart voice, his jeering laugh, and remembered the way he had gouged with his spurs, punishing not the horse but something else, something that Red Dillon represented. He had punished it, gouged and fought and mastered it, *rode* the horse to death. And Red Dillon's voice and grating laughter were still right here beside him.

He began to feel queasy again and wished Red would shut up. He was light-headed and sweating. Red sensed something wrong. He turned and looked at Tom and asked, "What's the matter with you?"

Tom shook his head and said, "Nothing," and knew he was going to be sick. He stopped his horse, got off, and fell to his knees and began to retch.

Red grinned. "You're kind of shook up, I guess. Feel better now?"

Tom got to his feet and stood, holding to the saddle, till his head began to clear. Finally he mounted again. They rode on, and Red said, "I'll stop in Blanco and get a bottle of tonic. That'll settle your guts." He laughed.

Blanco was only a couple of miles ahead. They rode up to the store and Tom waited while Red went in. He came back with three bottles, undid his bedroll and stowed two of them inside. Then he opened the third bottle and took a long drink from it. He wiped the neck on his sleeve and handed it to Tom. "Take a good swig. Clean the dust out of your throat."

Tom took a mouthful, swallowed twice and felt the burn of the liquor all the way to his stomach before he even tasted it. He took another mouthful, handed the bottle back to Red and shivered as he swallowed again. It burned all the way down, then seemed to fume back and fill his head. Red took another long drink, corked the bottle and got on his horse. They started on home.

Tom's head began to reel. He swayed in the saddle, had to hold on to the pommel. Red laughed at him. "Hold tight, Tom! Don't start flapping your wings or you'll fly right out of the saddle! Ain't used to wings, I guess, are you? Feel better now?"

"No."

Red uncorked the bottle and took another drink. "You will." He offered the bottle to Tom again.

Tom shook his head, and wondered why it didn't seem to be fastened to his neck. His body was down there somewhere, and it didn't ache any more, but his head was floating all by itself. Then he felt his body swaying and ordered his hands to grab the saddle and hold on. They got the order and obeyed. Then he ordered his eyes to look at his horse's ears and stop his head from spinning. His eyes looked, but the horse had four ears. Why? It didn't matter. He closed his eyes and let his head spin, and his hands gripped the saddle.

Darkness came and the horses plodded homeward. Tom slept, his hands still gripping the saddle, his chin on his chest. Red talked to himself, laughed from time to time. He began to sing. Tom woke up, almost fell out of the saddle, recovered and felt the queasiness again. Red's toneless singing rasped at his ears.

"Shut up," Tom shouted, and his own voice echoed in his ears. "Shut your damn big mouth!"

Red laughed and went on singing, and Tom was asleep again.

It was almost midnight when the horses picked their way down the trail along the bluff and crossed to the barn. Tom wakened and wondered where he was. The horses stopped. Red bellowed, "Meo! Meo, come here, you damn old chili-eater!"

A light appeared in the house. The door opened and Meo appeared, lantern in hand. He came to the barn and Red said, "Meo, you old chili-eater, I took 'em!" His words were slurred, thick. He laughed. "Put the horses away. We got to celebrate." He waved the bottle, now empty, and dismounted. Meo steadied him or he would have fallen. Red tilted up the bottle, said, "All gone. Dead soldier," and tossed it aside. He tried to untie his bedroll. Meo undid it for him, got it over his shoulder and Red started to the cabin, weaving as he went.

Tom dismounted carefully, each motion deliberate. His head still swam and he wasn't sure of his feet. He held to the saddle until he had his equilibrium, then took off his bedroll, put it on the ground and loosened the latigos. He almost fell as he pulled the saddle off, but carried it into the barn and got it onto the pole where it belonged.

"I'll finish," Meo said. "Go get some coffee."

Tom almost fell as he leaned over to pick up his bedroll, but he got it into his arms and carried it to the cabin. Red was sprawled in his bunk, already asleep. Tom put the bedroll at the foot of his own bunk, went to the hearth and poured a cupful of hot, black coffee. He sat down at the table, the cup in both hands, and tried to drink. He burned his lips but couldn't feel the scald inside his mouth. His mouth, his whole gullet, was numb. He set the cup down and was sitting there, staring at it, when Meo came in.

Meo glanced at Red, then came to the table. He filled a bowl with beans and chili, set it in front of Tom and put half a dozen cold tortillas beside it. "Eat," he ordered. "Put something in the belly."

Tom had no hunger, but he rolled a tortilla and scooped at the beans, took a mouthful. It felt good, though he could hardly taste it. He scooped another mouthful from the bowl.

"You won?" Meo said.

Tom shook his head. "I lost."

"Then you rode again?"

"Yes." Tom wondered how Meo knew. "I rode again. I rode a horse to death."

"Ah-h-h." Meo nodded. He glanced toward Red, snoring in his bunk, pointed with his chin. "*He* won."

Tom nodded.

Meo went over to Red and went through his pockets. He took all the money he could find, counted it, then put back a few bills. He folded the rest of it carefully and thrust it into his own pocket. Then he came back to the fireplace and filled Tom's chili bowl again.

Tom's head was beginning to clear. He could taste the bite of the coffee, the flavor of the chili. Meo sat down opposite him with a cup of coffee. "Tell me about it," he urged.

Tom told him. Meo listened, nodding, sipping coffee, making no comment. At last he jerked his chin toward Red and said, "Some day they will kill that one. Or he will kill himself." It was an unemotional statement, his only comment. He finished his coffee. "Tomorrow," he said, "we will harvest the frijoles, you and I. Go to bed now."

# 25

They harvested the beans in the old way, pulling the vines, piling them on a tarp, flailing them with a stick. Then they took away the broken vines and winnowed the beans, scooping them into a flat basket, holding the basket high and slowly pouring the beans onto a fresh tarp. The wind blew away the broken pods and chaff.

It was slow work and Meo never hurried. "The frijole," he said, "takes its own time. It waits for the sun and the rain, then grows one day at a time. Why should I tell it to hurry now? If I do not eat this frijole, it will wait and grow again. It does not need me to tell it what to do." He scooped another basketful and poured the beans slowly, watching the broken pods drift away and the dry, hard beans flow in a pattering stream onto the tarp. "We know these things, you and I. Our people were not born last year. We are of the old people."

They threshed the beans and winnowed them. Then they sat on the ground and sorted them, handful by handful, picking out the bits of stem and the small brown pebbles before they put the beans into storage bags. The sun was warm, the air was mild, and even the magpies in the cottonwoods had ceased their noisy scolding. Life seemed as unhurried as the day, or as the beans.

Tom asked, "Why did you come here, Meo?"

"One must live somewhere." For a minute Meo was silent as he sorted another handful of beans, then he asked, "Why did you come?"

Tom answered in Meo's own words: "One must live somewhere."

"Where did you live before?"

"On the reservation. I herded sheep."

"Before that?"

"I lived in the mountains, in the old way."

"Why did you leave the mountains?"

"They came and took me away."

"Your father and mother?"

"They are dead."

They sorted beans in silence for a time. Then Meo said, "The mountains are still there."

"The old way is finished." Unconsciously Tom made the cut-off sign. "I have no one," he added.

Meo poured a handful of beans into the bag, picked up another handful and began to sort them. "So you came here, with him." He pointed with his chin toward the cabin. "Why?"

"To be a rider."

Meo grunted. "Why?" he asked again.

Tom wondered how to tell him what he had felt when he was riding the big bay at Aztec. But the words wouldn't come. It was something deeper than words. At last he said, knowing it was not the whole truth, but still a part of it, "To be the boss."

Meo slowly shook his head, then glanced toward the cabin again. "He is the boss."

"I am the boss, on the horse."

"Sometimes. When he tells you to be."

Tom shrugged. "That is the way it is. I ride, I eat. What else is there?"

Meo poured another handful of beans into the bag. It was almost full. He got to his knees, grunting at the stiffness in his joints, and tied the bag with a string. He got to his feet, motioned to Tom, who took one end of the bag. They carried it to the cabin, stowed it in a corner by the fireplace.

Red lay on his bunk, two empty bottles on the floor beside him. He heard them, half opened his eyes, and muttered, "Get out. Leave me alone."

They went back to sorting beans. After a few minutes Meo picked up a single bean and held it in his gnarled fingers. "Frijole," he said to it, "our young friend thinks he is the boss. He will eat you, Frijole. But you have a rumble to make, so you will make that rumble in his belly." He shook his head. "Our young friend will be eaten, too. We are all eaten. If he has a rumble to make, where will he make it? In the belly of the one who eats him." He dropped the bean into the bag and picked up another handful, began to sort them.

Tom shrugged, then picked up a bean, held it between his fingers as Meo had done. "Frijole," he said, "maybe Meo will eat you, not me. Then where will you make your rumble? Is Meo the boss, to tell you what to do?"

Meo went on sorting beans. Finally he said, "Life is the boss. We do what we can. Then we are old. We creep off in a corner and sit, and the tongue makes the rumble. But it is only noise, talk, talk, talk." He sighed and was silent.

They harvested the beans. Then they picked the chilies and made long strings of them and hung them from the roof beams to finish drying. But after that one afternoon of talk, Meo was his taciturn self again, saying little, keeping his thoughts to himself.

The fourth afternoon Red came out of the cabin, pale, weak-kneed and weaving. He made his way to the horse trough, doused his head in the icy water, then sat in the sun for an hour. At last he shouted, "Hey, Meo, make me some fresh coffee."

When Meo told him the coffee was ready, Red went back to the cabin. He was there at the table, silent and disheveled, holding his cup of strong, black coffee in both hands, when Tom and Meo went in to eat supper. Red made a nauseated face at the sight of their food. He left the table, threw the empty bottles out the door, and went back to bed.

He still had a hangover, but he was sober, the next morning. After breakfast he told Meo to bring the horses in, and when Meo had left he said to Tom, "You're going to ride, get the kinks out of you. Next week—what day is this, anyway?"

"Friday," Tom told him.

"Week after next we're going to hit the road. But before we go you're going to learn how to lose a go-round without getting thrown. Let a horse throw you, you may break an arm or something. Then we're out of business for a month."

Tom was staring at him, his mouth set angrily.

"What's the matter with you?" Red flared. "You got ideas? If you have, get rid of them. We're not in the hero business. You're going to lose a lot of go-rounds. Understand?"

Tom didn't answer.

"I said, do you *understand*?"

Tom nodded reluctantly.

"Heroes," Red said, "are a dime a dozen. Little two-bit heroes everywhere you go. And they all wind up broke. Especially if they are Indians or Mexes. Meo was a hero once." He laughed. "Now take a look at him. Just another broken-down old chili-eater."

Tom made no comment.

After a moment Red said, "There's a dozen ways to lose a go-round. You're going to learn them all. And you're going to learn how to look good doing it, look like you're doing your damnedest *not* to lose. Understand?"

Tom nodded.

"We're going down south," Red said. "They hold a lot of little rodeos down there, and they're awful proud of their heroes." He grinned. "Proud enough to back them with betting money. It'd be a shame to let that money burn holes in their pockets, wouldn't it? When we can take it away from them so easy." Then he saw the look in Tom's eyes, and he said, "And if you ever get any ideas about double-crossing me, get rid of them, too. Just remember who's the boss around here."

"I'll remember," Tom said.

"You forget it, I'll break your goddam neck. . . . Better put new latigos on the saddle. I'll be out as soon as I finish eating."

## 26

So Tom entered the world of small-time rodeo, a world of hot, dusty little cow-country towns, makeshift arenas, vicious, unpredictable horses, ambitious country riders and jealous third-rate professionals. And, with Red Dillon, a world of noisy saloons, smoky pool halls, ratty little hotels, fly-specked chili parlors, conniving bettors.

They went all the way to Bernalillo for their first stop. It was a four-day ride, but Red wanted to be sure they were out of range of anyone who might have been at Aztec. They traveled light, with only their bedrolls, and didn't even take the bronc saddle. "It's a dead giveaway," Red said. "They see that saddle and they know one of us has done a lot of rodeoing. If the competition's fast and the horses specially bad, we can always borrow a bronc saddle. Sometimes," he added with a grin, "it's healthier not to wait around and get your own saddle after a ride."

They rode into Bernalillo two days before the rodeo and went to the livery stable. Red, looking like just another trail-worn saddle bum, asked what all the excitement was about. The liveryman was eager to talk about the rodeo. Finally Red said, "Hear that, Tom? The man says they're having a rodeo. Want to stay and have a go at it?"

"You ride, or rope?" the liveryman asked.

"A stove-up puncher like me?" Red laughed. "No, sirree! I'm an old man. I like my women wild but my horses gentle. But the boy, here, thinks he can ride. Maybe this is his chance to find out."

The liveryman looked at Tom. With his ragged haircut, faded work shirt and Levi's and his battered boots Tom looked like just another Indian kid. The liveryman smiled. "They aren't running any juvenile events this year."

Red grinned. "Tom talks big, almost man-size." And he made a deal with the liveryman to put up their horses and let them spread their bedrolls in the hay.

They stalled their horses, left their gear in the hayloft, then went out to size up the situation. They made the rounds of the saloons, pool halls and cafes, and Red told the same story he had told in Aztec. By the next morning the word had got around. The Indian kid thought he could ride. And as though that wasn't enough of a joke, the saddle bum seemed to think the boy could, too, and apparently had a little money to back him. The trap practically laid itself.

The night before the rodeo opened Red summed it up and gave Tom his orders. "These wise guys have got it all figured. So we'll just play along with them. You're going to make a fair to middling ride in the first go-round. Then in the second go-round you're going to foul out. Understand? We'll play them fair and square, give them what they expect. But in the finals you're going to go to town, and we'll give them the works. We'll take their shirts." He grinned. "Fair and square. Can't ask more than that, can they?"

Tom followed orders. Red placed a scattering of small, cautious bets on the first go-round and Tom made an awkward, amateurish ride. Red paid off his bets, got odds on the second go-round, but still kept his bets small. And Tom pulled leather, fouled out. Then Red played the drunken braggart. He still thought Tom could ride, thought he was the best damn rider of them all. Tom had just had bad luck up to now. Bet on the final go-round? Damn right he would! And when he got the odds he wanted he made half a dozen big bets. So Tom made a spectacular final ride, clean and clear all the way, and Red collected his winnings. They got out of town before the bettors knew what hit them. It was, as Red said, as easy as falling out of bed dead-drunk.

That set the pattern. For the next two months they shuttled back and forth across the state, Red picking only the little rodeos that offered purses too small to lure even the third-rate professionals from any distance. The system wasn't foolproof. Once Tom made such a flagrant foul-out that the judges barred him from the finals. Red ranted at him for two days after that one. And once Red tried to set up the deadfall, only to have the local betting crowd catch him in it by refusing to go for the extra ride. But it averaged out, as Red said. They worked seven rodeos and Red cashed in at five of them.

Then they went to Carrizozo, and everything went wrong. Trying to make a losing ride look honest in the first go-round, Tom was thrown and landed heavily on his left shoulder. His arm was so lame he had to ride right-handed in the second go-round. Off balanced, he grabbed the saddle and fouled out to spare himself another fall. The situation was hopeless, and Red agreed that there was no use even trying to ride in the finals. And to cap it all, Red got roaring drunk that night, started a brawl and landed in jail. It took him a week after he sobered up to argue himself out of jail by paying a fine and promising to get out of town.

By then, Tom's arm had begun to heal. But he was ready to call it quits. Tom was tired. He had averaged one rodeo a week all fall, with long, hard rides between. He was young and strong, but the beating he took in the saddle was beginning to tell on him. And he wasn't even getting the satisfaction of winning on horses he knew he could ride. There were a dozen ways to lose a round, and he knew them all by now. But every one of them took something out of him. When he rode loose in the saddle, his spine took a beating. When he broke rhythm, his neck was jerked. And his arm still throbbed and his whole shoulder ached night and day. He wanted to quit and go home.

Red, however, had been rolled and robbed of better than a thousand dollars during the big drunk in Carrizozo. Red wasn't quitting. "There's a little jerkwater called Felice," Red growled, "down the road a piece. They're putting on a show next week. Probably some of the riders at Carrizozo will be there, but that'll just help the setup. We're going to work Felice. And I mean work it!"

Felice was a hard-bitten little alkali-water town with equally hard-bitten bettors. As Red had suspected, they had heard about what happened to Tom at Carrizozo. And, as he had said, that helped rather than hurt. Red began working toward a deadfall.

Everything went according to plan for the first two go-rounds. With his lame arm, Tom couldn't be a power rider. He couldn't keep pressure on the rein. So he had to be a rhythm rider, giving the horse its head. It didn't take much faking to lose the number-one ride, and he was glad to grab the saddle and foul out on the second go-round. Red's plans couldn't have worked out better.

But before the finals Red said, "We'll just saddle our horses and tie them in those cottonwoods back of the stands. Just in case. There's a couple of loudmouth know-it-alls that may start trouble. You ride like I told you in the finals, and then I'll set up the extra. And when you've rode the extra horse into the ground, get ready to run. Things start popping, like they may, you get the hell out and bring the horses to the main gate. I'll meet you there."

So Tom made his final go-round ride, and lost it as Red had ordered him to. Then Red put on his drunken braggart act, set up the extra ride and got the bets he wanted.

The horse the bettors chose was big and mean, but Tom knew after the first few seconds that he could ride him even with that sore arm. There were horses in the bucking string that could have given him plenty of trouble, horses that kept shifting rhythm. But this one was a pattern bucker, full of fight and meanness but predictable. Tom rode him clean for the first ten seconds, then raked and roweled and loosened up with all his tricks. It wasn't the best ride he ever made, but it was good enough. He rode the horse to a standstill.

But even as he dismounted he heard the rumble of trouble at the chutes. He stepped out of his chaps and saw the fighting start. Two men jumped Red, Red knocked one of them down, then began to retreat toward the gate. Then the sideline crowd surged out into the arena, toward the chutes. Tom ducked into the crowd. Nobody paid any attention to him, all intent on the fight. Tom squirmed his way, finally got clear and ran to the gate. He got outside, got the horses and rode back toward the gate. Just as he got there, Red came charging through the crowd. He had reached the gate and was almost in the clear when someone grabbed him by the shirt. Red slid out of the shirt like a snake out of its skin, yelled, "Get going!" and grabbed the horn of his own saddle. He slapped his horse in the flank, pulled himself up and both horses lunged into a run.

As they raced through Felice's dusty main street Tom saw Red trying to stuff wads of money deeper into his pockets. Several green bills fluttered free and Red grabbed at them, then began to laugh. He slapped his horse with his rein ends and they went out of town in a cloud of white dust.

They rode almost a mile and came to a brushy gully. Red led the way into the brush. A few minutes later half a dozen men went pounding past, spurring their horses. Red watched them go and grinned. "They'll be halfway to Alamogordo before somebody gets the bright idea that maybe we didn't go that way." Red had a big bruise under his left eye, his nose was skinned, the knuckles on both hands were bleeding, he had lost his hat, and his naked torso was grotesquely white from his neck to his belt. But he had set up the deadfall, and won it.

When the posse was out of sight they rode up the gully for a couple of miles, came to a creek and followed it for almost an hour. By then Red's naked skin was beginning to sunburn, so they stopped in a grove of box elders till sundown. Then they went on, heading west into the hills.

Toward midnight they came to a little rancho where the woman, probably tired as well as careless, had left her washing on the line. Levi's, work shirts and underdrawers flapped in the dying moonlight like dismembered ghosts. Red chose a shirt, put it on, then pinned a five-dollar bill to the clothesline. As they rode on he said with a laugh, "That woman will leave her washing out every night for the next six months, figuring some well-heeled saint did this for her and may come back."

At dawn they came to a sheep camp just as the Mexican herder was getting up. Red picked up the rifle the herder had carelessly left standing against a tree and ordered him to cook breakfast for them. When they had eaten, Red appropriated the herder's hat, and when the herder called him vile Spanish names Red took the rifle to the second hilltop, emptied the magazine and jammed the weapon muzzle-down into the sod.

They worked north, keeping to the hills, eating at sheep camps and little ranches, until the money in Red's pocket and the thirst in his throat got the better of him. "To hell with this!" he said, and they rode in to Socorro. Red found a saloon and a poker game and Tom waited out his spree in a shabby little hotel room. And at last, haggard with a hangover and his pockets almost empty, Red said, "Let's go home."

## 27

The next spring they worked the early rodeos in eastern New Mexico and the Oklahoma panhandle, and that fall they worked little Colorado towns. It was the same story over and over. Tom won or lost, pretty much as Red told him to. Tom had learned most of the tricks, but now and then a horse outguessed him, and occasionally he was thrown when Red had ordered him to win. Red was furious each time, accused him of the double cross, but in his sober, good-natured intervals he said things evened out pretty well. "We're still eating, and I always say a man's doing all right as long as he don't go hungry or thirsty too long at a stretch."

Tom's life settled into a pattern of long rides between rodeos, when he just drifted and didn't even think; of days and nights in shabby hotels, third-rate cafes and noisy little towns where he slept, ate and waited; of hot, sweaty, horse-smelling, crowd-noisy arenas; of hard-riding go-rounds when he really lived. Those were the times for which he endured everything else, especially the winning rides that Red eventually ordered at every rodeo. The other riders paid him little attention. Time after time some gay-shirted, arrogant rider mistook him for a stable boy or a gangling kid who had sneaked into the arena and either ordered him out or tried to send him on some errand. That was inevitable. Tom had grown a couple of inches, put on twenty pounds of muscle and sinew and was almost as big as Red, but he still played the part of a back-country Indian kid with ragged hair and shabby work clothes. The other contestants, even the local amateurs, wore gaudy shirts, bright neckerchiefs and fancy-stitched boots. Tom looked like a rusty, bedraggled crow in a pen of peacocks.

Another winter and, when spring came, Red said he guessed they'd better try north Texas this time around. It was a long ride there and rodeos were far apart, bettors cautious. Red became sullen and surly. "No profit in this," he said. "We got to find some way to cover more ground." But Tom was riding well when he rode, and by early June Red decided to make a killing in one of the better shows up near the Oklahoma line. He picked up a fair-sized stake of winnings along the way and they moved in on the show Red had marked.

Red sized things up and decided on a final go-round win with big stakes. Tom made his routine rides in the first two go-rounds and was all set for the finals, when he would not only win Red's bets but would have the satisfaction of a really top-form ride.

When he went to the chutes before the finals, Tom wondered why Red was so pleased with the world. Finally Red said, "I've got a surprise for you." Tom asked what it was, but all Red would say was, "You just go out there and do your stuff and we'll go home in style!"

Tom had drawn a big roan that had thrown the best of the local riders in six seconds on the first go-round. It looked like the worst horse Tom had drawn all spring. Red said it was a tight bucker to the right, and fast. "Keep a short rein, power the bastard all you can, and you can ride him till hell-and-gone."

Tom settled himself in the saddle, dried his hands, measured a short rein and threaded it between his fingers. He set his spurs. The judges signaled ready and Tom gave the signal to the gateman. The bucking strap was jerked tight around the bronc's flanks, the gate swung open and the roan lunged out, bucking viciously. Tom powered the rein, hauled the horse's head around, and it went hog-wild. It bucked twice, then ran straight across the arena and slammed into the fence as though it were stone-blind.

Tom didn't even have time to kick free of the stirrups. His right leg was caught against a fence stringer and the stab of pain was like a lightning bolt through him. But he kicked free as the bronc went down and he sprawled on hands and knees. He got up, took three steps and fell, just out of reach of the bronc's thrashing hoofs. The horse had broken its neck.

The crowd groaned. The pickup men galloped up, swung out of the saddle and helped Tom to his feet. He tried to step on that right leg and would have fallen again if the men hadn't held him up. Red came running from the chutes, cursing like a devil, and helped Tom hop back to the chutes and sit down, dizzy with pain. A doctor came, a tall, leathery man, and after a quick probe with his fingers he said, "I think your leg's broken, son." He looked up at Red, standing by and still damning everything in sight. "Are you this boy's father?"

"Hell no!" Red said. "He's an Indian."

"I didn't ask the color of his skin," the doctor snapped. "Are you responsible for him?"

"I run things, if that's what you mean."

By then they had brought the stretcher. "Get him over to my office," the doctor said, "where I can make a proper examination."

The office was only a block down the street. The doctor gave Tom a shot to ease the pain, made a thorough examination and said, "The tibia's broken. That's the big bone in your lower leg. You're through riding for a couple of months, son."

Red, who was scowling and muttering to himself, exclaimed, "That's a hell of a thing to do to me!"

The doctor swung around, furious. "Whose leg is this, his or yours? Get out of here, you damn fool, and get a pair of crutches for this boy. There's a drugstore down at the corner. Now git!"

Red snorted, "I had close to fifteen hundred dollars on that ride!" But when the doctor turned on him again, Red left.

The doctor fitted splints and bandages. When he had finished he said to Tom, "I want you to stay out of the saddle till next fall. Understand?"

"How am I going to get home?"

"Where do you live?"

"In New Mexico, over near Aztec. I've got to ride home."

Just then Red came back, with the crutches. The doctor adjusted them, then asked Red, "How is this boy going to get home? He can't ride a horse."

"He'll get home all right," Red said.

"How?"

"I said he'll get home all right. Come on, Tom."

"Just a minute," the doctor said. "There's a little matter you are forgetting. My bill."

"That," Red said angrily, "is on the rodeo!"

"No, that's on you."

Red tried to argue, got nowhere. Finally he paid the doctor's bill and they left. Out on the street, Red demanded, "Why in hell, if you had to do something like this, couldn't you do it yesterday, before I put my money on you?"

Tom didn't answer. He was still dizzy and he was having trouble with the crutches. He hoped Red had left the horses in front of the arena. He didn't know how he could get into the saddle, but he figured he could ride, once he got on.

They went up the street to the arena's main gate, Red still snorting and snarling. Tom looked for their horses. They weren't anywhere in sight. Then Red cut across the street toward a battered green pickup truck with a two-horse trailer. He turned and shouted to Tom, waiting uncertainly at the curb, "Come on over here."

Tom hobbled across to where Red stood beside the truck, a half grin on his face. "Where are the horses?" Tom asked.

"In the trailer." Red gave a short, bitter laugh. "I said we'd go home in style, but I didn't figure I'd go home broke." He was both proud and angry. Pride won, for the moment. "I bought this outfit this morning, off of that calf-roper that broke *his* leg yesterday. He was hard up for doctor money. Get in." And he turned away.

"Where are you going now?" Tom asked.

"To get your chaps. And see if I can find that stakeholder and get my money back." Red crossed the street and went into the arena, truculent as a dog looking for a fight.

Tom crutched around the trailer. The horses were restless, nervous on the trailer's quivering floorboards. He saw the two saddles and the bedrolls in the back of the truck. He knew little about cars, but this outfit looked as though it had been over a lot of roads. And at last he opened the door, pulled himself up and settled himself in the well-worn seat and waited.

Red was gone fifteen minutes. He came back with a stormy look, tossed Tom's chaps in the back with the saddles, got behind the wheel and started the motor. He ground the gears, jerked to a start and snorted, "Goddamned thieves!" Obviously, he hadn't recovered his bet money.

Red wasn't much of a driver, but he did keep the outfit on the road and he avoided other cars and trucks, some of them by inches. Before they got to Albuquerque he stopped and bought a box of groceries for Meo and a case of whiskey for himself. Then he waited till late at night, when the streets were deserted, to drive through Albuquerque. Even at that, he needed several drinks to make it. A few drinks called for more, and by the time they reached Bernalillo, just before dawn, he didn't care which side of the street he drove on. He got through Bernalillo, though, and out into the open country before he was too drunk to see the roadside fences. There he pulled up and slept till late afternoon. Then they went on home. Red still had enough for a weeklong spree, and when

Meo went through his pockets he found almost a hundred dollars.

Meo took over the care of Tom's leg. He massaged it, urging the circulation, and when the bone began to knit he kept the ankle from going weak and stiff. By midsummer the leg seemed as good as ever. But, despite Red's objection, Meo insisted that Tom should stay out of the saddle till August. Then, Tom got on one of the gentle horses and rode out on the flats a few hours each day, getting the feel of the saddle again. Two weeks of that and he was ready to ride the broncs. They brought in the rough string, Tom began testing his skills and his timing, and by mid-September he was ready for the fall rodeos.

## 28

They went northeast, into Colorado again, but Red couldn't get things going his way. When they found a town with free money, the bettors were suspicious of Red or of Tom. When betting money was tight and Tom rode for purses, the purses were small. Red wouldn't admit it, but Tom had outgrown the look of a country boy, an awkward Indian kid. On the street or even on foot in the arena, he might look like a novice, but once in the saddle his skill and experience couldn't be hidden. He knew all the tricks, all the slick ways to lose a go-round, but even the judges seemed to sense that something was wrong. They didn't disqualify him once, but the bettors were suspicious and refused to walk into Red's setup traps.

With the truck they could cover more ground, so when they had no luck in Colorado they went up into Wyoming. Red made two good cleanups there. Then they moved into lower Idaho and from there turned south into Utah. Finally Red said, "We're not getting anywhere, and the season's about over anyway. We're going home."

So they went home, to rest, to eat Meo's beans and chili, to wait for spring and a new season.

Late February and Red was full of plans again. This time they would go to southern Arizona, where Red said there always was plenty of sucker money. But it was the same old story except that there were fewer rodeos in southern Arizona. They played only four shows between Gila Bend and Bisbee and Red won less than a hundred dollars. "A man could starve to death here," Red said. "We're going to Texas."

They stopped in Deming for a show and Tom picked up enough purse money to buy gas and hamburgers. El Paso,

Fort Stockton, Sonora and Fredericksburg treated them little better. Red couldn't raise a bet. They kept going east, and finally they passed Austin and Red brightened. "Now we're getting over in God's country, my old stomping ground. My old man had a cotton patch over east, near Crockett, and when I left home I worked this whole country with Doc Barlow, from Trinity River to Eagle Pass. Now we'll be eating high on the hog."

But it turned out to be a scrawny hog. Things had changed, apparently, since Red was there with Doc Barlow. But finally they hit a town where the pool-hall crowd had been winning race-horse money from the bookies, and Red set them up for a final-round killing. Tom did his part and Red collected close to a thousand dollars, his first real triumph that spring. But after that even Tom's luck began to run out. He couldn't seem to win even when Red ordered him to.

Finally Red demanded, "What the hell's going on?"

"I'm getting tired, I guess. My timing's off."

"Timing, hell! You can ride, or you can't. I know you can ride when you want to, and you damn well *better* ride in this next show."

They were in Duval County, west of Corpus Christi, and it was June. The show opened and for two go-rounds Tom's luck seemed to be coming back. He made good, clean rides, scored high. Then in the finals he drew a particularly mean horse and he knew he was going to lose as soon as he got in the saddle. He not only lost, he was thrown for the first time that season.

Red was furious. Tom wondered if Red was going to try to trounce him, and for the first time he wasn't afraid. He half hoped Red would try because he believed he could at least make a fight of it. But Red didn't make a pass at him. Instead, he cursed and demanded, "What happened this time?"

"I don't know. I was going all right in the first two go-rounds. Then I seemed to lose my timing. I don't know what happened."

"I was away ahead of you," Red snapped. "I figured you might throw it, so I laid off, didn't bet a dime on you. But you should have took the purse."

"I'm tired, Red. Let's go home."

"Home? We're not going home broke! No sirree! There's a show up in Uvalde County next week. We're working it. Understand? If we win, then we'll go home. But if you lose—" Red rubbed his fist and laughed, a short, ugly laugh.

So they drove north, to Uvalde County. They took a room at the hotel and Red said, "I'm going out and set things up. You stay here till I get back. Get rested up, if you're so goddam tired."

When Red hadn't come back by suppertime Tom went to a nearby cafe and ate alone. Red still hadn't come back when Tom returned to the room, so he went to bed early. It was after midnight when Red came in, stumbling and obviously drunk. Tom pretended sleep and Red fell into bed. He was still sleeping the next morning when Tom went out to breakfast. Then Tom went out to the arena to look at the horses and listen to the talk of the riders and hangers-on.

Nobody paid any attention to him. He wandered about the arena, paused at the chutes and listened to the men loafing there. It was the old, familiar talk about horses and women, the same old stories. He listened a little while, then went over and climbed into the empty stands and sat in the sun. And the questions came: Who am I? Where am I? Where do I belong?

Back in his memory, like a dream, he saw a boy he once knew, a boy called Bear's Brother. A boy who lived in the mountains, in the old way, a way that was now past, gone, cut off. Then, also far back in his memory, there was another boy, Thomas Black Bull. A boy who lived on the reservation, braided hair ropes and bridles, rode ponies in the creek-bed sand, herded sheep for Albert Left Hand.

He had known those boys. He remembered them. But he wasn't Bear's Brother, and he wasn't Thomas Black Bull.

Then he saw another boy, in the corral at Red Dillon's place, learning to be a bronc rider. Learning how a bucking horse acted, how to ride clean, how to ride dirty, how to win, how to foul out. Learning to do what he was told to do. That boy was partly himself, but still a stranger. That was the boy to whom old Meo once said, "You want to make a rumble in the belly of life."

He sat there, remembering, and he saw a little whirlwind pick up a puff of dust down in the arena and swirl it past the loafers sitting beside the chutes. The dust hid the men for a moment and he saw a crowd of riders there, shouting to each other, swearing at the horses, laughing, arguing. He heard the horses puffing, grunting, squealing, making the planks of the chutes clatter and groan. Saddles creaked, stirrups rattled, spurs jingled. The pickup men rode into place. The crowd cheered, stamped, whistled. The ten-second horn bellowed. Hoofs drummed, bat-wing chaps slapped like handclaps.

His nose quivered at the smell of horse sweat, man sweat, at the smell of the corrals, fresh pine oozing pitch, fresh hay, manure, urine. The choking alkaline smell of dust churned up in the arena, and the hot, clean smell of sunlight, the cool, clean smell of a cloud shadow. The smell of hot, sweaty leather, the horse smell, the sweat-and-wool smell of saddle blankets. The smell of old boots, dirty Levi's, sweaty shirts. The leather-and-horse smell of your own hands, the sour smell of your own hatband.

He saw the horses, rolling their dark eyes till the whites showed, baring their yellow teeth, laying back their angry ears, rippling a shoulder or a flank nervously, switching a tense tail. Hunching under the feel of the saddle in the chute, tensing every muscle as you let yourself down into the saddle, felt for the stirrups. The big horses, long-legged, bow-necked. The blocky ones, short-coupled, big in the barrel, hard-muscled in the hips and shoulders. The bawlers, the squealers, the silent ones that saved their wind for the bucking.

He felt the tightness in his belly as he sat in the saddle, braced, just before the gate opened. The quiver in his legs, spurs hooked just ahead of the horse's shoulders. That first lunge, the jab of the cantle in the small of his back, the thrust of the pommel in his lower guts. The feel of the horse you got through the rein, taut in your left hand. The feel of his ribs beneath your calves, his shoulders beneath your thighs. The feel of the stirrups, the rake of the spurs, the rhythm. The jolt of the ground through the horse's stiff legs, like a hammer blow at the base of your spine. The way a horse eases off just before the ten-second horn; the way another horse makes a final, desperate lunge just as you relax. The bellow of the horn, the grab for the pickup man, the vault from the saddle. The feel of the ground again, the ride done and over, and the weakness of your knees. The exhilaration, the sense of mastery. The contest won, not over the other riders but over the horse, the violence, the elemental force. The sense of triumph, of mastery, and then the slow letdown. . . .

The sun was beating at him. The arena lay hot and quiet, only the few loafers there at the chutes, still talking, still laughing at the same old woman-jokes. The empty stands around him.

He left the stands, went back to the hotel.

# 29

Red was up and dressed. "Where have you been?" he demanded truculently.

"Out at the arena," Tom said, "looking at the broncs."

"They've all got four legs, haven't they?" Red was bleareyed with a hangover and in an ugly mood.

Tom didn't answer him.

"Get over being tired? You'd damn well better. I've paid your entry fee and we're going for broke. I'm setting up the deadfall, so start figuring how to lose the first go-round and make it look good."

Tom shook his head. "No, Red."

"What did you say?"

"No. Bet it straight."

Red gasped. "Who the hell's giving the orders around here? I said I'm setting up the deadfall!"

"No, I'm going to—"

"Don't you say no to me!"

"I'm going to ride this one clean and for keeps."

"Why, you dirty, lousy, double-crossing little Indian bastard!" Red made a lunge at him.

Tom sidestepped the blow and knocked Red down. He scrambled to his feet and Tom knocked him down again. Red was slower getting up that time and Tom turned and left the room. Red didn't follow. Tom went downstairs, through the lobby and out onto the street where he walked for half an hour, letting his anger cool. Then it was almost noon so he went into a cafe and had a bowl of chili. When he had eaten he went back to the hotel room.

Red wasn't there. Tom waited ten minutes, then went out

to the rodeo grounds, got his gear, checked the saddle and took it out to the chutes. Red was nowhere in sight.

He had drawn the number-four ride so he sat down in the shade of the chutes and waited. Then his horse was in the chute, a short-coupled black with rolling eyes and quick movements. There still was no sign of Red, and when an old man with a gimpy leg asked if he wanted help saddling up, Tom said, "Yes, I can use some help."

The old man held the horse's head down while Tom set the saddle in place. He tightened the cinches, shook the saddle, let off a notch on the back cinch, took up a notch on the front one. "He's a fast bucker," the old man said. "Don't give him too much rein." Tom nodded and hitched up his chaps. He let himself down into the saddle and the old man handed him the rein. The first two rides were over and the third rider got the signal and went out on a hard-bucking bay. Tom glanced up, then looked for Red once more. Still no sight of him. He laced the rein through his fingers.

The third rider was over. Tom saw the rider limping back to the chutes, slapping at the dust on his shirt, and knew he had been thrown. Then the announcer bellowed, "Coming out of Chute Number Three, on Black Star—Tom Black!" The bucking strap was jerked tight, Tom set his spurs and braced himself. The gate swung open and the bronc lunged into the arena.

For the first few jumps Tom didn't know whether he could make it or not. Then something happened inside. He wasn't riding a bronc. He was riding a hurt, a hate. He had walked away from Red Dillon this morning because, though he hated him, he didn't want to kill him. Now he wanted to hurt and maim. All his tiredness was gone. His timing came back, all his skill. He raked and gouged with his spurs. He fought every pitch and lunge, punished the horse every way he could. And the horse fought back.

The stands roared, but Tom didn't hear them. He didn't

even hear the ten-second horn. His spurs kept gouging and the horse kept fighting. Then the pickup man was yelling, "Time! Time, you damn fool!" He grabbed the rein and Tom automatically reached for his shoulder, swung out of the saddle and pivoted off the pickup man's horse onto the ground.

He unbuckled and stepped out of his chaps and went back to the chutes. A waiting rider asked, "What are you trying to do? Kill off the livestock?" Then he saw the look in Tom's eyes and turned away, silent.

They brought his saddle and Tom left the arena, not waiting to hear the score for the round. He had made his ride. The score didn't matter.

He went back to the hotel. Red was there on the bed, deep in a drunken sleep. Tom started to leave the room, then turned back and went through Red's pockets. He found more than seven hundred dollars. He took all but ten dollars, then went back downstairs. He walked along the street and came to a candy store. On impulse, he went in, bought a bag of gumdrops, and went on up the street, his mouth full of candy. He came to a clothing store, its windows full of bright shirts, neckerchiefs, Levi's, jackets, boots. He stared at the display. He started to walk on, then saw himself in a corner mirror in the window. He stopped and stared, unbelieving, as though seeing himself for the first time. With his beat-up old hat, his long, ragged hair down on his shirt collar, his faded work shirt and his worn Levi's, he looked like an overgrown reservation kid. He stared for several minutes, then looked at the clothes in the window again.

He went inside and he bought a whole new outfit, cream-colored hat, pink-striped silk shirt, purple neckerchief, copper-riveted Levi's, fancy-stitched boots. He put everything on, left his old clothes in the fitting room, and paid the clerk. As he started to leave, the clerk said, "If those boots pinch, come back and—"

Tom dashed back into the fitting room and salvaged his

old boots, the one thing a bronc rider never throws away. You feel the horse, sense every move he makes, through your feet in the stirrups, through your old, soft, worn boots. New boots are stiff, hard, slick in the stirrups.

The clerk wrapped the old boots for him. "Throw everything else away?" he asked. Tom nodded. "Now," the clerk said with a smile, "all you need is a barber."

Out on the street, Tom saw a barber's striped pole. He went in and sat in a barber chair for the first time in his life. When the man in the white coat had finished, Tom just sat there, staring at himself in the mirror. The barber grinned at him in the mirror. "You sure needed a shearing," he said with a laugh.

Tom looked at the man, then at himself in the mirror again. He was no longer a boy. He was a man. He looked like a ranch hand fresh in town, shorn, slicked, and with two months' wages on his back. He looked to be eighteen or nineteen years old.

Still marveling, he went out on the street again. But he had to get used to this new self. He found a pool hall, went in and chose a stool opposite a big wall mirror. He sat there an hour, vaguely watching the players but mostly looking at himself in the mirror. Then it was suppertime.

He went to a restaurant. The waitress smiled at him. He couldn't understand why. Waitresses usually gave him one look and turned away, sniffing. The girls back of the counter watched him, talked among themselves, laughed, tried to catch his eye. When he had eaten, the girl at the cash register asked if he had enjoyed his meal, trying to get him to talk, to keep him there at the desk a little longer. But he paid his check and went out.

It was late dusk. As he walked along the street toward the hotel he saw two girls watching him. Wondering what was wrong with him, he paused at a store window, looking for a mirror. One of the girls came and stood beside him, making a show of looking in the window. He glanced at her and she smiled, asked, "Don't I know you? Isn't your name—" She paused, her eyes inviting.

He didn't know what to say. He wanted to run, and yet he wanted to stay.

"What *is* your name?" she asked.

"Tom," he said, but his tongue was slow and thick. "Tom Black."

"Tom! Of course! Don't you remember! I'm Kitty."

He didn't know anybody named Kitty.

She put a hand on his arm. "My," she said softly, "you are sure good-looking. I'll bet you're here with the rodeo."

He nodded. "Yes."

"I just love rodeo men!" She smiled. "And I'm not busy tonight."

He looked at her again and his sensitive nose caught the scent of strong perfume, a musky smell. His pulse throbbed in his temples. Then he saw the crow's-feet around her eyes, the slight pouchiness under her chin, the little blotches beneath the make-up on her face. He saw the hard, calculating look in her eyes, the provocative smile on her lips. And he knew what she was. He turned away.

She caught his arm again, pressed her body against him. "Tom, honey, don't go away. I've got a room—"

He pushed her from him and hurried up the street to the hotel. He got the key at the desk, went up to the room, hoping Red would be there. The room was empty.

He went to the window, looked out, then turned off the light and stood at the window a long time, letting his pulse throb and slowly ebb. There was only one thing that mattered to him—the arena, the battle with the broncs. Deliberately he went back over his ride today. It was a good ride, clean, skillful, with perfect timing. He was tired now, very tired. But tomorrow he would ride again. His draw was a leggy bay called Sleepwalker. A big horse, probably as mean as they come. Which suited him right down to the ground. Mean horse, spectacular ride.

Then he heard her voice again, remembered the smell of her, the feel of her as she pressed against him. "To hell with them!" he said aloud. "All of them, Red, and the women, and . . . all of them!"

And after a little while, dog-tired, he went to bed.

## 30

He slept late, and when he wakened there still was no sign of Red. He went down and ate a leisurely breakfast, went out to the arena and killed the morning doing nothing. He ate the noon meal near the arena, then got his gear and went out to the chutes for the second go-round.

The old man who had helped him the day before came looking for Tom again, didn't recognize him at first with the haircut and the new clothes. Then he grinned, whistled softly, hunkered down beside Tom and watched the calf ropers. "What happened to your redheaded sidekick?" he asked. Tom shrugged and made no answer. The old man asked no more questions.

Tom had drawn next to the last ride for the go-round. Even in the chute, while he was being saddled, Sleepwalker was just as mean as Tom had thought. When the gate swung open Sleepwalker put on a spectacular battle, and Tom made one of the best, most brutal rides of his life—rough, hard and punishing. The crowd didn't recognize him at first, then remembered his ride of the day before and began to applaud. Then it fell silent, awed at the cold viciousness and superb skill Tom showed. The horn blew and the crowd exploded in a roar of cheers. The horse was snorting bloody foam as the pickup men rode up and Tom pivoted out of the saddle. He kicked out of his chaps and went back to the chutes, the crowd still roaring, and the men at the chutes stepped back, making way, watching him in silence. Even the old man with the gimpy leg said nothing.

Then the last ride made his ride and the day's totals were announced. Tom Black was top man again. He was packing his gear when the head judge, a gaunt old-timer with a white mustache, came over and said, "You've got a crawful of cocklebure, son. Any special reason?"

Tom looked at him and shrugged.

"What are you trying to do? Kill yourself, or kill every horse you straddle?"

"I rode clean, didn't I?" Tom demanded.

The judge sucked his teeth a moment. "Look, son, forget it, whatever it is. Yes, you rode clean. You could be a champion in the big time, maybe. But if you keep on the way you're going you won't live to see the day."

"Does it matter?" Tom asked.

The judge saw the look in his eyes and walked away.

Late that night, around midnight, there was a banging at the door. Tom roused slowly, went to the door expecting Red to lurch in. Instead, there stood the gimpy-legged old man. "Your redheaded partner," he said, "is in the hoosegow."

"Drunk?"

"Drunk as a fiddler's bitch."

"Thanks."

"You going to leave him there?"

"Yes."

Tom closed the door and went back to bed.

The next morning he went to the stable and looked at the two saddle horses, debated for several minutes, then went out to the truck and trailer. He unhitched the trailer and drove the truck downtown to a garage. He traded it in on a secondhand black Buick convertible, paying the difference from the money he had taken from Red's pockets. He had them put the trailer hitch on the Buick, loaded the saddles and bedrolls in the car's trunk, and drove back to the livery stable. He hitched on the trailer and left the outfit parked there while he ate lunch. Then he went to the arena for the final go-round.

He won the finals with the same kind of all-out horse-killing ride he had made twice before, and he clinched top spot in the averages by a big margin. The old man helped him pack his gear, then went with him to the office to get his purse money. He gave the old man twenty-five dollars; then they went to the livery stable, loaded the horses in the trailer, and Tom drove downtown and parked at the jail. The jailer sent him to a justice of the peace and Tom paid Red's fine and got an order for his release. Red was still in a drunken stupor in a cell, but the jailer helped Tom wrap him in a blanket and load him into the back seat of the Buick. Then Tom headed for home.

He drove till about ten o'clock that night, then pulled off the road, got a blanket for himself, and slept in the front seat till dawn. Red was still dead to the world when Tom took to the road again. It was late morning before Tom heard him groaning and glanced back to see him hunched on the back seat, holding his head in both hands. Another half hour and Red tried to climb over into the front seat. He almost fell out, and Tom stopped the car long enough to let Red get in beside him.

Red's hands were shaky and his face was the color of an old gray blanket with two smoldering spark holes for eyes. He licked his dry lips and asked, his eyes shut, "Where are we?"

"We passed Fort Stockton a little way back."

Red opened his eyes and looked at Tom, then closed them tight before he looked again. His mouth fell open. "My God! Who are you?" He stared and licked his lips again. "You are Tom, aren't you?" Then he grinned, a silly grin. "You got a haircut. And a pink shirt. You goddam dude!"

Tom drove in silence.

Finally Red asked, "What happened?"

"I paid your fine and got you out of jail."

"That's right. They locked me up. Got to fighting, I guess."

"Probably."

Another silence. Then Red looked around, felt the upholstery, put his hand on the dash, and asked, "Whose car is this?"

"Mine."

Red tried to turn and look behind, but winced and held his head between his hands. "What'd you do? Sell the horses and the trailer?"

"No. They're hitched on. I didn't even sell your saddle."

"Good." Then Red asked, "You ride?"

"Yes."

"You win?"

"I won."

Red straightened up, felt in his pockets. He searched them, one by one. Finally he said, "Somebody rolled me."

"I did."

"When?"

"After the first go-round."

"I must have still had a pretty good wad, didn't I?"

"Quite a bit."

Red was silent a long time. At last he said, "Meo used to roll me. I don't know how much that old chili-eater took off of me, but plenty. Now you're doing it." He shook his head, winced again, covered his eyes with his hands. "I never could save a dime," he said. "Somebody always took it off of me. When I was a kid it was my old man. When he didn't have field work for me he hired me out, then took my wages. Then it was Doc Barlow. He paid me a dollar every Saturday, and if I didn't spend it before bedtime he stole it out of my pants. Then it was Meo. Now it's you." Red wasn't complaining. He was stating sad, unemotional fact.

They went through Pecos and kept going northwest. The sign said Carlsbad was 85 miles ahead. The Delaware Mountains loomed off to the left, on the skyline, with the Guadalupes beyond, to the north.

Red sat staring ahead, unseeing. Finally he said, "Doc Barlow had billy-goat whiskers and he wore a top hat and a fancy vest and a big gold watch chain across his belly. No watch, just that chain. I ran away from home and was a twelve-year-old squirt working for my keep at the Madisonville livery barn, and Doc Barlow came to town and gave me a job helping him sell Kickapoo Elixir. Great stuff, that elixir. Half raw corn liquor, half branch water and strong coffee, with a handful of quinine in every tubful to make it taste bad. We bottled it and sold it at every crossroads in south Texas."

He sat in silence several miles, then went on. "We sold Kickapoo Elixir two years hand-running. Then the Doc turned to revivaling. And working cures by laying on hands. He preached the loudest sermons you ever heard, and I passed the hat. But it was laying on of hands he was best at, especially with the women. The young, pretty ones, mostly. Then one night he laid hands on the wrong woman, and her man caught him at it. After that I had to take a job as a cowhand. Till I met up with Meo and took to rodeoing." He sighed. "If Doc Barlow had just stuck to the elixir, we'd have made a fortune."

He looked at Tom again. "We'd have made a fortune, back there in Uvalde County, if you hadn't got so stiff-necked, Tom."

"No, Red."

"You won, you said?"

"I won."

"I guess you're getting pretty good, Tom."

Another silence. Then Red said, "We'll go home and rest up. Then after the hot weather we'll go to California."

"No."

"We could clean up, out in California."

"No, Red. I'm through with that. All through."

"What you got in mind, Tom?"

"I'm riding for keeps, from here on."

"The big time?"

"Yes."

Red sighed. "Always wanted to see that Odessa show. And Fort Worth, and Texarkana." He reached for the big names. "Nampa, Torrance, Wolf Point, Calgary, Denver, Albuquerque." He was silent again. Then he said, "I'm glad you didn't sell my saddle, Tom. Fellow sells his saddle, he's just about at the end of his rope."

The spidery legs of a water tower, sign of a small town, were visible on the skyline eight or ten miles ahead. Red saw the tower and said, "Could you maybe stop up there, Tom, and let me get a bottle of the old elixir? I've got a hell of a hangover."

"I'll stop."

Red reached in his pocket, found nothing there, glanced at Tom, then sat disconsolate. When they reached the edge of town Tom slowed up and eased down the dusty street till he came to the local bar and grill. He parked and gave Red a five-dollar bill. Red went in, was gone five minutes, and came back with his bottle.

Then they went on home.

## 31

July passed, and August, simmering hot. September came and Red wanted to go somewhere, do something, find a rodeo or a poker game, anything for excitement. "Just a couple of shows," he urged Tom. "Keep you sharp for next spring." But Tom said no.

Red became surly, then silent. He finally saddled a horse and rode away. He was gone a week, came back with a hangover and was mean as a rabid coyote. Tom and Meo ignored him and harvested the beans and chilies, and September passed.

October came, and first frost. Tom brought in the horses and spent a week working with them in the corral. Red, Meo said, was still *malo,* meaning either sick or mean, or both, but he came out to the corral and growled, "Damn shame, you doing this when you could be riding for money and both of us having fun." Tom paid no attention to Red. When he felt that he was doing something wrong he asked Meo. Meo said, "You work too hard. Save your arm," and when Tom asked what he meant, Meo pointed out that he tended to power the rhythm horses. It was a shrewd observation. You powered the duckers and dodgers that kept changing rhythm, but the pattern buckers didn't need all that pressure on the rein. You rode with them, not against them.

He rode the rough string until he had satisfied himself. Then, the last week in October, Red rode off again. At dusk a week later a stranger rode down to the cabin, a little dark man on a scrawny mouse-colored horse. Tom went out to see what he wanted, but the man spoke little English. Tom called Meo. They talked in Spanish and Tom heard Red's name several times. Finally Tom asked, "What's the matter with Red? Trouble?"

"He is sick, this man says," Meo told him.

"Did he get shot, or carved up?"

Meo shook his head. "Sick." He patted his belly. "Very sick."

"Where is he?"

"Aztec. In the hotel there."

Tom went back into the cabin, got his hat and coat. When he came out, Meo and the stranger were at the barn saddling a horse for him. "No, Meo," Tom said. "I'll take the car. It's quicker."

"I forgot," Meo said. Then he said, "Wait!" and hurried to the cabin. Tom started the car's motor, and Meo came back and handed him a roll of bills. "Get the doctor," he said.

It was dusk and the road was only a trail, but Tom knew every turn, every gully. He made the thirty miles to Aztec in less than an hour, parked in front of the hotel and went in to the desk. A little, bald man was there. "Where's Red Dillon?" Tom asked.

The man looked up, frowning. "You come to get him out of here?"

"Where is he?" Tom demanded.

The man's white eyebrows jumped. He jerked his head toward the stairway and then came around the counter. "I don't like them to die in my beds. It's bad for business. You going to pay his bill?"

"I'll pay what he owes."

They went upstairs and along the hallway and the man jerked a thumb toward a door. Then he turned and hurried off.

The room was dark, but by the faint glow from its one window Tom saw a bed and someone in it. He moved toward it and stumbled over a chair.

"Who's there?" It was Red's voice, hoarse and rasping.

"Me. Tom. Where's the lamp?"

"On the dresser, over there."

Tom found the lamp, lighted it, and in the glow saw the chipped iron bed, the grayish sheet, the worn brown blanket, the streaked yellow wallpaper. And Red, his face gaunt and dark with a week's stubble, his eyes deep-sunken, red-rimmed. His hands lay listless.

"What happened to you?"

"I'm a sick man, Tom. Doc Wilson—" He gasped, caught a shallow breath. "Take me home. Don't let me die in this rathole."

Tom took one of Red's hands. The fingers gripped his with desperate strength. They felt hot. "How long have you been sick?"

"I lost track." Red tried to sit up, sank back on the dirty pillow. "Help me put on my pants and take me home."

"Pretty soon. After I see the doctor."

Red's eyes lighted in anger. He pushed Tom's hand away. "Just like the rest of them!" He tried for a jeering snarl, managed only a whine. "God damn all of you!" Then he reached for Tom's hand again and his fingers worked convulsively. "I didn't mean that, Tom. I didn't mean it." He pushed Tom's hand away again and growled, "Go on. Get the hell out. I don't need you, or anybody else!" He lay wheezing for a moment, frowning in pain. Then he whispered, "But come back, Tom. Come back and take me home."

Tom went downstairs. The man at the desk said Doc Wilson lived two blocks down, in the white house. Tom found the house, went in the door marked "Office" without knocking.

A thin, dark man with a florid face sat in his shirt sleeves at a rolltop desk littered with pill bottles, rolls of bandage and adhesive tape, bottles of dark medicine. He was smoking a handmade cigarette and flakes of tobacco polka-dotted his shirt front. He looked up, scowling. "Who are you? What do you want?" His voice was a tired growl.

"I'm Tom Black. I want to find out how sick Red Dillon is?"

The doctor took a deep puff on the cigarette, slowly let out the smoke, then dropped the butt into a cracked soup bowl already overflowing. He stamped out the coal with his thumb and wiped it on his blue serge pants. "Dillon," he said, "has a bad heart, his kidneys are riddled, his liver is shot to hell, and he's got a double hernia. That answer your question?"

"Is he going to die?"

"Yes."

"How soon?"

The doctor shrugged. "I saw him three hours ago and figured he'd be dead by dark. He's still alive, I take it."

"Yes. I'm going to take him home."

"You'll have a corpse before you get halfway there."

But Tom had turned toward the door.

"Wait a minute, son," the doctor said.

Tom paused. Doctor Wilson got up, wearily shouldered into his coat and put on his hat. "I'll go with you, have another look." He picked up his black bag, tucked in the dangling stethoscope and snapped it shut.

They went back to the hotel, ignored the man at the desk and went up to Red's room.

Only Red's eyes moved as they came in. He watched them a moment, his eyes vague, then rasped, "Where's Meo? Tell the old chili-eater to make a fresh pot of coffee. Got a hell of a hangover." He lifted one hand, let it fall limply and licked his lips.

Tom glanced at the doctor, who took the stethoscope from his bag, thrust the ends into his ears and held the diaphragm to Red's chest. "Leave me alone," Red growled, gasping. He lifted a hand, tried to push the stethoscope away. The doctor stepped back, slowly shaking his head.

Tom took Red's hand. It clutched desperately. Then Red's eyes seemed to clear. "Take me home, Tom," he ordered. He tried to sit up. Tom put an arm around him, supporting him, and Red stared at him and whispered, "Better luck next time." He swallowed hard and his eyes closed, then opened again as with a great effort. His lips moved, whispering again, and Tom leaned close. "Game's over," Red said. Then Tom couldn't catch the words until Red gasped, ". . . dirty deal." Then the breath seemed to ease out of him.

Tom let him back gently onto the pillow. He glanced at the doctor, who held the stethoscope to Red's chest a moment, waited, listened again. "That's it," he said. "He's gone." And he drew the sheet up over the lifeless face.

They went downstairs. The man at the desk looked up, questioning. "He's dead," the doctor said.

"Goddam it!" the man cried. "Another bed ruined, and—"

"Shut your foul mouth," the doctor snapped. "Isn't there any decency in you?"

"Where's the room key?" the man asked sullenly.

"In my pocket. And if anybody goes in that room before the undertaker comes, you'll answer to me." He turned to the door. "Come on," he said to Tom, and they went out into the street.

Tom hesitated. "I'd better go back and pay for the room."

Dr. Wilson put a hand on his arm. "Let the damn fool wait. I'm the coroner, and I'm running things now. Where's your horse?"

"I drove in." Tom nodded toward his car.

The doctor got in and they drove back to his house. "Come on in," he ordered.

They went into the doctor's office and he got a bottle and two glasses from a cabinet, poured two drinks. He handed one to Tom, said, "You can use this," then lifted his glass and said, "*A los muertos,* as they say." He took a gulp, then glanced at Tom. "But you're not Mexican, are you? No. Well, anyway, to the dead. Just like the rest of us, he didn't want to die. And, like the rest of us, he was mortal." He sat down at his desk and deliberately rolled a cigarette, brushed the spilled tobacco from his shirt front and struck a match. He smoked for a moment, then said, "Weren't you the kid Dillon used to take the gambling crowd to a cleaning at the rodeo here a few years back?"

"Yes."

"What do you do now?"

"I'm a bronc rider."

"You any good?"

"I'm a good rider."

The doctor nodded, then sighed and took another gulp from his glass. "At your age, we're all good. Or think we are. Then life catches up with us, no matter who we are." He sat silent a long moment, then said, "I suppose Dillon didn't leave a dime."

"I guess not."

"Just that hideout of his, out on the river. He didn't even own that. Or didn't you know? Just a squatter. He have any livestock out there?"

"A few bad horses, buckers. That's all." Then Tom realized what the doctor was saying. "I'll pay to bury him," he said.

The doctor looked at him, surprised, but all he said was, "I guess he deserves a coffin and a prayer. He was a human being, no matter what else. Want me to notify the undertaker?"

"Yes."

"What are you going to do now?"

"Go home and tell Meo."

"I mean from here on. Get a job as a cowhand, or a wrangler?"

"I'm going down to Odessa the first of the year, to ride."

"Rodeo?"

Tom nodded, and the doctor glanced at him and said,

" 'Time is the rider that breaks youth.' " He slowly shook his head. "A man named George Herbert said that almost three hundred years ago, and it's still true. Most of us are a long time learning it." He sat silent, considering, as though wanting to say more. Then he said again, softly, "A long time learning," and he sat staring at the glass in his hand.

Tom set down his glass, half finished, and got to his feet. The doctor looked up, and Tom felt that he was a lonely man, reluctant to see him go. But he got up and went to the door with Tom and out onto the porch. He said, "I'll get the undertaker."

Tom got in his car and started the motor. The doctor was still there on the porch, his head tilted back a little, staring up at the stars. He was still there as Tom drove away.

Tom drove home, wondering whether Red would care whether he was buried in the graveyard, or out on the flats, or wrapped in a blanket and left in a cave somewhere in the bluffs along the river. Probably the graveyard was best. With a coffin and a prayer, as the doctor said. Maybe Red would be at peace there.

He went home and found the stranger, the man who had brought the message, still there, asleep in Red's bunk. He didn't rouse, but Meo did when Tom went in. Tom told Meo that Red was dead.

Meo sat up and crossed himself. "So," he said. He asked no questions. He sat there on his bunk for several minutes, then lay down again, turned his face to the wall and went back to sleep.

Two days later they buried Red in the dusty little graveyard, just Tom and Meo and the undertaker and his helper and the preacher. The preacher, a tired little pinched-face man in a shabby black suit, said the service by rote and read a short, impersonal prayer. Meo crossed himself and muttered something in Spanish, and Tom whispered part of an old chant in words he had almost forgotten. Then the undertaker's helper began shoveling the dirt into the grave, the clods thumping hollowly on the black coffin.

Tom gave the preacher five dollars and would have given him a ride back to town if he had as much as said thank you. He didn't, so Tom left him to walk or go back with the undertaker. He and Meo drove back into town, paid the doctor and the bill at the hotel. The undertaker had already been paid, before the funeral, so that closed matters. They headed for home.

Meo sat silent for a long time. Then he said, "It costs money to die."

Tom nodded. Most of the money had come from the roll of bills Meo had given him the night they got word Red was sick. Red's own money, in a way, money that Meo had taken from Red's pockets. And he thought of Red's words: "I never could save a dime. Somebody always took it off me." Well, some of Red's money went to give him a decent burial."

A little later Meo said, "Now it is my place."

"Yes," Tom said. "It's your place now, Meo."

Meo gave him a quick glance, as though surprised at having no argument about it. "When my time comes," he said, "then it is your place."

"Don't worry about that, Meo. I won't be here long."

"You going away?"

"I'm going to Odessa in a few more weeks."

"Odessa?" The name seemed to mean nothing to Meo.

"Odessa, Texas. That's where the big rodeos start the year."

"So. You make the big rumble."

"I'm going to make the big rumble, yes. Do you want to come along?"

Meo shook his head. "I rode my horses. I am an old man."

It didn't matter to Tom whether Meo went along or not.

Nobody else can live your life for you. You have to ride your own furies.

He said, more to himself than to Meo, "I've got a lot of riding to do."

"What?" Meo asked.

"I've got a lot of horses to ride," Tom said.

## 32

Odessa was just a small southwestern Texas town, but because its rodeo opened the season it drew big crowds and long rolls of contestants. Veteran riders and ropers went to Odessa to test their skills and reflexes and weigh them against the inevitability of time. Newcomers went there to see if youth and hunger for glory could outweigh experience in the arena. Many newcomers were weeded out at Odessa. Some persisted a few more weeks, as the circuit moved across the Southwest and crept slowly northward with spring. A few, the fortunate, skillful few, stayed and rode to glory.

Tom Black was one of the newcomers, and at first he was lost in the detail and the routine. But he found a hotel room, paid his entry fees, studied his draws and had time to appraise the horses and listen to the talk. He had heard most of the talk before, but the horses were new, trained buckers, big, mean, and natural outlaws whose violence was fostered and encouraged. The veteran riders discussed them and swapped stories about them. Tom listened and looked and drew his own conclusions, knowing that all talk ends when you are astraddle a bronc and the chute gate opens.

He had ridden enough horses, heard enough crowds, been in enough arenas, that he thought he wouldn't be tense or nervous when his turn came. But his hands were sweating and his legs were quivering as he sat in the saddle awaiting the signal for his first go-round ride. The signal came, the bucking strap was jerked tight, the gate swung open. The horse lunged twice, ducked, the rein slipped and Tom was almost thrown. Fortunately, the horse was a rhythm bucker. Tom recovered and finished the ride clean, but as he walked back to the chutes he knew it was a mediocre ride. He hadn't been thrown; that was all he could say for himself. But his first ride was over, his first ride in the big time.

He lay awake that night going over every wrong move he had made, and he did better the next day in the second go-round. But he still was too tense, trying too hard, and he knew it.

Then in the finals he drew a horse so mean and full of fight that he had no time to think of anything or do anything but ride. For the first time at Odessa, he rode the way he knew he could. When the scores were announced he placed second in the final round, won enough place money to pay his hotel bill. The money mattered little. He had begun to find himself. That *did* matter.

The Odessa show closed and he went on to the next show, and the next, and the next. The lists began to thin out as the newcomers dropped out. But Tom Black was still there, doing better in each show. Then, in Fort Worth, he made two spectacular rides and knew the glow of satisfaction, the triumph of mastery. That was the turning point.

In the next two months he rode eight shows and finished in the money in six of them. The crowds began to know him by name, to watch for him. He was talked of as the best first-year man on the circuit. Then, before he realized it, he began to lose. He finished out of the money in three shows in a row before he remembered Red Dillon's bitter words: "You start riding for the crowd and you forget what you're there for." He was no longer riding to Red's orders, but he was riding for the crowds, trying to be a hero. He stopped listening for the cheers and became a rider, a man fighting it out with a horse. He began to win again.

The weeks settled into a pattern. There was the long drive to a strange city, the strange hotel room, the strange arena. There were the events that meant nothing to him, the bull riding, the calf roping, the steer wrestling, the trick riding, sometimes the inconsequentials of a horse show. There was the waiting, the long, dull hours of waiting. Then the one thing that mattered, the bronc riding, the battle between man and horse. Three rides, three brief moments when he came fully to life. Then the pattern started all over again.

The weeks became months. Summer passed. The circuit reached Albuquerque and for some reason, he didn't know why, everything went right for him. He drew the worst horses he had drawn all season. His timing was perfect. He made three all-out rides, and he won every go-round, placed top in the averages, took the big purse.

The night the show ended he decided to skip the next show, drive home and see Meo, take a few days off. The break, he decided, would do him good. The next morning he bought a new car. Then he bought two cartons of groceries and headed for home.

He reached the cabin in midafternoon. Meo was in the garden, pulling bean vines. When Tom went to greet him the old man peered at him and said, "Who are you? You bring news about Tom?"

"I am Tom, Meo," Tom said.

The old man shook his head. "Tom," he said, "is a boy, like this," and he held his hand at shoulder height. Then he bent to pull another bean vine.

Tom put a hand on his shoulder. "Boys grow up. Come help bring in the groceries, Meo."

Meo went with him to the car and they carried the cartons into the cabin. Tom set the jars and boxes on the table and Meo examined the label on each one, just as though he could read, before he put them carefully on the shelves beside the fireplace. When they had finished he said, "Get the cups," and he poured coffee and they sat down and looked at each other.

Finally Meo said, "You have been gone a long time. Too long. Tomorrow we finish harvesting the frijoles."

Tom tried to tell him about the big circuit, where he had been, what he had done, and especially about Albuquerque, which he was sure Meo would understand. But Meo only waited for a pause long enough to say, "And next week we harvest the chilies."

Before he went to bed that night Tom went out and hid all his money but ten dollars in his car. Sometime during the night he wakened and saw Meo going through the pockets of his pants, but the ten dollars was still there the next morning.

Tom helped with the beans for three days and they got them all harvested and threshed. The third evening Tom said he was leaving the next morning. Meo seemed to pay no attention, but at breakfast the next morning he said, "You come, you go, just like him." He smiled, wryly. Tom finished eating, put on his coat and hat, and said, "I'll be back late in November, Meo." And the old man said, *"Vaya con Dios,"* then added, *"y el diablo."* It was his farewell, "Go with God, and the devil," and Tom didn't know, or much care, whether it was a blessing or a curse.

He caught up with the circuit, rode it through, week by week, till the last week in November, then called it a season and went home. He felt entitled to a month's rest.

Meo made no pretense of not knowing him. He gloated over the groceries, as before, then set out the coffee. "Now you come back to stay?" he asked.

"For a month or so."

"Then?"

"Then I go back, ride some more."

"You win this time?"

"Sometimes I won, sometimes I didn't. It was a pretty good season." There was no reason to tell Meo that he had been named the best first-year man on the circuit.

Meo peered at him, speculating. "You bring a bottle?"

Tom knew what Meo was thinking. He had stopped out on the flats, before he came down to the cabin, and hidden most of his money in the car. "No bottle," he said. Then he reached in his pocket and drew out two hundred dollars in tens. He spread them on the table, divided then into two equal piles and pushed one pile over to Meo. Meo counted it, then asked, "This is what you win?"

"That's your share. And," he added, "you don't have to roll me for it."

Meo folded the money carefully and put it into his pocket. He shrugged, smiling to himself. "We do not tell all we know, eh? We are of the old people, you and me." He chuckled, then got up and set out bowls and dished out beans and chili. "Eat," he ordered. "The frijoles are good, big and strong. They make a big rumble, bigger than you make."

Tom stayed a month, then packed his gear and was on his way again, back to Odessa and the big circuit. He was a second-year man now. He took up where he had left off, won the number-two purse in the first show, then took top money in the next one. Nobody could win them all, but if his luck held he would break the tradition that a good first year is always followed by a poor second season.

For three months he was in the money in every show, and rodeo people began to say that Tom Black was on his way to the championship, something practically unheard of for a second-year man. Then in May he began to override the horses, pressing too hard. He finished out of the money in one show, took fifth place in the next, then was thrown for the first time that season. And realized that he had been playing to the crowd, trying to overpower every horse he straddled. He eased off and began to win again.

Then it was June, hot, sweaty June. The heat never bothered Tom, but it seemed either to slow down the horses or make them extra mean, depending on the horse. His first go-round horse was the mean kind, but he rode it clean and hard. For the second go-round he drew a horse he knew, one he had ridden six weeks before. It was a ducker and dodger that bucked a tight pattern close to the chutes.

As he saddled up he decided to power it from the start, try to work it out away from the chutes, then give it its head and let it give him the worst it had. He resined his chaps, dried his hands, eased into the saddle and measured his rein. The announcement blared. "Coming out of Number Two Chute, on Nightmare, Tom Black!"

The gate swung open. The crowd roared. The horse lunged out in the pattern Tom remembered, three quick jumps, then a duck and a dodge. He powered its head around to the left, to prevent its spin to the right and back toward the chutes. It made another lunge, tried to duck, and he powered it again, and it seemed to go crazy. It reared, danced, squealed wildly, then lunged right, toward the chutes, lunged again.

Number One Chute was empty, its gate swung back, a helper holding it. As the horse lunged toward the chutes, the helpers scattered. The horse plunged against the open gate, struck it with its shoulder. There was a crash and a splintering of planks and the broken gate swung loose. Tom tried to power the horse into the open, but it lunged wildly, reared, plowed into the broken gate and struck the chute full force. Tom, fighting the rein, was thrown heavily against the chute.

The horse screamed, kicked madly. Men shouted. The crowd groaned. Tom, on the ground inside the empty chute, saw blood spurting. In the lunge that threw him, the horse had impaled itself on a splintered plank. A sliver broad as a man's hand had pierced the horse's chest like a huge bayonet, then broken off. Still screaming, the horse went down, hoofs flailing, frantic head pounding the ground.

Pain stabbed through Tom's chest and he was gasping for breath, but he pulled himself to his feet and reached for the chute to steady himself. A new stab shot up his right arm. Then an official pushed through the milling riders and helpers and held a pistol to the doomed horse's head. The roar of the mercy shot was like a jagged prong through Tom's chest. The horse let out all its breath in one last long gasp, then relaxed, dead.

Someone was shouting in Tom's ear, "You hurt?" He turned and saw a youngish sandy-haired man with a black bag, the arena doctor.

Tom said, "No. Just . . . shook up."

The doctor watched his face, saw his quick gasps for breath. "Can you walk, or shall I call a stretcher?"

"I'll walk."

They went to the first-aid room and the doctor stripped back Tom's shirt and made a quick examination. He loaded a syringe, jabbed it in Tom's left arm. "This will ease the pain. Your right arm's broken and probably a few ribs." He turned to an older man. "I want X rays of his right arm and his chest. I'll be at the hospital by the time they've got the pictures."

Half an hour later Tom was in a hospital bed and the doctor was splinting his arm. "The radius is broken," he said, "the big bone. But the ulna's all right." He reached for the tape. "And you've got four broken ribs. I'll have to tape you. That's all I can do for them. But you're going to lie here a few days till we see how your guts are." He gave him another shot. "You're through riding for a while. I'll see you tomorrow."

The next day they took more X rays, and they kept him quiet with sedatives for three days. The fourth morning he refused all medication, and, when the doctor came in, Tom had his pants and his boots on and was trying to get into his shirt. "What do you think you're doing?" the doctor demanded.

"I'm getting out of here."

"All right. I came in to tell you you're all right inside, no internal injuries. But you can't go back to rodeoing till that arm knits. A couple of months or so. Where are you going?"

"I'm going home."

"Where do you live?"

"New Mexico."

"How are you going to get there?"

"Drive."

"Who's going with you?"

"Nobody."

"You're going to drive to New Mexico with one arm?"

"Why not?"

"Tough as rawhide, aren't you, and stubborn as all hell." The doctor stripped the tape from Tom's chest. "These ribs will be sore for a while and it will hurt to take a deep breath. But they're knitting. I'm telling you, though, stay off a horse for two months. Understand? And have a doctor look at that arm when you get home."

So Tom left the hospital. He got his car and his gear and headed west.

## 33

It was midafternoon when he came to the bluff and looked down at the cabin. In that first look he had the uneasy feeling that something was wrong. He drove on down the slope, parked the car and went to the cabin. He pushed open the door and saw that no one was there. He went out to the garden, found the beans and chilies choked by knee-high weeds, and returned to the cabin. Meo's bunk was made, the cooking pots were empty and clean, the dishes washed and in their places. Whatever happened, Meo had left the cabin in order. He went out to the barn. It was empty and Meo's saddle was missing.

Tom got in his car again and drove to Aztec. He went to Dr. Wilson's house, banged on the door and walked into the empty waiting room. The doctor came out of his office and exclaimed, "Tom Black!" and reached out to shake hands, then saw the splinted arm. "What happened to you?"

"Just a broken bone or two. Where's Meo? Have you see him? That's what I came about."

"Come on into the office."

They went in and sat down, and the doctor said, "Meo is dead."

"When?" Tom asked. "What happened?"

"About a month ago. He rode into town one afternoon and came to the office and sat out there in the waiting room for an hour, I guess, before I saw him. I brought him in here and asked him what was wrong, and he said, 'I am going to die.' He didn't look sick to me, but I took his pulse and blood pressure. They were normal. I couldn't find anything wrong."

"How was his mind?"

"Clear as a bell. I told him to go home and forget it, that he'd live another twenty years. But he just shook his head and said, 'No. Tonight,' like that, just as if he knew all about it. And he gave me a roll of bills and said I should see that he was buried right, with a coffin and a priest. Then I asked him if he had seen the priest, and he said no, so I took him over to the rectory and Father Gomez said he would take care of him. He sent a boy back to get the old man's horse and I figured Father Gomez would listen to him, put him up for the night, and the next morning he would stop in, pick up his money and go on home, satisfied."

The doctor paused for a moment. Then he went on. "The next morning, while I was eating breakfast, a boy came and said Father Gomez wanted me to come right over, so I went. Meo was dead. Father Gomez had put him up for the night and he'd died quietly in his sleep." He looked at Tom, frowning, baffled. "That's the story. I wish now I'd done an autopsy, but I'd swear there wasn't anything wrong with him. His heart was as good as mine!"

"He knew," Tom said.

"What do you mean, he knew?"

Tom shrugged.

"I've known some of these old people to wish themselves to death, but that was when they were dying anyway. He wasn't sick! I'm telling you, he wasn't sick."

Tom made no comment. Dr. Wilson shifted uneasily in his chair. "Anyway, I gave the money to Father Gomez and he arranged the funeral. Did it up right. So," he concluded, "that's what happened. . . . Now, let's have a look at that arm of yours."

He examined the arm, said it was knitting nicely, and readjusted the splints and bandages. He probed Tom's chest with his fingers, listened to it, and said as he put away his stethoscope, "Young bones knit fast. What are you going to do now?"

"Go out to the place till this arm's all right."

"That'll be another month. Better let me have a look at it again next week. You all through rodeoing?"

"No."

The doctor looked at him, speculating. "I'd think you'd want to settle down. You could buy that place cheap, I imagine. Put a little herd of sheep out there, or a few cattle—"

But Tom was shaking his head.

"Look," the doctor said, "I know you're a reservation boy, but you're smart and you could make something of yourself. You saw what happened to Dillon and old Meo. Dillon was a tinhorn gambler who drank himself to death. Meo Martinez was an illiterate Mexican just two steps away from a *jacal*. He still believed in *espíritu*. But you've got a chance, if you'll take it."

He stopped, wondering if he had said too much. Tom seemed to have retreated into himself. You talk to a Mexican that way and he smiles and nods and seems to agree, even though he goes out and does things the way he always has. But time after time he had seen an Indian just sort of draw the curtains and retreat, as though he was slipping back into the remote past, into a kind of pride that was all mixed up with hurt and resentment. Tom Black was doing that right now, retreating into an emotional cave. When that happened there wasn't a thing you could do. You could talk yourself blue in the face and get nowhere.

The doctor shrugged. "Well," he said, "it's your life. As George Herbert said, 'The wearer knows where the shoe wrings.' We've got our own demons and our own necessities, I suppose. There may even be a pattern all laid out for us. Who knows?" He got to his feet. "Come back to see me next week?"

Tom thanked him and left. What the doctor had said made him remember the agent at the reservation. But he shrugged it off. It was of no consequence. He didn't want to think about those things.

He went back to the cabin on the river, aired it out and tried to settle in. But the cabin, for all its familiar corners, was a strange place, alien. For two days he sat in the sun, going inside only to cook his meals and sleep. Then he looked at the garden, at the bean plants and the chilies being choked by the weeds. He was tempted to pull the weeds, as Meo would have done. Then he thought: Meo is gone. His sweat and his footsteps are almost forgotten. If the beans and the chilies cannot live with the weeds, they do not belong here. I do not hate those weeds. I do not belong here either, and now Meo is gone.

Instead of weeding the garden, he walked, to keep his legs strong. He walked upstream, and five miles up the canyon he saw four of Red's old rough string, the broncs. They were wild as deer, snorted, tossed their heads and ran at sight of him. He walked a few more miles, then went back to the cabin. Neither then nor in the next few days did he see the other broncs or the second saddle horse. They had either wandered off and joined some other horse herd, or a mountain lion had come down the canyon and made a few meals of horse meat. It didn't matter any more than the garden mattered. They had been Red Dillon's horses, and Red was gone.

Two weeks passed before he remembered the doctor. It didn't seem important to go and see him. His bones would heal. They were his bones, not the doctor's. He flexed his arm to keep the joints from stiffening, and he took off the bandages and the splints and massaged the muscles, forced the circulation to help the healing. He began using the arm, carefully.

Then he walked out onto the flats. He saw an occasional jack rabbit and a few pronghorns, and almost every day he saw a prairie falcon hunting ground squirrels. Then he found a small prairie dog town and he sat and watched the prairie dogs and the burrowing owls. He sat there, not thinking, feeling the sun on his back and the strength of the earth beneath him, and vague, cobwebbed memories came back, memories of Albert Left Hand. They drifted through his mind, like shadows, and they left a dull ache that brought back memories of Benny Grayback and Blue Elk. He pushed the memories away and got to his feet and walked back toward the cabin.

He was a stranger here. He had always been a stranger. All he had here was a hatful of memories. And what did the memories mean? Nothing. Less than nothing. They were like scars. You looked at them and remembered old hurts that had healed over.

He went back to the cabin, and it was a place full of strangeness. He knew every corner, and yet he didn't belong there. He cooked his supper and ate, and he went outside and sat in the dusk. Bullbats "peened" overhead and dived on roaring wings. The first stars came out and the cool dampness crept in from the river. The afternoon's memories came back, and he put them away again, and he looked at the corral, its poles now tumbling down, unused, neglected. He looked at the barn, empty, meaningless. Then he saw himself in the corral, learning to ride, to match and master the violence of the fighting, squealing broncs. Learning to punish with raking spurs, a vicious rein, a brutal ride.

He sat, and the late moon rose, and the shifting shadows and the thin moonlight seemed to set the rails in place again and he saw a deep-set snubbing post and a bear cub chained to it. And in the vague tree-shadowed light the barn became a barn where a boy who hated the smell of cows was forced to clean the stinking stalls, where a tormented boy was flogged for turning on his tormentors.

He sat there a long time. It was almost midnight. He

shifted his legs and felt the cramps in them, and the ache was in his arm. He got to his feet, eased the cramps and rubbed the ache, and then he went to his car, got in and drove it over to the foot of the bluff and left it there. He came back to the cabin and got an ax and a handful of matches and went out to the corral. He carried the fallen rails and piled them against the barn and he loosened the other rails with the ax and added them to the pile. Then he went into the barn, started at the far end and set a series of fires in the litter of old hay, and went back and sat down in front of the cabin.

The barn was tinder dry. Within fifteen minutes the flames were leaping through the roof. Then the roof fell in with a roar and a great billowing of embers. Some of the embers came all the way to the cabin and hissed and smoldered on the roof and died in the night dampness there. The grass, midsummer green and wet with river dew, steamed like fog in the blast of heat and shriveled and charred in a great circle around the barn and halfway to the cabin. The big cottonwoods rustled, and those near the barn sizzled and spat and set up little spurts of flame all along their coarse-barked branches.

Then the flames began to die down. They slowly subsided into a great bed of coals that winked and hissed and spurted in sudden, angry life. The darkness crept back, now twice as dark as before, with the huge torch burning out. The valley was gray with acrid smoke, held close by the night's damp air, the smolder of old hay adding its sour stink to the woodsmoke and the smell of charred green cottonwoods.

At last Tom got to his feet and went inside and to bed.

It was midmorning when he wakened. The cabin smelled of smoke and smoldering hay, and the ashes of the barn still fumed and sent up curls of white smoke. He cooked and ate breakfast, then packed his gear. He brought the car to the door, loaded it and took it back and left it at the foot of the bluff. Then he returned to the cabin, split a big armload of kindling and piled it carefully in the middle of the floor. He moved the table and benches over beside it, then set fire to it and went back to his car and sat down in the shade and waited.

The windows began to glow with the flames inside. Then the smoke threaded out through the cracks and began to billow out the doorway. A window fell in and flames reached out and licked at the eaves. The flames burst through the roof and towered, hissing and crackling. When the roof fell in, a great shower of fine white ash was carried high into the air by the blast of heat and, drifting on the breath of a breeze, fell like fine snow around him and on the car, harmless white ashes, fine as dust.

The big cottonwoods beside the house withered and seemed to shrink and curl, and flames crept up their big limbs like hungry red tongues. The trees hissed and spat, then began to pop like gunfire. The weedy garden withered as though under a sudden frost, and the tall weeds crumpled and fell and the whole garden disappeared, leaving only a patch of charred ground. The grass seemed to melt away in a spreading circle that met the circle scorched last night in the moonlight, and flaming embers fell there and blossomed briefly—red flowers that bloomed and faded in a few minutes. Then one wall tottered, sagged, fell with a fresh showering of embers and a new surge of flame.

Tom waited almost an hour, watching the flames consume the cabin, log by log. Then the fire subsided into a great, smoldering heap of ashes with the chimney thrusting up like a stubborn black thumb. He got to his feet, brushed the fine white ash from his clothes and was aware for the first time of the deep, dull ache in his arm. he kneaded the muscles, accepting the pain almost gratefully. Then he got into his car, found the circuit schedule, saw that he had missed four shows. He had been here two days over a month. The next show was at Wolf Point, on the Missouri River up in the northeast corner of Montana. He had four days to get there, find a place to sleep, make his entry.

He took one more look at the dying fire that had been the cabin and at the scatter of char and white ashes that had been the barn. Then he started the motor and drove away.

## 34

Before Tom's ride in the first go-round at Wolf Point the announcer said, "The next man out is just back in business after a month out with an assortment of broken bones. A bronc put him in the hospital, and could be he's out for revenge. Anyway, here he comes, out of Chute Number Two, on High Tension—Tom Black!"

The crowd applauded as High Tension came lunging out. Three jumps and Tom was dizzy with the streaking pain. Every jolt drove the pain deeper, but he fought it down with raking spurs. He made a hard-driving ride all the way, then stumbled back to the chutes, rested ten minutes and went to his hotel room. The throbbing arm and the pains that racked his ribs kept him awake most of the night, but the next day he made the most punishing ride the Wolf Point crowd had ever seen.

He spent another sleepless night and went to the arena for the finals dizzy and blear-eyed, queasy and stumbling with weariness. But he steeled himself, saddled his horse, grimly waited out the riders ahead of him. Then he eased into the saddle, measured his rein, set his spurs and watched for the signal.

The announcer bellowed, "Well, folks, this is it. I said before the first go-round that the next man might be riding for revenge. I didn't tell you that the horse that put him in the hospital a month ago had to kill itself to do it. But it did! You've seen him make two all-out rides, and now he's set for his final. Is he still out for blood? My guess is yes! So here he comes, the old devil-killer himself, out of Chute Number Four on Red Devil—Tom Black!"

The crowd roared, the chute gate swung open, and the

big bay called Red Devil lunged out, fighting. Tom was swaying in the saddle as they left the chute, but he summoned strength from somewhere and he rode Red Devil like a fiend. It was an even more brutal ride than the one the day before. Tom demanded the worst the horse could give, got it, took it, and demanded more. The horse was in a bawling frenzy and snorting bloody foam when the horn blew, and Tom was so spent that he could scarcely pivot out of the saddle and off the pickup man's horse. He stumbled and went to his knees twice on the way back to the chutes. The crowd was in a turmoil of applause.

He sat for half an hour before the pains eased enough that he could go to his hotel room. There he fell into bed and stayed till the next afternoon, utterly exhausted. Then he went down and ate and went back and slept another twelve hours. On the second day he got his car and took off for the next show on the circuit.

He rode the next show, and the next, and the physical pain eased off. But his riding style had changed since that month off. He was still the slick, skillful rider who could pile up the points when he wanted to, but now he wasn't riding for points. He was riding for the ride, for the punishment he could give a horse. He still won enough purse money to pay his expenses, but if it was a choice between a clean, high-scoring ride and a rule-defying ride that brought out the worst in a horse, he ignored the rules. The rule book forbade a rider to touch horse or saddle with his free hand, but if he drew a horse that reared and danced instead of bucking he slapped it across the ears until it fought back. If he drew a quitter he asked for a reride on the same horse and came out of the chute raking and gouging in defiance of the rules, goading the horse to violent, malevolent action. He knew a dozen ways to drive a horse into a frenzy, and in show after show he let the points fall as they might and made the most racking, punishing rides ever seen on the circuit.

He didn't win the championship that year. He didn't even come close. But he left no doubt that the glib announcer at Wolf Point was right—he rode for revenge, though nobody was quite sure why. He was the devil-killer, and nobody worried or wondered about who was the real devil he was trying to kill.

He finished the season in California, spent a few weeks waiting, restless and resentful of the inactivity, then was on his way to Odessa again. The next season passed, and the next one. Wherever there was big-time rodeo, Tom Black's name was known, Killer Tom Black. The crowds waited for his name to be announced, applauded wildly at the announcement, then sat in tense silence while he made his ride. They cheered some riders in the arena, and now and then they booed a rider, but they neither cheered nor booed Tom Black when he was fighting it out with a bronc there in the arena. He rode in a silence so tense, so profound, that those in the far bleachers could hear the grunt and wheeze of the horse at every frantic lunge. Some even said they could hear Tom Black cursing the horse he rode, but that wasn't true. Tom Black rode in tight-lipped silence, even more quietly venomous in the saddle than he was on foot. And he was known as a hostile, silent man at the chutes, on the street, in the hotel lobbies. He had no friends, wanted none, needed none. He lived for only one thing—the violence of his rides in the arena—and the crowds sensed it. They sat silent when he rode because they were awed and morbidly fascinated. Tom Black was more than a rider. He was a kind of elemental force, a primitive scourge and a raw challenge that summoned diabolic violence from every horse he rode.

Tom Black didn't always master the horse; but that, too, was an element in the fascination. His losses were as viciously spectacular as his brutal winning rides. In Calgary one season he was not only thrown but stomped by a horse and carried unconscious from the arena. A week later he was riding again, "stuck together with tape, catgut and bandages," as other riders said. In Denver, two years later, a horse crashed into an arena barrier with him and broke his right leg again. But he was back in action with a steel brace on his leg a month later.

His worst accident was the one at Nampa, when his horse lunged over a pickup man's mount just as the horn blew. In the melee of men and horses, one horse broke a leg and had to be destroyed, and Tom's left shoulder was smashed by a flailing hoof. The shoulder healed so stiff he couldn't trust the rein in his left hand. But even before it had healed, he was riding again, an unorthodox right-handed rider. The combination of the forced change in style and the wrenching pain in his left shoulder made him awkward and off balance for almost two months. In anger at himself and to ease the pain, he began drinking. But the liquor slowed his reflexes as well as dulling the pain, and it made him more moody and truculent than ever. After half a dozen brawls in which the worst he got was a broken nose, he got into a Chicago saloon fight that sent him to the hospital with a concussion from a blow with a bottle and a knife slash across his shoulders that required thirty-seven stitches. After that he recalled Red Dillon's advice of long ago: "Take it out on a horse, where you've got a chance to win." He stopped drinking, became more of a recluse than ever, and rode with cold and ruthless fury.

## 35

Nobody knew what drove Tom Black, but he became a living legend. When rodeo folk gathered to swap stories, in hotel rooms, in hotel lobbies, or at the arena waiting for a program to start, the conversation always came around to saddle broncs, which always have been and always will be the heart of rodeo. So, when they gathered and talk began, during Tom Black's spectacular years, somebody would mention Steamboat or Midnight. Somebody else would speak of other legendary broncs—Iron Mountain, War Paint, Tipperary. And as the names were mentioned everyone—steer wrestlers, bull riders, calf ropers, even the acrobatic girls who were trick riders—paused to listen. Only the oldest of the old-timers had ever seen any of those fabulous broncs in action, but their names were as firmly embedded in the lore of the arena as are the centaurs and the Minotaur in Greek mythology.

They would talk of the horses, and they would mention the great riders. And before more than three names were said someone would say, "Well, for my money, Tom Black. . . ." And there would be a pause. Men would lift their heads and look around. Tom Black was never there in person, since he avoided such gatherings, but his presence was. And his name was always spoken with respect that verged on awe.

A first-year man, brash in his ignorance, might ask, "What year did Black win the championship?" And one of the veterans would say quietly but with rebuke in his voice, "Tom Black never won the championship. He never went after it." And if the first-year man was brash enough to persist,

"Why not, if he's so good?" the answer would be, "Old Man Satan never had to win a title to prove how good *he* was."

The comment was ambiguous, and intended so, and the reference to Satan was inevitable. Tom Black was sometimes called Devil Tom, and a kind of demonology, a Satanic folklore of fantastic stories, had grown up around him. One such story said that Tom Black and the Devil were first cousins, but that they had a quarrel and a fight and the Devil chopped off Tom Black's tail. Tom Black was so enraged that the devil had to turn himself into a bronc to get away. And, so the story went, Tom Black became a bronc rider and tried to kill or maim every bronc he rode, just to be sure he got the right one, since nobody knew which bronc was the Devil.

Another story said that Tom Black and the Devil once were partners, joint owners of Hell. The Devil wanted the place all to himself, so he challenged Tom Black to a pitch game with Hell as the stake. Tom wasn't a pitch player, as everybody knew, but he learned fast. He matched the Devil, trick for trick, three days and three nights. Finally the Devil fell asleep, worn out, and Tom stacked the deck, but when the Devil woke up for the final hand he switched decks and dealt himself the winning cards. The Devil won clear title to Hell. But he told Tom he'd take him in as partner again after he'd ridden five thousand broncs. Then, to make a devilish joke of it, he said he would knock off five hundred for every horse Tom Black rode to death. That, the story went, was why Tom Black rode the way he did.

That story always led to speculation. Working a full season, the way he did, Tom Black rode at least a hundred and fifty broncs a year, a full thousand every seven years. At that rate, it would take him thirty-five years, give or take a year or two, to ride five thousand. Take off five hundred for every bronc that had died under him, and where did you come out? The tallies didn't agree, but the veterans said Tom had killed at least five broncs, six if you counted that one in Denver the time Tom Black's shoulder was smashed.

"Call it six, then. Take off three thousand for the dead broncs. That still leaves two thousand he has to ride."

"Fourteen years of riding."

"How long has Tom Black been up?"

"I couldn't say. He was here when I came up, six years ago."

"Hell, I saw him ride at Odessa eight years ago! And he'd been around a while, even then."

"Well, all I can say is that Tom Black hasn't found the right bronc yet. If you ask me, he'll outlast all of us."

"He can't! He's human, isn't he?"

"I've heard it argued both ways, son. But, like I was saying, when you talk about great bronc riders—well, Tom Black's name belongs right up near the top."

That's the way the talk went.

If anyone had asked Tom Black himself, he would have had to stop and figure before he said how long he had been riding on the big circuit. Even then, he might have been wrong by a year or two. Time no longer mattered to him. Nothing mattered except those intervals in the arena when he, like the broncs themselves, was a fighting creature wholly devoted to punishment and violence. Between shows he merely went through the motions of living, waiting, almost passive. Driving from city to city, moving from hotel room to hotel room, going from one arena to another. Then those brief spans when he came fully to life, when life had meaning. Nothing else mattered because there was nothing else. Ride three times, pack, go. Ride three times, pack, go. Ride three times. . . . It was a rhythm, almost like the rhythm of a pattern bucker. Someday the pattern might break, but meanwhile he rode with it as he rode the pattern buckers.

Time had no meaning. Put it that way. Forget time.

That's the way the years passed.

## 36

It was almost noon when he wakened, and for a few minutes he didn't know where he was. All cities sounded pretty much alike. Especially from a hotel room. Los Angeles and New York had a beat, a throb, that you felt beyond the noises actually heard. Chicago had a confusion of beats. Denver and Dallas lacked the throb.

He lay listening and heard the sounds of construction across the street. This must be New York. Somehow, he always picked a New York hotel just across the street from a new building going up or an old one coming down. In Philadelphia he always seemed to choose a hotel where they were tearing up an old street or putting down a new one.

This was New York. He remembered now. He rode at the Garden last night, a white bronc called Forked Lightning. There weren't many white horses in the bucking strings, maybe because they weren't supposed to have the fight, the stamina. Forked Lightning was plenty mean, though. Gave him a battle. And tonight he would ride a bronc they called Sky Rocket. A big roan, maybe the same one they called Lights Out a few months ago. They kept changing names. Sky Rocket tonight, and tomorrow a dun they called Suicide. Then he would pack his gear, get in his car, drive. Sleep in another hotel, ride in another show. . . .

He stared at the ceiling of the room. It was sky blue. The drapes were a darker blue, the furniture still darker. Blue, the female color. He was surprised to think of that. He hadn't thought in the old way in a long time. Blue for the south, the gentle, the female. Black for the north, the harsh, the male. . . . He put the thought away from him. Blue was blue.

He yawned and stretched, and felt the deep, old aches. His right knee throbbed, the knee that was smashed in Denver six years ago. Or was it seven? No matter. There was a dull ache in his left shoulder, the stiff one. The aches you live with. But neither of his collarbones ached this morning. His right ankle was sore, but a hot shower would loosen it up and somewhat ease the other aches.

He got up, showered, shaved, dressed. He went downstairs, and on his way to the dining room stopped at the newsstand and bought an evening paper. He leafed through it after he had given his order and found the feature story on an inside page. The scowling photograph, with the slit mouth, the crooked nose, the wide cheek bones, the scar across the chin. The headline read, "The Killer Rides Again."

The first few lines were so familiar he could have read them with his eyes shut:

"Tom Black is back in the Garden with the rodeo, and the crowds are waiting for him to kill another horse. Black, a full-blooded Indian, is known to rodeo buffs as Killer Tom, Devil Tom, and an assortment of other grim nicknames. He has earned them all. A veteran bronc rider, Tom Black has ridden nine horses to death in the rodeo arena, and at every performance the spectators expect him to kill another one."

The story went on for another half column, full of vivid detail of which the greater part was only half true. Tom had read that story a hundred times. Apparently the rodeo publicity men kept it mimeographed to hand out to reporters.

The waitress brought the steak and eggs he had ordered and he put the paper aside and ate. Actually, he had been involved in the death of only six horses, counting the one at Aztec. And that one wasn't even in the records. But several other broncs had to be retired, wind broken or spirit broken, after he rode them. He had to admit that, to himself at least.

He finished his meal, paid his check and went out onto the street. He walked aimlessly until his right knee began to throb. Then he caught a bus and rode to the end of the line, far uptown. He got off, found a bench at the edge of a tiny patch of fenced grass, and watched the pigeons. Two small boys were chasing the pigeons, and when they flew they made a whistling sound that reminded Tom of the doves that used to pick up waste grain in the corrals and sit on the ridge of the barn at the place on the San Juan. Red used to try to shoot those doves with his .30-30 rifle, but so far as Tom knew Red never killed a dove. Meo used to say Red couldn't hit a horse inside the barn with the door shut, and Meo probably was right. Red wasn't much of a marksman.

The pigeons flew and circled and came back, and the boys chased them again. Finally the boys tired of that game and came and gawked at Tom. One shouted, "He is too! He's that Indian that kills horses in the rodeo!" The other one shouted, "That's a lie! If he's an Indian, where's his bow and arrow?" The first one cried, "Stupid! Indians use guns, just like anybody else! If I had my gun I'd shoot him right now! Bang-bang! Powie!" And the other one came up to Tom and demanded, "What's your name? Are you an Indian?"

Tom ignored him. The pigeons came back and the boys went to chase them again. Tom got up and went over to the bus stop and took the next bus downtown. He could have gone to the arena, like the other riders, but he preferred to be alone. The others spent the whole afternoon at the arena, just talking. Talking business, talking horses, talking women. He had heard all their talk, long ago.

He got off the bus, walked back to the hotel and sat in the lobby for an hour. A hotel lobby was the only place you could be alone in a crowd, alone and unnoticed. Then it was almost suppertime, his suppertime, since he always ate early.

He went to the dining room and ate another steak. Then he left a call at the desk, went to his room and lay down and slept. When the phone call roused him and the girl said it was seven-thirty, he got up, showered again to ease the aches and the stiffness in that right knee, and sat relaxing for another half hour. Then he went over to the Garden.

## 37

The night show was getting under way. He got his gear and made his way out to the chutes. The bull riding was going on. Bull riding left him cold. Brahma bulls were mean buckers, but the rider had a surcingle to hold on to. Even at that, bull riding was at least half a matter of luck. And that cowbell on the surcingle made the whole thing seem absurd to him. He began checking his gear, cinches, stirrups, rein, boots and chaps.

The bull riding clamored and clanked to a conclusion. The announcer made his spiel, and the trick riding started. The girls who did the trick riding might just as well have been Broadway showgirls, except that they had learned to ride a horse and do stunts on a special saddle. He had seen all their stunts, and he knew all their faces, whether he had ever seen them before or not.

Finally the last of the girls left the arena and the bronc riding was the next event. The broncs were in the chutes. Riders and helpers were saddling them in a babble of talk, laughter and good-natured curses. Tom had drawn tonight's number-three ride, two others ahead of him.

He always took his time about saddling, not liking to wait too long before he rode. He went over to Chute Number Three as the number-one rider was announced. A helper was there, holding the big roan's head. Tom stepped up onto the chute runway, saddle in hand, and let it down easily, cinches dangling. The roan flinched, but didn't even try to hunch its back. Saving its strength. Some broncs tried to fight the saddle. Others saved their fight for the rider.

The helper reached between the chute's planks with the wire and fished for the front cinch, got it, handed it to Tom. He snugged the front cinch while the helper fished for the other ring, on the back cinch. Tom took it, jerked the back cinch tight to force the roan to let out its breath. It wheezed, eased for an instant, and Tom hauled up the front cinch a couple of notches before the roan could catch another breath. Then he let off on the back cinch, kept it just tight enough so the saddle wouldn't rock.

The crowd was roaring. The number-one rider, a newcomer who had made a spectacular ride last night, apparently was doing all right for himself again. Tom didn't even look up, but he could hear the stomp of the bronc's hoofs, the grunting wheezes, the slap of the rider's chaps. Then the horn blew and the crowd cheered and whistled. Tom glanced up then and saw the rider pivot off the pickup man's horse, grin at the crowd and wave his hat. Then he unbuckled his chaps, stepped out, slung the chaps over his arm and came back toward the chutes, almost strutting. He was good, and he knew it, a boy on his way up. The pickup men chivied the bronc toward the exit and the announcer started his spiel about the number-two rider.

Tom shook his saddle, testing it, and took up the front cinch another notch. He resined his chaps, remembering when he was a boy on his way up. When the crowds cheered and whistled and stomped for him. When he was riding for points. A long time ago. He checked his spurs, dried his hands on his shirt and got ready to ease himself down into the saddle.

The gate opened at Number Two Chute and out went a hammerheaded black with a rider in a yellow shirt. The crowd began to roar.

Tom let himself down into the saddle and the roan didn't even hump its back. He felt for the stirrups, felt the hard curve of the metal through the thin soles of his boots. He sensed the taut muscles of the bronc beneath his calves—hard, tense, ready to explode into action. He dried his hands again and glanced at the number-two rider. The hammerheaded black was ducking and side-jumping, and the rider had too short a rein and couldn't seem to slip it.

A helper laid the bucking strap across Tom's horse's back, fished the buckle and fastened it loosely, ready to jerk tight. He handed up the rein, on the left side.

"No." Tom snapped. "The other side."

"I forgot," the helper apologized, and brought the rein around for Tom's unorthodox right hand.

The crowd groaned. The number-two rider was in trouble. His short rein had jerked him loose in the saddle. The bronc knew it, lunged viciously, side-jumped, and the rider was thrown. The pickup men closed in, drove the bronc toward the exit, and the unlucky rider slowly got to his feet, shaking his head. He dusted himself and walked unhappily back toward the chutes.

The announcer was bellowing, "And now, ladies and gentlemen, here comes a rider you all know, at least by reputation. Some call him the Killer, some call him Black Death—he has a whole string of names like that. And he's earned every one of them!" The crowd had begun to cheer. The announcer waited for the cheers to ease off, then went on. "I don't have to tell you any more about him, I see. Anyway, here he is, coming out of Chute Number Three—I give you Tom Black, on Sky Rocket!"

The crowd roared again, louder than before, then tensed into silence.

Tom got the signal. The bucking strap was jerked tight around the roan's flanks. Tom set his spurs well forward, leaned back against the rein, took a deep breath and let it out. He nodded to the gateman, and the gate swung open. The roan called Sky Rocket went out with a lunge and a bellow. Rein taut, spurs raking, Tom Black began his ride.

He had made that ride a thousand times. Sky Rocket was a pattern bucker, three lunges, a side jump, a half spin, then three lunges again.

Tom rode with the rhythm, concentrating on punishment with his spurs and being brutal with the rein at every side jump and spin. Three times the roan followed the pattern, lunge,

lunge, lunge, side jump, spin. Then the punishment made it frantic. It tried to duck left, shaking its head, bellowing. Tom hauled its head around, and it lunged again, then tried to duck again. Tom shifted his weight for leverage, and a stab of pain shot through his right knee and streaked to his ankle. In fury at the pain, Tom jerked the bronc's head up and around by sheer strength. The ankle went numb, and to keep from losing the stirrup he jabbed his foot deeper. The roan squealed and came up, pawing the air. It reared, danced, still trying to spin left, and again he jerked its head around to the right. Neck bowed, it came down fighting, bunched for another lunge.

His right leg now numb from knee to ankle, Tom was jerked forward as the roan struck the ground, head down. It lunged, and he powered its head around as it left the ground. Off balance, it seemed to tangle its feet in the air. Tom felt it begin to fall, still fighting for its feet. He knew it was going, knew he had to get clear. He kicked his left foot free of the stirrup, but his right foot didn't respond. He grabbed the pommel of the saddle with his left hand, tried to thrust himself clear, but he was still in the saddle as the roan came down with a crash on its right side, rolling with its own momentum.

Tom felt one crushing blow across his hips before his head struck the arena. Then the whole world seemed to explode in a burst of light and pain. Then darkness, nothing.

He had a brief span of semiconsciousness before they moved him, enough to know the sensation of floating in a choppy sea of pain and hear voices all around him. His head was a throbbing balloon and his vision was blurred. Spasms of nausea wrenched at him. Then they gave him injections and the sea of pain began to quiet, even the pain in his chest that almost stopped his breathing. Then he was unconscious again. He never knew how they got him on the stretcher, put the stretcher in the ambulance, took him to the hospital. He never knew how thin was his thread of life for a night and a day and another night.

## 38

Most of the first week he existed in the half-world of the critically hurt where there is neither night nor day, time nor reality, but only the overlapping periods of confused consciousness and dreams and nightmares. His body fought its battles quite apart from his mind; the transfusions, the injections, the X rays and the merciful surgery were performed on flesh and blood and bone temporarily cut off from the normal processes of awareness. He roused enough from time to time to sense his hospital surroundings and feel the deep, insistent throb of pain in his head and the dull, remote pain elsewhere, but reality never quite overcame the dreams and nightmares. Dreams of boyhood, of his mother and the mountains, of the reservation, Red Dillon's place and the back-country rodeos. And always the dreams came to a chilling nightmare of falling, of being trapped in the saddle on a bronc that was forever falling but never landing.

Slowly his vitality reasserted itself. As his awareness increased he was restless and resentful. The stir and activity of the ward rasped at his nerves, and when he was lucid enough to enforce his demands they moved him to a private room six floors above the street. There, the first morning of his second week, he wakened at dawn and saw the flame of sunrise in the small patch of sky beyond his window. He watched it, and the memory of another dawn came to him, the dawn when he and his mother, on the flight from Pagosa, bathed in the icy pool of a brook, then sat naked on the rocks and sang the chant to a new day. The rhythm of that chant throbbed in his memory like his own heartbeat for a few moments. Then he tried to move and pain stabbed at his chest and hips and bitterness rose in his throat like his own gorge. He was no longer a boy or a breechclout Indian. He was a grown man in another world, a bronc rider trapped by his own injuries in a world of pain and helplessness.

He was still rankling when a nurse came in. She was plump and had coppery hair and blue eyes and looked to be in her mid-30s. She said, "Good morning! How are we today?" and he immediately resented her ready smile and bubbly air. He frowned at her and did not answer. She lowered the window shade and started to put a thermometer into his mouth.

"Put up that shade," he ordered.

"But the sun is right in your eyes."

"I like the sun. Put it up!"

She laughed at him, raised the shade again, then took his temperature and his pulse. She straightened his bed, deft and efficient, then said, "You must be starved. What would taste good for breakfast?"

"I'm not hungry."

"How about poached eggs?"

"I said I'm not hungry."

"You will be. Nothing tastes good in a hospital, but you have to eat. And poached eggs go down easy." She filled his water glass and left the room. A little later she came back with a tray of toast, poached eggs and coffee, arranged them on the bed table, saw that he took two capsules—"Happy pills, to sweeten your disposition"—and went away.

The coffee tasted the way burning hay smelled, and he had a flash of memory of the night he burned the barn. Then he remembered the strong, bitter coffee Meo used to make, and the bite of Meo's chili, and the whole remembrance of the place on the San Juan came back to him. He thrust the memories away and ate the toast and the eggs, hungry as the nurse had said he would be. Then he slept.

The next morning when the copper-haired nurse came in

and asked him how he was, he demanded, "What's your name?"

"Mary Redmond." She moved to lower the window shade.

"Leave that shade alone! Where are you from?"

"Massachusetts." She came back to his bedside.

"That's New England, isn't it." It was an accusation.

"About as New England as you can get." She put the thermometer into his mouth and counted his pulse. When she took the thermometer again he said, "I used to have a mealy-mouthed school teacher who looked a little like you, and talked like you. She was from New England."

She laughed. "You're talkative this morning. You must be feeling better." She began making his bed. When she had finished and folded the blanket across the foot of the bed she asked, "Where did you know this charming school teacher from New England?"

"In Colorado, on the reservation."

"Oh?" She went to get him a fresh glass of water.

When she came back he repeated sharply, "On the reservation."

"I heard you the first time."

"Well?"

"Look, Chief, you'd just as well put away your tomahawk and take the feathers out of your hair. This is a hospital, not a reservation, and you're just another man to me. . . . Anything else I can do for you?"

"No. Leave me alone."

That afternoon Dr. Ferguson, the surgeon, came in to see him. Dr. Ferguson was a tall, lean man with a lean face and a clipped voice that Tom remembered vaguely, but this was the first time he had been well enough to ask questions. While the surgeon was taking his pulse Tom asked, "Ribs?"

The surgeon nodded.

"How many?"

"Several. . . . Follow my hand." He moved his hand from side to side in front of Tom's face. Tom followed it with his eyes for a moment, then closed them, dizzy.

"How's the nausea? Thrown up today?"

"No. . . . What else besides the ribs?"

The surgeon watched him for a moment, then said, "A lung puncture, a deep concussion, a broken femur and a broken pelvis."

"Is that all?"

"Isn't that enough? Do you want a broken back too?"

"How long will I be laid up?"

"Till your pelvis knits. Six weeks or so. We've pinned your femur—that's the big bone in your thigh. You can walk again as soon as your pelvis knits."

"How soon can I ride again?"

"Never, if you take my advice."

"I didn't ask for advice."

"Well, you got it. As far as the injuries go, the lung puncture is healing properly. You're almost over the effects of the concussion. But broken bones don't knit overnight, as you must know. I see from the X rays that you've had quite a few in the past. But you seem to heal fast and your bones probably knit fast."

"They do."

"Well, in another six weeks you should be able to walk out of here. Beyond that, it's up to you."

"I'll walk out and I'll ride again."

Dr. Ferguson shrugged and left the room.

That night Tom had the dreams and nightmares again. He wakened and tried to remember that last ride. All he could remember was right there in the nightmare, being trapped in the saddle and the big roan falling, falling, never coming down.

## 39

When Mary Redmond came in the next morning, cheerful as always, he watched her with rising resentment. She was the most skillful of the nurses, the most solicitous and helpful, the most friendly. But her very efficiency and gentleness emphasized his helplessness, his need for care. She represented this whole infuriating situation, the fact that he was trapped in the hospital, unable even to get out of bed, let alone stand on his feet and walk. And the fact that her voice reminded him of Rowena Ellis brought back all the bitterness of his memories of the reservation and the school.

Finally she said, "So you're from Colorado. I hear it's beautiful out there."

"You wouldn't like it. Where I came from it's all mountains and trees and rocks."

"I like mountains and trees."

But he wasn't talking. The other nurses had told her that he was grumpy as an old bear and didn't appreciate anything you did for him. But most men were that way when they were sick. Then they began to get well and they saw how much you were doing for them. Some of them appreciated it, or seemed to, even though they did forget you as soon as they left the hospital. She filled his water glass, made his bed, fluffed his pillow, humming softly to herself. She adjusted the ventilator in the window and came back to the bed and asked, "Now, what more can I do for you?"

"Get me a glass of fresh water."

"I just filled your glass. See?"

He reached for the glass, drank the water and held out the

empty glass. "I said I wanted fresh water." His voice was testy.

She took the glass, filled it again and set it on his bedside table. "There you are. Anything else?"

"Don't you know who I am?" he demanded.

"Of course I do. You're the man who rode ten horses to death." She made a face. "But you aren't proud of being cruel, are you?"

"Why not?" Then he asked, "So they say it's ten now?"

"Yes, ten, counting the one you killed in the Garden, the one that put you in here. That's what the papers say, anyway."

"So that one's dead too? I didn't know."

"Well, now you know." She said it sharply. He didn't seem to be sorry at all, and suddenly she was angry at him, not only for his callousness about the horse but because he didn't appreciate anything that was being done for him, by her or anyone else. "Now," she said, "you can cut another notch in your saddle, or whatever you do to keep score!"

But he wasn't listening. He was thinking about the big roan bronc, the one they said brought his score up to ten. Even with that one, the tally was only seven, really, and all but one or two of those seven had killed themselves. Seven or ten, though, what did it matter? He didn't want to think about them, put the thought away from him.

But that night he had the nightmare again and wakened in the cold sweat. Lying there in the darkness, for the first time he remembered the ride from the moment the chute gate opened right through to the end. He remembered the bronc's pattern, how he shifted his weight, how the stab of pain in his knee numbed his whole leg. He remembered his anger, then his fear, the fear that made him so desperate he yanked the roan's head around and jerked it off balance. He remembered the fall, the crushing blow on his hips, the agony just before his head struck, just before the knockout.

And now he knew why he hadn't been able to remember anything of the ride but that sensation of falling. He had refused to face the fact that he had panicked, that he had forced the fall. Now he faced it, and the nightmare came at last to its conclusion. Coldly analyzing it, he knew his own fear had forced him to fall. And there it was. Fear. Facing it, admitting it, he could start from that point and think straight. But he had to start there because, according to the code of the arena, a bronc rider wasn't afraid of man, beast or devil. Especially Tom Black, Killer Tom Black. But you don't ride as long as he had ridden without knowing a few times when fear does share the saddle. You don't admit it, even to yourself. You get up off the ground and back in the saddle, and you ride the bronc to a standstill, and the fear with it.

Well, now he would go back and ride again. He would be better than ever, with all his skills and experience and with the knowledge that he had panicked in the saddle, forced the fall that almost killed him. Knowing that, he would never do it again. It was as simple as that. He had known he had to go back and ride again, but until now he hadn't known why, hadn't admitted it. Now he did.

He slept, free of the nightmare at last.

Mary Redmond did not appear the next day, or the next. He wondered why, but he didn't ask. It wasn't important, and he had plans to make. He had to heal himself and get back on his feet. He had to get out of here. He would go somewhere for a while, take it easy, rest up, get himself back in shape. Then catch up with the circuit. It would take a while, he knew that, but he would be back in the saddle by the end of the summer.

He thought of the place on the San Juan. If the cabin was still there, that's where he would go. But that was out. The cabin was gone and some sheepman probably had moved in by now and taken over the whole canyon. He wondered how Red and Meo found it in the first place, if Meo went there to recover and rest up after his smashup, planning to go back to the arena. He never went back. He stayed there, puttering in his garden, talking to his beans and chilies, even to himself, an old man with a hump on his broken back who once was a rodeo rider.

Red's words came to him now: "Meo was a hero once. Now look at him! Just another broken-down old chili-eater." And then Red's comment: "Heroes wind up broke. Especially if they are Mexes or Indians."

Tom hadn't tried to figure it before, and even now he could only guess, but he wouldn't have much left when he got out of here and paid his bills. He had never saved his money. He lived it up when he had it, spent it on hotels and clothes and expensive cars. And these past few years a good deal of it had gone for doctors and hospitals. He wouldn't be flat broke, but he knew there wouldn't be much left this time.

Then he had a wry thought. Red, who had called Meo a hero who wound up broke, was the one who died penniless. Meo paid for his burial. Meo, who rolled Red every time he came home drunk, accumulated enough not only to give Red a decent burial but eventually to shrive and bury old Meo himself.

Life plays strange tricks. Tom, too, was a hero of a sort. Not the kind the crowds come to cheer, but the kind they watch with morbid fascination, hoping to see him kill a horse—or a horse kill him. A dark-souled hero. He knew that. And after this brush with death the crowds would be more than ever fascinated, more morbidly curious. That was another reason to go back. To defy the cruelty and the death wish of the crowd. After all, he was Killer Tom Black, wasn't he, the devil-hero?

But first he had to get back on his feet, get out of here.

Mary Redmond was there again the third morning. She came in with her ready smile and asked, "How are we this fine morning?"

He wasn't in a fine morning mood. "Where have you been?" he demanded.

"Why, Chief!" she exclaimed. "Don't tell me you missed me. The last time I saw you, you hated everybody in sight."

"I still do."

"Then we can start right where we left off." She put the thermometer into his mouth. "Maybe if patients had two days off each week, like nurses, it would improve their disposition." She took his pulse, then read the thermometer. "I guess," she said with a smile, "you're going to get well after all. You're looking better."

"What do you do on your days off? Go around patting little kids on the head, just to keep in practice?"

"Some folks," she said as she began to make the bed, "are just too mean to die. On that basis you'll live a long, long time."

Now she knew who he reminded her of—Bart Huntley. Bart was taller and slimmer, but he had the same dark, resentful eyes. Maybe the fear of never being able to walk again had something to do with it. Women were afraid of being disfigured, but men were afraid of being crippled, dependent. Bart was terribly mangled in the auto accident, but they saved both his legs. And it was her massaging that got him walking again. She could have got him off the crutches, too, in time. But she saw him only twice after he left the hospital, once when he took her out to dinner, once when she asked him up to her apartment and cooked dinner for him. He was arrogant and defensive at the restaurant, and at her apartment he was bitter and resentful. She finally came right out and told him what she could do for him, and he accused her of wanting to marry him for his money. That was the thanks she got. She never saw him again, never even heard from him.

She decided Tom didn't look like Bart Huntley at all, except for his eyes. He had a crooked nose and high cheekbones and a broad, square jaw. *He's mad at life,* she thought, *not at me.* She finished making the bed and said, "If I had time I'd give you a massage. But this is one of those days. Maybe tomorrow."

He didn't answer.

"A massage will do your legs a world of good."

Then he looked at her, frowning. "Massage? No, I don't want a massage. Leave me alone."

"You didn't hear a word I said." She laughed at him. "I said I didn't have time to give you a massage today. . . . Well, ring if you need anything. I've got to run. We're shorthanded today."

The next morning she gave him the massage. Her hands were firm but gentle and knew instinctively where the deep aches lay and how to ease the bed-stiff muscles. He made no comment, but she knew from the way he relaxed that it did him good.

That afternoon, Dr. Ferguson came in with a strange nurse and took the stitches from the incision they had made to insert the intermedullary nail in Tom's femur. When the nurse had left, Dr. Ferguson said, "You're healing nicely. In a few more weeks you can go back home and rest a while. I understand you're from Colorado."

"I was born there."

"Nice country. I'd like to retire there myself some day."

"Retire? I'm not retiring!"

The surgeon smiled at Tom's resentful tone. "Still got a lot of gravel in your craw, haven't you?"

"Yes."

"Well, maybe that's to the good, too. The will to get well. Keep on at this rate and we'll have you up in a wheel chair by the end of the week. Then, after you've toned up your muscles a bit in the chair, we'll let you try the walker. Get your legs under you and see how you manage. I said we'd get you out of here on your own two feet. You didn't believe it, did you?"

"I told *you* I'd walk out of here," Tom snapped.

"That's right, you did."

"And I said I'd ride again!"

The surgeon slowly shook his head. "Damned and determined, aren't you?" Then he chuckled. "A lot of *rough* gravel in your craw," he said, and he left the room.

## 40

Looking forward to the wheel chair, to something beyond the imprisoning bed and the confines of the room, eased the next few days. Then the morning came when Mary Redmond triumphantly brought the chair and said he was going for a ride. She helped him out of bed, gentle as with a child, settled him in the chair and took him down the long corridor to the sun porch, deserted at that time of day. She showed him how to manage the chair, and he wheeled himself up and down the room for ten minutes, rested and did it again. She said he learned faster than any other patient she ever had. Finally, aching from the unaccustomed exercise, he let her take him back to his room. She helped him into bed and massaged his complaining, unused muscles and told him again what a wonderful patient he was.

It was easier the next morning, still easier the next. She exclaimed at his determination, his growing strength, and his quick skill with the chair. "You've still got a long way to go, but you just don't know what it is to give up, do you?"

"I never did. Why should I start now?"

She laughed. "I suppose you've always been this way, tough and determined. But you would have to be. It takes courage and determination to ride a bucking horse, doesn't it? Did you always know how, or is it something, like learning to walk again, that you have to learn?"

He was resting between sessions with the chair. "Look," he said; "broncs are mean. They're outlaws. You either learn how to ride or you get hurt. I learned by riding broncs."

"Oh. Didn't you ever have a pet bronc, as you call them?"

"A pet bronc?" He laughed at her. "I just told you broncs

are mean. They're not like dogs. Give them half a chance, they'll kill you."

"I had a dog once. I was just a little girl and it followed me home and I had it all afternoon and I wanted to keep it and take care of it, but my mother said it was just a dirty mongrel. And when my father came home he called the dog warden to come take it away. I cried all night."

"Over a stray dog?"

"Don't you know what it's like to grow up without anything or anyone to love and take care of? No, I guess not. I guess only girls feel that way."

"Didn't you ever have another dog?"

She shook her head. "I finished school and went into training, and—" She shrugged. "Some get married, some turn into sour, cat-loving old maids, and some just try to help people. I guess I'm that kind." She laughed self-consciously. "Besides, I don't like cats. They're too independent."

He wheeled the chair away, down the room, and resumed his exercise. He was going to walk out of here, and he wasn't going to wait too long. He wheeled himself up and down the room, making plans.

Tuesday came, Mary Redmond was off duty, and he called another nurse to bring the chair and help him into it. They went to the sun porch and he dismissed her, said he would be all right alone. When she had gone he moved the chair to a place where he could grasp a window frame and lift himself out of the chair and onto his feet. He stood there for several minutes, then sat down and rested and did it again. His legs were weak and his hip joints stiff and painful, but he took a few tentative steps, holding to the window frames. He rested again, then made his way with halting steps halfway down the room and back. He almost fell twice, but caught himself, holding to the window frames. Then he returned to the chair, sweating with the effort, and was staring out the window when the nurse returned.

The next morning he managed a dozen steps without holding on to anything, balancing carefully on his weak legs. He could walk again.

Mary Redmond came back after her days off and said, "You look pleased with life today, Chief. As though something nice happened."

"I'm getting well."

"Of course you are." She gave him a frowning look and started making his bed. "You begin to get well and you get impatient. You feel better and you think you're all well. Even though you're not."

"I'm going to walk again," he said. "And ride again."

"Not right away. You will need taking care of for a while, even after you leave here. You know that, don't you?"

He didn't answer and she asked. "Was Dr. Ferguson in to see you yesterday?"

"No."

"I thought maybe he said you could try the walker in another week or so." She finished the chores and left, and came back half an hour later with the chair. "Now you go for your ride, your daily dozen." She helped him into the chair, even more solicitous than usual. They went to the sun porch and she sat and waited while he wheeled the chair to the end of the room and back. She wanted to talk, but he shook his head. "Just leave me alone a while. I'll be all right. Go give somebody an enema, or a massage, or something."

Reluctantly she left him. As soon as she was gone he got out of the chair, walked carefully down the room and back. He rested for a few minutes, then walked again. He was halfway down the room, taking his third walk, when Mary Redmond came back.

"What are you doing?" she exclaimed, running toward him.

"I'm walking."

"You can't! You're not supposed to leave the chair!" She tried to take his arm. He shrugged her off, almost lost his careful balance, caught himself and slowly walked back to the chair. She hovered beside him, wanting to take his arm but afraid he would lose his balance and fall if she tried. He reached the chair and let himself down into it.

"You mustn't do that! You mustn't!"

"I did it."

"You," she said severely, "are going right back to your room. You're not ready yet to walk. You are still weak. Suppose you had fallen."

"I'd have picked myself up."

She angrily piloted the chair back down the corridor and ordered him into bed.

"Who do you think you are, ordering me around?" he demanded. But he let her help him back into bed and lay there, expecting her to calm down, give him a massage and admire his achievement. Instead, she took the chair and left the room, bristling with indignation. Fifteen minutes later she was back, with Dr. Ferguson.

They came in and the surgeon looked at Tom, appraising. "So," he said gruffly, "you pulled a Lazarus." Then he smiled. "Knowing you, I'm not surprised."

"But he isn't—" Mary Redmond started to speak, then bit her lip as Dr. Ferguson glanced at her with a frown. He looked at Tom again. "All right, let's see you do it again. Think you can get out of bed and walk over to the window?"

Tom threw back the covers and carefully moved his legs over the edge of the bed. Mary Redmond hurried toward him, but Dr. Ferguson waved her away. "Let him do it alone." To Tom he said, "Go ahead. If you've done any damage to those bones, a few more steps won't make it any worse."

Tom felt for the floor and stood up. He was still tired from his walk on the sun porch, but by watching each step and balancing carefully he crossed the room to the window, turned, and came back to the bed. His forehead was beaded with sweat from the effort, but there was both triumph and defiance in his eyes.

Dr. Ferguson nodded. "Not bad. Not bad at all. You're a week ahead of schedule."

"How soon can I get out of here?" Tom demanded.

"That depends. If you tried to walk out of here today you'd fall flat on your face in ten minutes. Your muscles are still weak. Right now you're walking on sheer will power and your sense of balance. But you are walking, no question about that." He considered. "Before I can release you I want some X rays and I want to run a few tests. That will take a few days. Meanwhile you can get those muscles toughened up and those legs working a little better. Just being in bed as long as you have takes a lot out of anyone."

"How long?" Tom insisted.

"Well, let's plan on next Tuesday or Wednesday. Unless the pictures or the tests show something. How does that sound?"

"All right."

"After you leave here, though, you'll have to take it easy for a while. You're not well yet. You'll need a few weeks in some place like a convalescent home. Where you can walk and rest and be well taken care of. We have a list of good places at the office. I'll tell them to send a list up." He held out his hand. "Stout fellow."

They shook hands and Dr. Ferguson started to leave, then turned back and said, "I'll set up the X rays for tomorrow. Then we'll set up the other tests."

Mary Redmond was still there after the surgeon left. She looked at Tom almost accusingly, seemed about to say something. Then she changed her mind and left him alone. He lay back in bed and every muscle in his body seemed to scream as the tensions began to let down.

# 41

He was looking at the list of convalescent homes the next morning when Mary Redmond came in. He didn't like the sound of any of them. She came in, bright as always, and said, "Well, stout fellow! I expected you'd be up, have your bed made and be out taking a constitutional."

"Where is White Plains?" he asked.

"Out in Westchester. Why?"

"Where's Stamford?"

"Connecticut." She looked over his shoulder, saw the list and said, "Oh, those places." Then she said. "You won't want to walk this morning, I guess. There won't be time after you've eaten your breakfast. You are scheduled for X rays at a quarter of ten."

"I had breakfast early so I would have time. Bring the chair and I'll go out on the sun porch while you straighten things up in here."

"You can't rush things that way. Maybe this afternoon—"

"Go get the chair," he ordered.

She brought the chair and would have gone to the porch with him, but he said firmly, "I'm going alone."

"You heard Dr. Ferguson say you'd fall on your face in ten minutes."

"If I do, I'll get up again." He wheeled the chair into the corridor and went to the sun porch alone. He alternately walked and rested for twenty minutes before Mary Redmond returned. When he sat down again she said, "Those homes on that list—some of them are pretty terrible. And the really good ones have long waiting lists."

He didn't answer.

"What you really need," she said, "is just a quiet place and somebody to look after you and see that you get good meals and plenty of rest. And you should continue the massages. That's what really got you on your feet this soon. I hope you realize that."

He wheeled his chair back to the windows and resumed his walking, slowly, carefully. He still had to concentrate on every step. He had never tried it, but he imagined walking a tight wire was something like this, demanding almost as sure a sense of balance. He walked and he rested again, and Mary Redmond said, as though there had been no interruption, "You need a place where you can walk several times a day, too. Oh, I wish you had a place like my apartment! It's just two blocks from the Drive. Did you ever walk along the river and look at the water and watch the gulls?"

"Gulls? Those birds that never sing, just squawk and fight over garbage?"

"They don't squawk. They cry, like lonely children." She looked at her watch. "It's after nine and you'd better rest before your X rays."

"One more walk," he said, and went back to the windows and walked to the end of the room and back. Then they returned to his room, she helped him into bed and gave him the daily massage. Her hands seemed even more deft and gentle than usual and she gave him a long, thorough rub before the orderly came and took him to the X ray laboratory. That afternoon, after Mary Redmond had gone off duty, he called for the chair, and a strange nurse took him to the sun porch. He walked, rested, and walked again for almost an hour.

The next morning Mary Redmond came in triumphant about something, but she kept it to herself till they were on the sun porch and he had walked his first round. Then she said, "I've found just the place for you."

"Where?"

"Near Nyack."

"What's Nyack/ It sounds like a fish or a disease."

"It's a town, just up the Hudson. This place is out in the country and you'll love it. I know the woman who runs it. I used to work for her. I called her last night and she has a room she'll save for you."

"Oh."

"Isn't that wonderful?"

"I'll have to think about it." He wheeled the chair away and started walking again. Something in this situation added up wrong. He tried to puzzle it out, forgot to concentrate on his walking, lost his balance and would have fallen if he hadn't caught hold of a window frame. Mary Redmond was watching and ran to take his arm, steady him. He shrugged her off and snapped, "Leave me alone. I'm all right." He was angry at himself, not at her; but when she said, "You're tired. You'd better rest," he flared, "Leave me alone, I said. I know what I'm doing."

He walked, and rested, and refused to talk, and walked again, driving himself. And finally he sat down in the chair and ordered, "Take me back to my room."

She took him to his room, but before she had a chance to massage him an orderly came to take him for the other tests.

It was noon before they finished with the tests.He ate a late lunch. Then, worn out, he slept. He had just awakened when Mary Redmond came in, about to go off duty. "I have to call my friend in Nyack this evening," she said. "Do you want me to tell her to hold that room for you?"

He had to think for a moment to remember what she was talking about. When he didn't answer she said, "I'm not trying to talk you into anything. It's just for your own good." She hesitated, then hurried on. "When I mentioned my apartment yesterday I didn't mean a thing. I was just thinking of you and a nice place to walk. So don't get any wrong ideas. If you go to Nyack I may go up there on a day off to see that you are getting the right kind of massage. But beyond that—"

Then he remembered and the whole pattern fell into place. Blue Elk, Benny Grayback, Rowena Ellis, Red Dillon—they had trapped him, every one of them, tried to run his life, make him do things their way. And now Mary Redmond.

"Tell your friend," he said, "I've made other plans."

"But—but what happened?" She stared at him, then asked, "Did Dr. Ferguson find a place for you?"

"No. I found it all by myself."

"Oh. . . . Well, I hope it's what you need."

"It is."

There didn't seem to be anything more to say. She turned and left the room.

When she had gone, he got pencil and paper and set down figures and added them up. He knew how much he had in the safe at the hotel, the money he had left with the clerk for safekeeping. He estimated the surgeon's bill and the hospital charges. He made a guess at what he could get for his car. He hated to sell the car, but he had to pay the bills, and he could get another car when he was in the money again.

He added and subtracted and decided that after he had paid train fare and bus fare he would have a hundred and fifty, maybe even two hundred dollars. Enough for a while. At least, he wouldn't be flat broke. Then he smiled wryly. "Heroes die broke." Well, he wasn't dead, and he wasn't broke. Not quite.

That evening he sat for a long time in the chair beside the window and he remembered another night, long ago, when he sat beside the window in a shabby little Texas hotel, waiting for Red. Red didn't come in. Red was drunk. And the next day, when Red tried to tel him what to do, how to ride, he had knocked Red down, twice, then walked out because he knew he would kill Red if he had to, to get free. He had only one regret now, about Red. Red never saw him ride on the big circuit.

He sat there a long time before he finally went to bed and to sleep.

The next morning Mary Redmond came in almost as gay as ever. She made his bed, straightened his room, and though she looked at him from time to time she didn't say a word about the place in Nyack or ask where he was going. She chattered impersonally and when she wasn't talking she was humming to herself as though afraid of silence between them. Then she brought the wheel chair and let him get into it alone.

"I'll bet you could *walk* to the sun porch this morning," she said. "But you'd better not try. You're still listed as a chair patient, and if the supervisor saw you we'd both catch hell."

He went to the porch and she left him there alone for almost an hour. Then she came back and waited for him to say he was ready to go to his room. She gave him a thorough, efficient massage, but she seemed as impersonal about it as though he were someone who had just walked in off the street. She made him feel like an absolute stranger.

When she had finished and left him alone in his room he was tempted to call her back and say he had changed his mind. That he would go to that place in Nyack, that he wanted to be taken care of, comforted, eased, protected. Then he said to himself, angrily and aloud, "You fool! You damned fool! You've been taken care of for almost six weeks."

He pushed Mary Redmond out of his thinking. He had plans to make.

That afternoon, just before she went off duty, Mary came to his room again. He was sitting in the chair beside the window and he started to get to his feet as she came in.

"Don't get up," she said. "I just stopped in to say good-bye."

"Good-bye?"

"I do with all my patients before they go."

"I'm not leaving till tomorrow."

"I'll be off duty tomorrow. Tuesdays and Wednesdays. Remember?"

"That's right." He had forgotten.

"Well—" She hesitated. "Well, good-bye. And good luck."

He was still listening to her footsteps down the hall when Dr. Ferguson came in. He had the reports on the X rays and the tests. Everything, he said, was all right. "I'll sign your release and check you out before I leave. You can go any time tomorrow. Where did you decide to go, by the way?"

"I'm going back home."

"Good! Get out in the open air. Eat and sleep and walk. Best exercise you can get, walking. Check in with a doctor out there once a month or so. By the end of summer he'll probably let you ride again, if it's a gentle horse. Gentle, I said."

Tom made no comment. He asked what he owed, and Dr. Ferguson said the records were at his office, but he gave an approximate figure. Tom took the office address. The doctor wished him luck and they shook hands and said good-bye.

Alone, Tom looked around the room and knew he was a stranger here. A total stranger. He didn't belong here. So he was getting out, going back to the life he did belong to. All he had to do now was close this out and get ready to take up where he left off. By this time tomorrow he would be on the train heading west.

He turned to the window and stared out at the patch of sky beyond the buildings. Blue sky, the calm, gentle, comforting female color. Then he thought of his own name, Tom Black. Black, the harsh, ruthless male color.

He went out into the corridor and walked toward the sun porch, without the wheel chair and with no one at his elbow. He almost wished the supervisor, or someone, would try to stop him. But nobody did.

# IV. The Mountains

## 42

He was the only passenger for Pagosa. The bus stopped, he got off and the bus roared and went on toward Bayfield and Durango. He stood for a long minute looking up and down the street, which wound along the valley with its shops and stores on only the one side, facing the sharp slope at the foot of which flowed the San Juan. It was a tumbling mountain stream here, not really a river; it didn't become a river till it was joined by the Piedra, down at Arboles at the southern edge of the reservation, and began to canyon its way into New Mexico. He looked up and down the street, wondering why he had come. It was only vaguely familiar, like a place in a long forgotten dream. It wasn't home. But he had to come somewhere.

He picked up his clothes bag and walked up the street, limping slightly. He was stiff and full of dull aches from the long ride in the bus. He wondered if he should have stayed another week in Denver, shrugged and dismissed that thought. Four days had been long enough, four days to recover from the train ride. He couldn't afford to stay in Denver, even if he had wanted to.

He looked for a restaurant, saw the sign and mentally corrected himself. The Cafe. He went in, set his clothes bag against the wall, hung his hat on the peg above it, and chose a stool at the counter, well away from the four men already there. The waitress, middle-aged, plain, friendly, and with obviously aching feet, brought a glass of water and a menu. He glanced at the menu, ordered coffee and a hot roast beef sandwich. She started toward the kitchen and he called her back. "Cancel the sandwich. Make it a bowl of chili."

She gave the order and brought a spoon and a paper napkin. He glanced down the counter at the other four men. They were watching him. All were in Levi's, work clothes. He was conscious of his own clothes, the tan sport jacket, the brown-striped shirt, the tailored gabardines, the fancy-stitched boots. For years he had been stared at, on the street, in hotels and restaurants, and it hadn't mattered. It was part of being what he was. Now he felt self-conscious.

The waitress brought his chili, pushed the bowl of oyster crackers toward him, and the big shaker of coarsely ground red chili peppers. She brought his coffee and asked, "Come in from the east?"

He nodded.

"The washout all fixed, up the canyon?"

"All fixed."

"There's a long detour between Bayfield and Durango."

"I'm not going any farther." He smiled at her. "I'm here."

"Oh?"

"I used to live around here." Unconsciously, he was trying to make contact with somebody, something.

"Come back for a visit?"

"I may stay a while."

"There's worse places." She smiled and moved down the counter.

The chili wasn't very good. Too bland, even when he doctored it with the ground peppers. He tasted the coffee. Restaurant coffee. No, cafe coffee. But he drank it and he ate the chili. The waitress came back and he ordered more coffee and lemon pie. It was cafe pie, too.

He finished and went to the desk, and the waitress came to take his money. "Is it all right if I leave my clothes bag here a while?" he asked.

"Nobody will bother it."

He put on his hat and went out onto the street again. Two men, Indians, were sitting on the curb in front of the hardware store. One glanced up, stared at him for a moment. He glanced at them and walked on past before he thought that the one who had looked up was someone he knew. He reached back, finally found a name. Luther. Luther who? He glanced over his shoulder. They were both watching him, saying something about him to each other. And the name came: Luther Spotted Dog. His one-time roommate, the boy he had thrown out of the room, with all his gear, and later had beaten up in that fight in the cow barn. Luther Spotted Dog! In worn, dirty Levi's, looking like a skid-row character.

He went on, came to a market, Thatcher's Market, the sign said. Thatcher? Then he remembered. He stared through the big window. The place was all changed, a market now, not just a store. And another memory came back, of a boy and a bear cub and a crowd of men here in the street, right here, the men threatening to kill the cub. And Jim Thatcher coming out and warning them to leave the two alone, both the boy and the cub.

He was tempted to go in, see if Jim Thatcher was still there. Probably not. It was a long time ago. Even if he were there, Jim Thatcher probably wouldn't remember. What would it matter, even if he did?

Tom turned away, went on up the street, then came back. Luther Spotted Dog and the other man had gone. He crossed the street to a bench, started to sit down, then went on down the slope a little way toward the stream and sat down on the ground. A startled magpie flew squawking from a nearby aspen, long-tailed and strikingly black and white. He watched the water, glinting in the sun as it splashed along its rocky bed.

He had wondered all the way from Denver to Wolf Creek Pass what it would be like. Then, as the road wound steeply down from the pass through the pines and aspens the smells began to touch the quick of his being, the resinous pine smell, the damp woods smell, the clean smell of fast water, and it was almost painful, the way it cut down through the layers of the years. He finally had to close his eyes and make himself aware of the bus smells to ease it, the odors of people and dust and hot oil and exhaust fumes. Then the bus began to pass small ranches and streamside fishing camps and cabins and he could look again, smell again. Now, sitting here in the sun, watching the flashing stream, he found himself blocking out the sounds and smells of the street behind him.

He sat there half an hour, then decided he'd better find some place to stay. A cheap room somewhere. But first he had to get some other clothes. In these he looked like a millionaire dude. There weren't any cheap rooms for anybody dressed like this.

He went back across the street to the clothing store. A clerk, dressed like New York or Chicago, greeted him and Tom said, "I need some work clothes." The clerk looked him over, head to foot, and asked, "What did you have in mind?"

"Levi's."

The clerk led him to a counter, showed him a pair of tight-cut, fancy-stitched denim pants. Tom shook his head. "Work clothes," he repeated, then glanced at himself. "I've got the dude kind," he said with a smile.

Another man came in, a man in dusty Levi's and a black hat mottled with sweat stains. He stood at the desk while the clerk took Tom toward the back of the store, to a pile of folded Levi's cut for ease, not style. He chose a pair in Tom's size, held them up. Tom nodded. "And a couple of shirts and a brush jacket."

The clerk asked his shirt size, brought the blue work shirts and a short denim jacket. Tom tried it on, asked for more shoulder room. Then asked, "Have you got a place where I can change?"

The clerk took him to a fitting room and Tom put on the

work clothes, then came out and told the clerk he wanted a pair of plain work boots. While he was fitting the boots the clerk asked, "You staying around here?" It was a conversational question.

"I used to live around here." Then, with a smile, "I used to herd sheep, over near Bayfield."

The clerk chuckled. It was a joke, but he would go along with it. The dress boots Tom had just taken off cost eighty-five dollars a pair, and the clerk knew it. And that mohair jacket must have cost at least a hundred.

They went back to the desk and the clerk carefully folded the mohair jacket, the gabardine slacks, the striped shirt, and packed them with the spare blue work shirt in a box. He wrapped the eighty-five-dollar boots. Tom paid his bill and turned to leave.

The man who had come in while Tom was choosing the Levi's said, "Did I hear you say you used to herd sheep?"

"That's right." Tom smiled, sharing the joke with him.

"You wouldn't know where I could find a good herder, would you?"

Tom shook his head. Then, following the same impulse that made him talk to the waitress, he asked, "What do you need a herder for at this time of year? Your flocks must all be out on grass by now."

"They are. Up on summer range. But I lost a herder last week. Damn fool shot himself in the foot. Had gangrene when my supply man found him. May lose his leg."

"Where is this flock?"

"On the Piedra, up on Horse Mountain."

"Good grass up there. Used to be, anyway."

"Still is. You know that country?"

"I've been there."

"Your face is familiar. Do I know you? My name's Jim Woodward."

"I'm Tom Black Bull." He said the name without thinking.

Woodward shook his head. "No, I guess not." He turned to the clerk. "You know a herder looking for a job, Henry?"

Tom left them, went out and started down the street. Then, on impulse, he turned back and met Jim Woodward as he was leaving the clothing store. "I'll take that flock for you," Tom said.

"What!" Jim Woodward stared at him, unbelieving. Then he asked, "You mean that?"

"Yes."

"Well, I'll be damned!" Woodward laughed. "In the cafe, a little while ago, I said you probably were an actor from that movie crowd over at Durango. If you don't mind my asking, what do you want to herd sheep for? The job is yours, but I'm just plain damn curious."

"I've been laid up a while, sick. I want to get out in the hills doing something that's not too hard work for a while."

"How soon can you go?"

"Any time. Right now."

"Well, come on! I've got a man from the home ranch up there holding the flock, but I need him in the hay field. Throw your things in the pickup over there while I get a couple boxes of .30–30 shells. I'll be right with you."

## 43

They headed west on the highway. Woodward asked only a few questions, and Tom gave short answers.

"I've been back East. . . . A broken leg. But they pinned it and it's all right now to walk on, the doctor says. . . . I'm Ute, not Navaho."

Tom asked questions and Woodward said the home ranch was in the San Luis Valley, over near Antonito. He ran twelve to fifteen thousand head of sheep, parceled them out in flocks of two thousand head or so and sent them into the high country for summer range. Fed out his own lambs in the fall, wintered his ewes on the home ranch. He had three flocks between Pagosa and Durango. "Trail them out to summer range, back in the fall. My supply man makes the rounds once a week. If a good herder wants to stay on, I've got work for him at the home ranch all winter. If you know that Horse Mountain country, you'll make out. Only, for God's sake, if you got to shoot yourself, do it in the head and make a clean job of it." Woodward laughed wryly. "God, how gangrene stinks! Just like a flyblown sheep carcass."

At Piedra Town they turned north, up the river and into the hills, following a track that couldn't even be called a wagon trail. Woodward was so busy driving he had no time to talk. The track crossed the shadow Piedra half a dozen times and zigzagged up the valley, much of the way slow going for the pickup. Remembering his own trips up and down the valley long ago, Tom thought they made incredibly fast time. Before he could believe it they were at the foot of Horse Mountain, making their way around it. Then they climbed a sharp slope, topped out on a flat shoulder and came to a big natural meadow edged half a mile away by aspens and scattered pines. The flock was grazing at the far edge, just this side of the timber. The herder wasn't in sight, but a saddled horse lifted its head from grazing and watched them.

Woodward drove past a gray pyramid tent beside a small creek, gave it a nod, and drove slowly out across the meadow toward the sheep. A man got to his feet, waved, and two dogs barked. The man walked toward them and Woodward drew up beside him. "Dave," Woodward shouted above the roar of the motor, "this is Tom. He's going to take the flock. Come on in and show him where things are and we'll head for home."

Dave nodded to Tom. He was a tall, sinewy farm boy in his late twenties. He went to catch up the saddle horse, and Woodward drove slowly along the edge of the flock, appraising, then turned and drove back to the tent. They got out and Tom saw that Dave kept a neat camp. The Dutch oven beside the flat stones at the cooking fireplace was clean, the coffeepot was airing, the skillet had been scoured. Dave rode up, the dogs with him, and showed Tom the tin-covered grub box, the cooler in the creek with meat and butter, the kerosene can for the lantern. He flipped open the tent flaps, pointed to the blankets neatly drawn up on the folding canvas cot. "No bugs. Anything I hate is a lousy bed. I finally got them all cleaned out." He turned to the dogs. "Shep and Spot know the hand signals, good dogs. And old Mac—" nodding toward the bay gelding—"is a lazy old plug, but he doesn't wander. You don't have to hobble him."

Woodward was getting restless. He handed Tom his clothes bag from the pickup, then picked up the boxes of .30–30 shells. "Almost forgot these. You may need them."

Dave nodded. "There's a bear or two around. I haven't seen one, but Manual said he did. The rifle's in the saddle boot. She's sighted in at a hundred yards and shoots good and flat." He, too, was eager to be off. "That about cover things?"

"I think so."

Dave and Woodward got into the truck. "Anything comes up, ask Charley, the supply man. He'll be around Thursday," Woodward said. "Or is it Wednesday up here, Dave?"

"Thursday." Woodward was gunning the motor. "Good luck!" Dave shouted as Woodward swung the pickup around, headed toward the valley.

Tom watched them out of sight, heard the motor a few minutes longer, then just stood and listened to the silence. It was unbelievable. He had forgotten. Then he heard the burbling of the creek, the whispering of the aspens just across the creek, but those sounds were like a part of the silence, the peace.

One of the dogs nosed his hand. He rubbed its ear, then looked at the flock, beginning to loosen up, scatter into the edge of the timber. He ordered the dogs to go pull the flock together, but they were baffled by his words. Without thinking, he remembered the hand signals Albert Left Hand used, made them, and the dogs raced across the meadow toward the sheep. He looked at the saddle horse, was tempted to mount and follow the dogs, but decided against riding. He walked, leading the horse, and the grass underfoot felt strangely soft. It had been a long time since he walked on grass. His legs were stiff and his hips were sore from the pickup ride, but he walked all the way to the flock. The dogs had pulled them together again. He looped the reins loosely over the saddle horn, let the horse graze, and sat down to rest. He was breathing fast, unused to the thin air. It would take a few days to get acclimated again.

He sat, savoring the pine-scented air, resting his eyes on the nearby green, the distant blue. Then he looked at his

Levi's, still new and stiff, and at his plain work boots, and knew he was an outlander, a stranger. He heard lambs bleating for their mothers, ewes blatting their answer, and he smiled at the irony. He had come west to rest, to start over. But he hadn't expected to go all the way back to his beginnings. He was a sheepherder again, right back where he started.

He plucked a blade of grass, chewed it, watched the sheep and welcomed the warmth of the sun on his back. Midafternoon passed and the sun began to slip down toward the peaks to the west. The sheep were working back across the meadow toward the creek. When the long shadows reached him he caught the horse, reached for the stirrup and swung into the saddle without thinking. Then he felt a twinge in his right leg and an ache across his hips, but there was no real pain. He reined the horse around toward the sheep, thinking it had been almost two months since he had been in a saddle, years since he had been on a gentle horse. He rode along the edge of the flock, the horse at a walk, following the sheep toward the creek. They took their time and when they reached the water they scattered along it and drank their fill, then turned back onto the grass. They would graze for another hour, until late dusk, before they bedded down.

He rode over to his camp, unsaddled the horse and hung the saddle from a rope over a low branch of a pine near the tent to keep it out of reach of porcupines. He built a fire, opened a can of beans and set them to heat in the frying pan, made a pot of coffee. By the time he had eaten and fed the dogs the sheep had bedded down and the first stars were out. He washed his dishes, put them away, then went with the dogs for a slow walk around the flock. The stars glinted, the air was cool, the aspens whispered to the night. The sheep were quiet. He went back to the fire, poured another tin cup of coffee and sat sipping it, watching the embers darken and die.

He sat for another half hour before the chill deepened the aches in his tired muscles and complaining joints. He got up, tempted to bring out a blanket and roll up in it under the stars, the night close around him. But he knew that was foolish. He went into the tent, undressed in the dark, got into bed and was asleep in five minutes.

It was dawn when he wakened. He pushed back the blankets, pulled on his pants and his boots, went outside. The dogs, sleeping curled up beside the stones of the fireplace, stretched and yawned and whined a greeting. He went to the creek, washed in the icy water and noticed the night's dew dripping from the bushes. He had forgotten how wet everything was in a mountain dawn, and how chilly. He filled the coffeepot, built a fire, set bacon to fry. The sheep had begun to leave their bedground. They would graze contentedly where they were for another hour.

He had a first cup of coffee, then he mixed batter and fried pancakes in the bacon grease. He fed the dogs and ate his own breakfast, and the sun came up over the range to the east and shimmered the morning mist that hung over the meadow. Jays began to scream and one came close to the fire, expecting a handout. He tossed it a piece of pancake. A long-tailed magpie scolded but didn't come near.

He fried the last of the batter in one big cake and flipped it onto the stones to cool for the birds and the chipmunks. When he had washed his dishes he got the packet of stew meat from the cooler and set it to cook with onions and potatoes in the Dutch oven. By the time he had made his bed old Mac came up expecting to be saddled. Tom obliged him, mounted, called the dogs and went out to gather the sheep, which had scattered all over the meadow. Once they were bunched, he rode a slow circle of the meadow, orienting himself.

He couldn't remember ever being here, in this particular meadow, though he was sure he had been in the valley just below. On the way up in the pickup he had seen a dozen places that looked familiar, but distances were distorted, the pickup at its slowest traveling two or three times as fast as a man would on foot. He was sure there were other places he would recognize, once he let the layers of time slip off. Time, he thought, was like the onions he had just peeled. Layer on layer, and to get down to the heart of things you let the layers peel off, one by one.

He circled the meadow, finding hidden gaps among the trees that led to other, smaller, meadows which he marked in his mind to graze when the sheep had grazed down the big meadow. Then he came to a place where the timbered slope fell away steeply and a wide vista opened to the north and the west. The mountains stood in deceptive ranks, scattered but looking like successive ranges, each with its own degree of shadow and distance. Two peaks, well apart, loomed above the others, the gray bulk of one perhaps fifteen miles to the northwest, the bald upthrust of the other half again as far directly north. He smiled, recognizing them. Granite Peak, the closer one, to the northwest, and Bald Mountain to the north. He sat in the saddle a long time, just looking. Then he rode back to the flock, sat in the grass, let the horse graze, and felt another layer of time slowly peeling off.

Noon, the sun overhead, and he walked back to camp and ate a plateful of stew. And all afternoon he sat in the sun or walked and let the peace and the silence soak into him. Evening, supper, a last walk around the bedded flock.

"Eat, and sleep, and walk," Dr. Ferguson had ordered. Remembering, he smiled. There wasn't much else for a sheepherder to do, even if he wanted to.

## 44

Charley, the supply man, came on schedule. He was wiry, curly-haired, in his late thirties. He was talkative full of gossip and stories, profane, vulgar and friendly. He stayed almost an hour, cursing the rocks and the difficult trail, talking of women and liquor. He said that Manuel, the herder who shot himself in the foot, had been operated on. "Took his leg off, right up to the knee, the poor bastard. He'll have a hell of a time chasing the women now." But the curses, the woman talk, even the sympathy for Manuel, were conversational, nothing more. At last he asked, "Got any problems I should report to the boss?" Tom shook his head. "See you next week," Charley said, and he got into the truck and went back the way he had come.

Tom put the fresh meat and the butter into the cooler, stowed the groceries, and was glad to be alone. But that night he dreamed about Blue Elk. The old man came to him in his dreams, with his derby hat and his well-oiled braids and his squeaky shoes and his insistent talk. "The old songs have been sung," Blue Elk said. "The old ways are gone."

In the dream Tom was no longer a boy. He was a man, come back after the long years. But Blue Elk talked as though he was still a boy. "You must learn the new ways," Blue Elk said. "You must learn to read the white man's reading and write his writing. You must learn to plow and plant the field as he says."

And Tom asked, "Did you learn to plow and plant, Blue Elk? Did you learn to read and write?"

"I am an old man," Blue Elk said. "I speak for your own good."

Tom said "I learned. Don't you know who I am, Blue Elk? I am Devil Tom Black, the Killer. I killed you, Blue Elk, and I killed Benny Grayback and the others. I would have killed Red Dillon, but he killed himself. Do you know that, Blue Elk?"

And the man in front of him wasn't Blue Elk at all. It was Red Dillon, and Red was laughing at him. "When you feel that way," Red said, "don't try to take it out on me. Take it out on the horses, where you've got a chance."

"I took it out on the horses!" Tom cried.

And Red laughed at him again and tilted a bottle and drank and wiped the bottle on his sleeve and offered it to Tom. Tom took a swallow and his head reeled, and Red was gone, and there was Blue Elk again. And Tom was a boy chanting an old song, a song long forgotten, of the earth rhythm and the water rhythm and the rhythm of the days and the seasons. He chanted and Blue Elk began to sway in the white man's highbacked chair, to sway and chant, humming the words he couldn't remember. His voice rose to a mournful pitch, a howl that swelled and faded and swelled again.

Tom wakened, roused by his own voice and the howling, and after a moment he knew he had been dreaming. The light of the late moon shone through the tent with dull radiance and one of the dogs was howling just outside. Tom got up, flung back the tent flap and spoke sharply to the dog. It wagged its tail, cringing at his voice, and came low-bellied to him and licked his hand. He rubbed its ears and spoke to it and it went back and curled up beside the fireplace. He went back to bed and, after a time, to untroubled sleep.

The next morning he went naked to the creek and bathed in the icy water. As he got out and rubbed warmth into his legs and body he wondered why he had done it. It was sheer punishment to bathe in the creek at dawn. He usually took his bath in late afternoon, when the air was warm. But when he hurried back and got into his clothes he felt the glow all over his body and was glad he had done it. He built a fire, cooked his breakfast and set his camp in order. Then he saddled the horse and rode out to the flock, remembering the dream and the howling dog. He knew why he had that dream. The supply man reminded him of Red, and thinking of Red he had thought back to Blue Elk. Nothing mysterious about that.

He rode out to the flock, and he walked and sat in the sun and came in for his noon meal, and went back and told himself it was just another day, another day of waiting. Getting paid for waiting and healing himself, to be ready to get back to the arena. Then he smelled the smells of the arena, heard the sounds. He felt the remembered jolt of a bronc as it lunged out of the chute. He sensed the pattern, lunge-lunge-lunge, half spin, side jump, lunge-lunge-lunge again.

And caught himself. He had made that ride on the big roan in the Garden plenty of times. No need to go over it again. He stretched his right leg, tensed his thigh, felt the soreness still there. Not much, but some. He got to his feet, walked along the edge of the flock. He still had a slight limp. He was entitled to that. It was as much a part of him as that stiff left shoulder. The gimps, the scars, they were the marks of his trade. He was a bronc rider.

Then he laughed at himself. Tom Black, Killer Tom, herding sheep!

The days passed, and weeks marked only by the arrival of Charley, the supply man. Jays came to share his breakfast each morning and chipmunks sat on his knee and ate crumbs from his hand at the noon meal. Then one afternoon he plucked grass stems and wove a basket half the size of his fist, his fingers remembering a forgotten skill. Having done it, he knew it was silly, childish. But he hung it in a bush where a field mouse looking for an abandoned bird nest might find it and line it with fluff for a winter haven.

He grazed the flock in the smaller meadows near by, and coming back one evening to the bedground he surprised two does and their four fawns watering at the creek close by the tent. Seeing that the fawns were losing their spots, he realized how swiftly the season was passing. The sun was moving south, the days shortening. And a few mornings later he saw a white cap of snow on Pagosa Peak, far off to the northeast.

Then Woodward arrived again.

Tom was eating his noon meal when Woodward drove up. He got out the other tin plate and cup, poured coffee and told Woodward to help himself to the stew. Woodward asked the expected questions, about the sheep, the supplies, the grass. He kept watching Tom, and finally he said, "Found some rodeo pictures the other day in an old magazine."

Tom went on eating, made no comment.

"One bronc rider," Woodward said, "was a dead ringer for you. His name was Tom Black. Ever know him?"

"Yes."

"Quite a rider, I judge."

"That's what they say."

"What ever happened to him?" Woodward asked with a smile.

"He's still around."

Woodward seemed pleased with his discovery and didn't press Tom for more information. He finished his coffee, set his plate aside. "Well, come on, let's have a look at the sheep. I'm going to move them down in another couple of weeks."

They got in the pickup and drove out to the flock, went slowly around them, Woodward stopping from time to time to look and appraise. "Let them get all the grass they can before the drive," he said. "I like to start them in good shape. I'll bring men up from the home ranch to help move them."

They drove back toward the camp and Woodward said, "I told you when I hired you that I keep good herders on for the winter. Want to stay?"

"I've got other plans."

Woodward smiled. "Think you're ready to ride again?"

"Yes."

"Huh! I knew when I hired you that you weren't a sheepherder. But I needed a man, and you seemed to know sheep and you knew this part of the country, so I took a gamble. I will say you've done a damn good job, at that."

Tom got out at the tent. Woodward said, "See you in a couple of weeks," and drove back down the valley.

## 45

Now that he had committed himself, Tom began to plan. He had the rodeo schedule in his clothes bag, but he hadn't looked at it since he left the hospital. He got it out and decided Albuquerque was the place to start. He'd always had good luck there, and it was close by.

Two more weeks. He would pick up his summer's pay, buy a used car, have enough to carry him a few weeks, and get going. He wished he had a string of horses to tune up with. But he hadn't, so he would have to start cold. You don't forget, though. The skills and reflexes are still there. After all, it was his reflexes and his sense of balance that got him walking again. And even with old Mac, the plug, he had the feel of the saddle. It would all come back, just as soon as he straddled a bronc.

But he increased his walking, to strengthen his legs, and he chopped wood to loosen his shoulders and back. He forced old Mac to a lope and a gallop, to know that his hips and that thighbone could take it. And he reminded himself that he had no pain, hadn't even felt a twinge of the deep aches for several weeks.

A week passed. He counted the days, impatient for Woodward to come and take the flock.

The second day of the final week he took the flock to a small meadow just north of the camp meadow, where the grass was specially lush. From the far edge of the little meadow he could see both Granite Peak and Bald Mountain, and he sat there in the grass looking at them, wishing he had time to go and see them close up again. In the fall, with aspen gold and scrub oak red. Another month or six weeks and they would be beautiful. Then the leaves would fall and you would be able to see forty miles in the clear autumn air. Those perfect fall days when you felt that the whole world was yours and you had been here forever. Mountains did that to you, these mountains. Then winter would come, snow and silence, and the deep, deep green of pine and spruce. He'd like to know winter here again, too.

Then he thought: I'll be in California by then. Winding up the season, taking a rest, getting ready to open the circuit again in January.

He turned from the mountains and looked at the sheep, scattered over the little meadow. It was past midafternoon and they would soon begin to move back toward the camp meadow. To water at the creek, graze another hour, then bed down. Another day almost over. Another day nearer the circuit.

He was looking at the sheep, not really seeing them, when old Mac snorted. The horse was a hundred yards away. It jerked up its head, pointed its ears and began to dance sideways, watching a tongue of brush that spilled out of the timber from a shallow gully that washed into the meadow from the uphill side. The dogs leaped up, bristling and growling, and Tom started to get to his feet. He was still on his knees when the bear lunged out of the brush. It moved with deceptive speed, sweeping into a little band of sheep. It slapped with one big paw. The sheep blatted and ran in every direction, but a fat lamb lay there quivering, its neck broken.

Tom was on his feet, shouting. The bear lifted its head, heaved itself up onto its hind legs for a better look, then dropped to all fours again and nosed the lamb. Tom ran toward it, a scant two hundred yards away, the dogs just ahead of him. The bear hesitated an instant, then picked up the lamb in its jaws, turned and went back into the brush.

Tom shouted to the dogs, "Bring them in! Gather them!" They hesitated, and he gave the hand signals, shouted again,

"Gather them, you damn fools!" and the dogs raced to pull the panicky flock together. Tom hurried on.

He came to the tongue of brush, heard the bear crashing through the underbrush up the mountainside. The trail was easy to follow. He went up the slope a hundred yards and came to a little opening in the timber, and there, not fifty yards away, he saw the bear. It had stopped, the lamb still in its jaws, and faced him across the little clearing.

He stepped into the open and paused. The bear peered at him, dropped the lamb and rumbled a deep growl that ended in a hoarse, coughing grunt. It took a few steps toward him and he shouted, "Stop! Stop that! Get out of here!" It stopped, seemed to bunch its muscles for a rush. He shouted at it again. It swung its head from side to side, backed away a few steps. Then it growled once more, picked up the lamb and turned and went on up the mountain.

Tom watched it go, then wiped his face as though wiping away cobwebs. He felt the sweat flowing down his neck, down his belly under his shirt. His legs were so weak he had to sit down. Then he heard the sheep blatting and the dogs barking, and he went back down the slope. He thought what a fool he had been, following a bear into the brush without a weapon, not even a belt knife. The rifle was still in the saddle boot, and the horse was all the way across the meadow.

The sheep were charging about and the dogs were trying desperately to bunch them, almost as frantic as the sheep. He called the dogs, signaled them to ease up, let the sheep quiet down, and he went across the meadow and caught old Mac. The horse was still so skittish it side-jumped and bucked a couple of times when he mounted, catching him by surprise and making him grab the saddle horn for an instant. Then the leaders of the flock began to move toward the gap and back toward the camp meadow. He circled to help the dogs gather the stragglers, but the horse wouldn't go near the place where the bear had been. Tom sent the dogs, but they too smelled the bear and the blood and forgot the sheep until he shouted them back to business.

Finally he had the whole flock lining through the gap. But even on the home meadow they continued to mill and run from their own shadows for another hour before they quieted down. Then, the sun already set, he went in, made a quick meal of bacon and eggs, and mounted again and rode around the bedded flock several times. The sheep reasonably quiet at last, he went back to the fire, picketed the horse still saddled, threw a blanket over his shoulders and sat sipping coffee and going over the afternoon's events. The whole incident now seemed like an outlandish dream. Even his own actions were incredible. The more he thought about them, the more annoyed he was at himself. He had acted like a damned fool, charging up the hillside barehanded after a bear that had just made a kill. Then walking right out into the open with the bear not fifty yards away and hollering at it. It was all very stupid.

He looked out across the meadow. The sheep were bedded quietly, like a vast gray rug shimmering in the moonlight. Here and there a nervous old ewe got to her feet, blatted, then lay down again. It was like almost any other night. The air was chill, the aspens whispered, there was the soft sigh of air moving among the pines. Everything was peaceful. Even the dogs were asleep. He should go to sleep himself.

But something nagged at him. Finally he told the dogs to stay, got on the horse and rode quietly around the flock and across to the gap that led to the little meadow beyond. It shimmered in the moonlight with rolling puffs of mist, white as smoke, in the hollows. The pines were almost black and the aspen leaves, quivering in the soft night breeze, reflected the moonlight like spangles. Everything was so peaceful that it seemed impossible that anything had happened there only a few hours before.

He rode slowly around the meadow until he approached the tongue of brush. Then the horse began to snort and fight the rein. He tried to force it close, but it shied and danced sideways, refused. The bear smell was still there. He gave up, let the horse have its way, and rode back the way he had come, back to the fire. At least, he had proved that it wasn't something he had imagined.

He picketed the horse again, took the rifle from the saddle boot, built the fire up and rolled up in the blanket beside it, the rifle close at hand. If there was any disturbance in the night he would hear the sheep, or the dogs would waken him.

But he didn't go to sleep at once. He went over the incident of the bear again, recalling details. It was a big bear, and it stood high in the shoulders. Its head was broad and he was sure its face was dished. It had a grizzled look, almost frosty.

Then he thought maybe it wasn't really grizzled. It might have been the light that made it look that way. Maybe its face wasn't dished. And he thought: *You fool! What are you trying to do? Tell yourself crazy stories? The herder who shot himself in the foot said there were bears around. Bears, not grizzlies. You made enough of a fool of yourself this afternoon. Forget it.*

And finally he went to sleep. But he slept fitfully, waking several times, once with such a start that he grabbed the rifle and leaped to his feet, only to see the sheep sleeping quietly.

Then it was dawn, and he got up for the day, washed himself awake, put the rifle in the saddle boot, and cooked and ate breakfast. And told himself he had been jumpy, seeing ghosts, imagining things. So he had seen a bear. The bear got a lamb. He had been so jumpy he hadn't even got one shot at the bear. It probably wouldn't come back, but if it did he would shoot it, and that would be that. *Tom Black,* he jeered at himself, *Killer Tom Black, who sees a bear and runs after it empty-handed and hollers, "Boo!"*

The sheep left their bedground, began to graze. He rode out to them, sat in the sun for an hour. Just a few more days and he would be through with the sheep, through with this stupid job. But it had been a good summer, in a way. He'd got over the smashup, which was the important thing. Now he could go back and pick up where he left off. He had got a few things in place, too. Old Blue Elk, for instance. He wished he knew what had happened to Blue Elk, though it didn't really matter. The old buzzard was dead by now, must be. And seeing Luther Spotted Dog, there on the curb in Pagosa the day he arrived, had been a kind of satisfaction. Luther obviously wasn't worth a damn, not even to himself. He did hope Luther recognized him, knew who he was and what he had done. But that didn't matter either. None of them mattered.

He sat for an hour, knowing that he was putting something off. Something he had to do, something he had to know before he left here. And finally he caught old Mac, mounted and rode to the little meadow of the afternoon before. He didn't try to force the horse all the way to the tongue of brush, but got off and let him graze and went on foot. He took the rifle, just in case, telling himself that a fool's luck might not be repeated. If he saw the bear again it might charge him.

He went on foot to the brush and he searched for tracks. There wasn't a track, so he pushed his way cautiously through the brush and began to climb the slope. He reached the little clearing, and there he found what he was looking for. In a patch of soft earth he found a paw print, the mark of a bear's hind paw. There was the long triangular sole print, the mark of five toes, and four claw marks. One claw had left no mark. The print was six inches across and at least ten inches long. The claw marks were well ahead of the toes. He looked at it a long time. Then he looked for more tracks, found two, both smudged and indistinct. And at last he went back down the slope, caught the horse and rode back to the flock. That, he told himself, was that.

But that evening, sitting beside the fire with his last cup of coffee, he admitted that he wished he hadn't found the track. Now things kept coming back, things he had thought were disposed of long ago. And he knew why he hadn't gone into Thatcher's Market. Jim Thatcher might still be there, and he might remember. Why rake up the old memories? Sure, he was an Indian. A Ute, as he had made it clear to Woodward. But he wasn't a clout Indian, or a reservation Indian. He'd made something of himself, forced them to accept him. He was Tom Black, the bronc rider they would remember a long time. *Killer* Tom Black, by God! He told Woodward his name was Tom Black Bull, but that was like telling the clerk in the clothing store he used to herd sheep, a kind of back-handed brag. If you said it first they couldn't say it back with a nasty twist.

Well, he had found the track, and he had gone over the memories, and that was that. He was sorry he had acted like a fool instead of killing the damned bear, but it was too late to do anything about the now.

He put the whole thing out of his head, called it a day, went into the tent and to bed. And dreamed about his mother and the lodge and the winter she died. And chanted the death chant and waked himself up. He went outside and looked at the peaceful night, talked to the dogs till the chill got to him, then went back to bed.

## 46

Woodward arrived in the pickup with two men from the home ranch. They would herd the flock on foot, Woodward said, five miles or so down the valley today. The big truck would meet them there with the horse trailer and mounts for the herders, and the crew would have camp set up. They would go ahead and set up camp each night along the way. The trip would take about ten days.

"The boys will start moving them right out," Woodward said. "You pack the gear and stow it in my pickup while I help them get started. They'll take the dogs but leave the horse, and you can catch up with the flock."

"You don't plan on my going all the way in with them?" Tom asked.

"Not if you want to get away. I won't really need you after we get them down out of here."

"I'd rather not go all the way in."

"O.K. I'm going on home tomorrow and you can ride along with me. To Piedra, or Pagosa, or all the way to Antonito, wherever you want to go."

"That'll be fine," Tom started packing and Woodward went to help the herders start the flock down the valley. When he came back Tom had everything stowed. "See you in camp this evening," Woodward said, and he drove off.

Tom mounted old Mac and started to follow, then turned back. He wanted one more look. He rode across the meadow to the place where he could see Granite Peak and Bald Mountain, and he sat in the saddle for some time, just looking. Then he turned and went back past the camp site and down toward the valley. He caught up with the flock about two miles below, the sheep strung out and grazing their way. He fell in behind them, said he would keep the drags moving, and the two herders on foot moved up to the flanks of the flock to keep the strays out of the deep timber.

They camped that night in a big meadow six miles above Piedra Town, where the rest of the crew had supper ready and bedrolls waiting. Woodward brought his plate and sat beside Tom to eat. "So you're going back to rodeoing?" he asked.

"Yes."

"Kind of gets in your blood, I guess. If you're really good. How long you been riding in the big time?"

"Quite a while." Tom didn't want to talk about it.

"Maybe I'll go in to Denver and see you, next time around."

Tom made no comment. They ate and Woodward went back for a second helping. When he came back he said, "Meant to ask, did you have any bear trouble up there?"

"No trouble. I only saw one bear. It got a lamb."

"Kill it?"

"I didn't even get a shot. It never came back."

"Probably the one Manuel was talking about. A big old cinnamon, wasn't it?"

"It could have been, maybe."

"What do you mean, maybe?" Woodward laughed. "It *was*! Had to be. There aren't any grizzlies left. Jim Boone shot the last one four years ago, out deer hunting over near Granite Peak. Emptied his .30-30 into it before he put it down. A big devil, old as the hills. Right, Charley?" he asked the supply man. "You saw its hide."

"That grizzly of Jim Boone's?" Charley asked. "Big as a horse barn! Scared the hell out of me, just looking at the hide."

"Every now and then," Woodward said, "somebody still reports a grizzly. Always turns out to be a big cinnamon. See one in the right light, though, he can fool you. Looks downright frosty. You ever see a grizzly?" he asked Tom.

"Years ago."

"Dish-faced, high in the shoulder. Leaves tracks that long." He held his hands a foot apart.

Someone spoke of the flavor of bear meat. The talk turned to wild game in general. Tom paid no attention, was almost unaware of either the talk or the men around him. Everything had changed. He didn't know why. All he knew was that things had changed and that he had no choice. He had things straight, as he had planned to have them, but they came out at another place. He knew what he had to do. It was all clear now.

Then he heard two of the men arguing over the merits of fat bear meat and fat elk, and he got up and went to his bedroll.

The next morning he told Woodward he would go only as far as Piedra Town. Woodward nodded. "Just as you say."

So they rode the few miles in to Piedra, Woodward paid him off and as they left the bank Woodward said, "Well, Tom Black, good luck. If things don't pan out and you ever need a job, look me up. But I'll plan on watching you ride in Denver."

They shook hands and Woodward headed east, toward Pagosa and the road over the divide to Antonito and the home ranch. Tom looked around for the grocery and the hardware store. Half an hour later, in the hardware store lashing his pack, he looked out and saw the big Woodward truck, Charley at the wheel and the empty horse trailer behind it, go down the street on its way to the next camp site.

He shouldered his pack, picked up his rifle, went out and up to the end of the street. There he turned to the hillside and followed the winding goat trails through the brush. He traveled northward almost an hour before he heard the flock in the valley below him. He sat down under a pine and waited, resting his shoulders from the unaccustomed pack, till the last straggling ewe and the last herder had passed. Then he shouldered his pack again, went down the hillside to the trail along the Piedra River and resumed his journey back to Horse Mountain.

## 47

He stayed at the old camp site the first night, but even with the sheep gone their smell persisted. He had been so used to it all summer that he hadn't noticed, but now it seemed to taint the air. Sitting by his fire that evening, smelling the light breeze that came to him over the old bedground, he had the wry thought that a good many things were like the sheep. You got free of them, or thought you did, but the smell of them kept coming back. Well, he told himself, that's why he was here. He had got rid of those memory smells, all but one, and he had come back to get rid of it. He had put off his return to the arena for a week or two just to get this done, to wipe the slate clean. He was going to run that bear down, and if it was a grizzly he was going to kill it.

He drank a last cup of coffee, ignored the sheep smell, rolled up in his blanket, and slept soundly. But the sheep smell was still strong on the damp air the next morning, so, after a quick breakfast, he packed his gear and moved to the little meadow. He had seen a seep spring there a few days ago, enough water for a one-man camp. He went there, slung his pack in a tree, safe from prowlers, and set out with only his belt knife and his rifle.

He climbed the old trail through the tongue of brush to the little opening where he had seen the bear track and began to range the mountainside. The trail was cold and the mountainside was a maze of rocky ledges and talus slopes with a scattering of scrub oak and twisted pine. He climbed and he looked and half a mile farther on he found the remains of the lamb, two hoofs, a scattering of splintered bones, several patches of skin that had been gnawed by mice and pecked by magpies.

He went on, circling, and in early afternoon he found a big pine with claw marks. The gouges were high on the trunk, as high as he could reach, but that proved nothing. A rock that had been at the foot of the tree had been rolled aside, probably for the bear to get at the ants and grubs beneath it. The bear could have stood on the rock and put its claw marks on the tree before it heaved the rock aside.

He completed his circle, came back to where he started. He hadn't found another sign, hadn't seen one clear track. It was late afternoon. He went down to the seep spring, made camp. As he ate supper he tried to figure it. If it had been a big cinnamon it should have left more signs. A cinnamon is just a black bear in a cinnamon color phase. All bears are wanderers, but the blacks and cinnamons keep to a smaller range than grizzlies, especially if they have a convenient source of food. An old grizzly will travel ten miles overnight, stop for a light meal, then go on another ten miles or more. A cinnamon will eat, sleep, then go back to where it got the first meal. If this had been a cinnamon, Tom reasoned, it would have come back for another lamb. At least, it would have stayed around for a few days, hopeful. If it was a grizzly it probably would travel until it made a big kill, such as a deer. Then it would eat, hide its kill, sleep, then gorge again before moving on.

It didn't add up either way. Tom had kept telling himself he had seen a grizzly. But he had had only two brief looks, first when the bear killed the lamb, then when it turned and threatened to charge him at the little clearing. He had been so excited that he followed it into the brush unarmed. Could he believe his own eyes? He had found that one track, but couldn't he have exaggerated its size?

Woodward said, and his men agreed, that the last grizzly

had been killed four years ago. Woodward could be wrong, of course. There might still be a grizzly around, a wise old bear that had outwitted them all. But the chances that it was the cub Tom had known were less than one in a hundred. A grizzly cub doesn't reach full growth till it is six or seven years old, and there would be hazards all along the way, special hazards for a cub that had once been a pet. Some grizzlies live to be thirty, maybe even more, but even if that cub lived to grow up, its chances of survival this long were slim, with persistent hunters and bear-hating ranchmen. All the odds said that the bear Tom saw kill a lamb was a big cinnamon.

But he had come back to run that bear down, identify it if possible, put an end to that last nagging hurt. This hunt had only begun. He finished his meal, cleaned his utensils, and slept.

The next morning he went halfway up the mountainside, made a big circle. Late in the day, down near the river not far from the forks, he found a patch of pines that had been taken down a few years before by a rock slide. Poking around in the tangle he found where a bear had rolled two rotting logs aside to get at the beetles, then had dug out a den of marmots or chipmunks. It must have been a big bear to have moved those big logs. It had been there several days before and the tracks it had left were all smudged.

He went up West Fork a little way and found a rotten stump that had been ripped apart, more of the bear's work. But again there were no recognizable tracks. By all the signs, the bear was going northwest, away from Horse Mountain where he had left his gear. He was two hours from his camp, and as he worked his way wearily back up Horse Mountain he decided that if he didn't want to spend half his time coming and going he had better move. Then he thought that if he was doing this the old way he would forget about camp, just take his rifle and his knife and maybe a small packet of food and stay with the trail till he caught up with the bear, sleeping wherever night found him. And, he thought with a bitter laugh, sing the bear chant! That's why he had come back, he told himself—to be free of such things, to kill those memories, that last remnant of the past.

The next morning he packed his gear and took it down to the Forks, went up West Fork a little way and set up a new camp beside the stream. That afternoon he worked on up the creek and found where the bear had dug quamash—camas roots—in a grassy opening. It had ripped up quite an area, flinging big chunks of sod aside, tearing them apart to get at the quamash in them. It had been there only two days ago, three at most.

He spent two more days working the lower end of West Fork, but all he found was another place, upstream, where the bear had dug quamash. The second afternoon a chill wind blew up and the sky clouded over, and when the rain began that evening he remembered several signs of bad weather coming that he had ignored. The rain was cold, probably was falling as snow on the peaks. From the look of things it could continue all night, perhaps for several days. He got soaked finding dry wood, and before he had eaten his supper the drainage from the slope began to seep through his camp. The place he had picked was all right in dry weather, but would be miserable in the rain. He moved up the hillside to the partial shelter of a clump of spruces, rigged an inadequate roof with his small tarp, finally got a new fire going in front of it and rolled up in his damp blanket. He spent a cold, uncomfortable night.

He wakened to a gray, chill, rainy day and got soaked looking for a standing dead tree with dry wood. With a fire going at last, he cooked breakfast and tried to dry his blanket. But the gusty wind whipped the fire and blew rain into his shelter. He spent a miserable day, feeding the fire and trying to dry his gear. And trying to make sense of what he was doing. He had been here a week on this bear hunt and as far as he could see he was no closer to the bear than when he started. Why, if it was a cinnamon, didn't it stay in one place? Why, if it was a grizzly, didn't it either move out or make a big kill?' There were deer around. He hadn't seen a deer, but he hadn't been looking for one. There were tracks.

Thinking of deer, he was hungry for venison. For a week he had been living on pancakes, bacon and trout, and his bacon was almost gone. Thinking of the soggy, half-cooked pancakes he had eaten today, his mouth watered at the very thought of venison. He told himself that he would take a deer tomorrow, if it stopped raining. Butcher out a loin and live high for the few days he would be here. One loin, that's all he needed.

Then something deep inside said that it wasn't right to waste meat. It wasn't even right to take meat unless you needed it. Waste meat, and what you take to use will soon begin to stink.

He shook his head angrily at the thought. Superstition! Who was he, anyway? A clout Indian?

He felt the chill of water trickling under him and moved to a drier place and put more wood on the fire, wet wood that smoldered and smoked. No, he decided wryly, he wasn't a clout Indian or he would have picked a better camp site when he had the chance. And seen to it that he had plenty of dry wood. And watched the weather signs. Instead of squatting on a creek bank with bad weather coming, like a fool on his first camping trip! All right, so he made a mistake. Another mistake. His first mistake was in coming back here instead of going to Albuquerque.

Why had he come back, anyway? Because he saw a bear that he thought was a grizzly and got the idea that he had to kill it. Why? Because he was Killer Tom Black and wanted to forget that he was an Indian, that's why!

He laughed at that, a snorting laugh of derision. Killer

Tom Black, the Indian who was a devil-killer, was just newspaper stuff, publicity. All right, so he had killed a horse or two. So he had a grudge—a lot of gravel in his craw, as Dr. Ferguson put it—and he took it out on the broncs. He made a reputation and he lived up to it, gave the crowds what they wanted. But that was all over now, over and past. He had got that out of his system. Now he was going back and ride for points, for money, and wind up his career in a few more seasons with a record they would be shooting at for a long time to come.

He felt the rain trickling under him again, and the smoke in his eyes, and he reminded himself that he wasn't in the arena or anywhere near it. He was right here, in this miserable camp, waiting for the cold rain to let up so he could go looking for that bear again. And the whole thing seemed very stupid. The more he thought about it, the more he felt like a fool. He had lived with everything that bear represented for a long time. He could go on living with it, he decided. As soon as this rain stopped he would dry his gear, pack up, and get out of here.

With that thought, a decision made, he felt more at ease. He built up the fire again, found a dry spot to sit, and dozed in the warmth. When he wakened in midafternoon the rain had begun to slacken. Another hour and it had eased to a drizzle and the sky had begun to clear.

He needed more wood. He picked up his ax and started to leave his shelter, and his eye was caught by a movement down at the stream. He stopped, looked again, saw a doe and two fawns come out of the brush. The doe sniffed the air, swiveled her big ears, curious. She was looking upstream. He carefully laid down the ax and picked up the rifle, got the doe in the sights. She was not fifty yards away. He fired, killed her with one clean shot. The fawns whirled, lunged into the brush, and he took his knife and hurried down the slope to bleed the doe, smiling to himself. He had been hungry for red meat, for venison, and here it was, practically in his frying pan.

He bled the doe clean, then butchered out one loin and took it back to his camp, exulting. He chopped dry wood from the dead pine, built up his fire, cut a slice of venison and set it to cook. He hung his blanket where it would catch some of the fire's heat, hoping to dry it out before he tried to sleep in it.

The venison cooked with a tantalizing odor. It had been a long time since he had eaten venison. Finally it was done enough. He put it on his tin plate, cut another slice and set it to cook, and began to eat. The first few mouthfuls tasted wonderful. Then the taste began to change, he didn't know why. He put more salt on it, and that helped. He finished the first slice. The second slice was ready, but he left it in the frying pan. Something was bothering him, and he was angry at himself for being bothered. Finally he exclaimed aloud, "I didn't sing the deer chant, either!" He said it defiantly, then was silent, abashed and somehow sorry he had said it. He took the second slice onto his plate, cut into it. It was too done, but he ate it, telling himself that at least he wasn't wasting cooked meat.

When he had finished he looked at the rest of the loin and decided to cook enough of it to last him on the trip out. It wouldn't spoil if it was cooked. Not so quickly, anyway. So he fed the fire and cooked several panfuls of slices and wrapped them and stowed them with his other supplies. By then the drizzle had stopped and the first stars were out in an open patch of sky off to the north. His blanket was still damp, but he rolled up in it and went to sleep, knowing he was going to get out of here in the morning.

He had a restless night with bad dreams, mostly about his mother and the old tales, that he refused to remember the next morning. He got up, shivering in the chilly dawn, cooked a breakfast of pancakes and the last of his bacon, closed his pack and was ready to go. He looked at the venison hanging in the tree, more than half the loin he had taken from the doe, and he took it down and left it on the ground, where the carrion eaters would soon dispose of it. Then he went along the hillside half a mile before he turned and followed the easy trail beside the creek, not even allowing himself to look at the doe's carcass.

The brush was dripping but the air was clear and crisp, as always after a rain. A few degrees lower and it would have been frosty. He thought of frosty mornings at the lodge his father had built, when his mother sang at her work and taught him little songs about the yellow leaves and the hoarding squirrels and the fawns that had lost their spots. Some of the words came back to him now. He could smile at them, remembering, because he was going away from here and probably would never come back. Then he came to a place where he could look off to the southeast and see Horse Mountain, shimmering in the clear morning air, and his mind went back to the frosty morning when he went down the valley from Bald Mountain and the charred ruins of the lodge and met Benny Grayback and the old man called Fish, waiting there at the foot of Horse Mountain to take him back to school. That was a bitter memory. He put it away from him.

He went down to the creek bank again, pushing that memory from him, and came to a place where the creek made a small mud flat. He went around it and started on, and turned back. His eyes had seen something that his mind had missed. He went back and looked again. It was a bear track there in the mud flat. It was full of water from the rain, but it was a big track. Then he saw other tracks, all of them full of water. They had been made during the rain, yesterday.

He looked around, crossed the creek, and in the soggy soil of a game trail he found another track, a track clean enough to show the long triangular sole mark, the round prints of the five toes, even the claw marks, all five of them. No, only four claw marks. It was the mark of a hind foot identical with the print he had seen on Horse Mountain.

He went on up the slope, finding a sign here, another there. A quarter of a mile and he found a stump that had been ripped apart, and beside it was the mark of a forepaw, the rough halfmoon of the palm, the round heel print, the round toe marks and their claws' prints. There was no doubt now that this bear was not a cinnamon. No cinnamon bear ever had such paws or such claws.

The trail wandered, zigzagging back up the mountainside, down through the gullies, doubling back on itself. It wasn't more than thirty-six hours old. He forgot time until it was midafternoon and he was hungry and the pack straps were cutting into his shoulders. He went to a nearby rise and took his bearings. Off to the southeast was Horse Mountain. To the northeast was Bald Mountain. He was on the first bench of Granite Peak, and the only sensible thing to do was to find a camp site, spend the night, leave his pack and pick up the trail again in the morning. Then stay with it till he ran the bear down.

He worked his way along the bench till he came to a place where a small creek bubbled across an opening with a thicket of lodgepoles pines at the back and a clear view to the east. The kind of camp site he should have chosen in the first place instead of squatting down there on West Fork in the rain. He picked a spot close beside the creek and sheltered by the pines. He cut poles and slung his tarp for a roof, quickly laid up stones for a fireplace, gathered wood and built a fire. He set coffee to cook, opened the packet of cooked venison and put a slice in the frying pan to warm up. It didn't taste the way it had tasted fresh, but it was meat, food. He ate while his blanket, still damp, steamed in front of the fire.

Then he smoothed a place for a bed, rolled up and slept, dog-tired.

The sun wakened him the next morning. He made a quick breakfast, stowed the remaining venison in a small pack, put everything else except his knife and rifle under the tarp, and went back to where he had left the trail yesterday. It was a cold trail and for the first hour he wondered if he could follow it at all. Then his eyes began to sharpen and he saw little signs that he had missed the day before. A broken bush here, a scuffed patch of gravel there. By afternoon he was able to lay out a line to follow, for the bear had stopped wandering at random and was going somewhere. He forced himself to stop thinking like a man and began to think the way a bear would think. It hadn't made a big kill since he had been on the trail. It was getting hungry for something more than grubs and squamash and chipmunks. It would go down into the valley and kill a deer. Go where the deer were, anyway. He laid out a line and followed it, and knew he was right. Going down the long slope he came to a pine tree with a low branch where the bear had stopped to scratch its back. A few white-tipped hairs were still caught in the rough bark. He would have missed that sign yesterday. Now he saw it. And a little later he found a small aspen that it had bent down and walked along to scratch its belly, breaking the brittle branches along one side.

Then it was dusk, and he made a cold camp, ate some of the meat. He didn't like the taste, or the smell of it, but he ate. Then he found a clump of low-hung spruce and crawled in among them and spent the night. The next morning he ate more of the meat, and went on. The trail led down across the valley to Los Pinos Creek. Following the bear's trail up the creek he began to have stomach cramps. Then his head felt light and he began to sweat. He had to stop and rest, and when he started on again the cramps were worse. He retched and vomited twice, cleaning out his stomach, and felt better. But before he went on he opened the packet of meat. It had begun to stink. He retched at the smell, and he threw the meat away. Then he found a serviceberry bush and chewed a few twigs. The taste cleaned out his mouth enough and cleared his nose so that he could go on.

Half a mile upstream and he found a mud wallow the bear had used the day before. From there the trail left the stream, and that afternoon it led him to the lower reaches of Bald Mountain. He thought he had lost it there, but just before dark he found a big pine where the bear had torn off strips of the outer bark to get at the sweetish cambium layer beneath. The tooth marks were still clear and the scar oozed fresh resiny sap.

He made another cold camp that night, going without food. The next morning the trail led him onto Bald Mountain's first bench. There, just before midday, he found where the bear had waited beside a deer run. It had made no kill, but it was hungry for red meat. Near by he found where it had slept, and there he found fresh scat it had made that morning. He knew he was getting close.

Early afternoon and he found where it had made the kill. It had hidden in the brush beside a deer run until four deer came along—a big doe, a smaller doe and two last spring fawns. They came to where the bear was waiting and the bear made its rush and struck down the big doe. The whole story was written unmistakably in frantic hoofprints, broken brush, a gout of blood still drying into the dust, in spatters of blood and loose deer hair on leaves and brush where the bear had dragged its kill up the mountainside.

He followed the trail, wary now, every sense alert. It was only a few hours old. Less than a hundred yards up the mountainside he came to an opening among the trees and saw the cache. The bear had eaten its fill, then crudely hidden the rest of the carcass under a heap of scratched-up dirt and leaves.

Cautiously he made his way around the edge of the clearing, feeling every step, making no sound. The bear was sleeping not far away, gorged. When it had slept off its first big meal it would return and eat again. Halfway around the clearing was a tumbled heap of huge boulders that had lodged there in some ancient slide. Moving like a shadow, he searched among them, making sure the bear wasn't there. Then he chose a hiding place among the rocks and settled down to wait. The cache was in clear sight, nor thirty yards from the rocks. His rifle would be deadly at that range.

## 48

At first the sun felt comfortably warm, but as the rocks caught and reflected the heat he began to feel scorched. His head began to ache and his eyes to burn, and his mouth felt parched. Thirst became a torture. He kept thinking of a small creek he had passed just before he found the place where the bear had made its kill. He should have drunk his fill then, but he didn't. He was hungry, too, but his belly didn't really demand food. He hadn't eaten since the previous morning, when his stomach had refused to keep the bad meat, but he had chewed twigs and a few dry berries, sucking but not swallowing them. He could fast, but thirst was a torture. He put a few pebbles in his mouth to suck on, but that was little help.

Then he began to feel the cramping of his muscles, the tension of lying in one position. He tried to stretch his legs and made a noise among the dry twigs that had lodged among the rocks, and lay still again, enduring the aches.

The afternoon slowly passed. Nothing came to the cache but a few magpies. They ate and squawked and flew away. Then the shadows crept across the opening, the sun slid down behind the shoulder of the mountain and the quick chill of early autumn evening began to make itself felt. The rocks still held the midday heat, but as the first stars appeared a cold breeze flowed down the mountainside like a chilly mist. He edged closer to the rocks to share their warmth.

Night came, full darkness. He tried to remember where the moon stood in its cycle, whether it was early or late, and knew that he hadn't really seen the moon in a long time, didn't even know when it came to the full. And knew that was wrong, since a man should have a sense of time, a friendship with the moon, the sun, the earth. He looked up and saw familiar stars. At least he hadn't forgotten the stars he once knew.

He waited, staring at the dark, shadowy mound of the cache. Nothing was there, nothing that moved. Staring at it, his eyes wearied, lost their focus. He looked at the trees, the clear line between earth and sky, at the stars beyond, forcing his eyes to see. The chill made him shiver and he hugged the rocks, and the warmth soothed him. He was very tired. He dozed, jerked himself awake and fought the drowsiness. He tried to shift his position, crackled the dry twigs and lay still again. He drifted into sleep.

He didn't know how long he slept, but when he wakened and stared at the cache he could see it clearly. Now there were shadows in the clearing, dim shadows. Then he saw the moon, a starved, irregular half-moon. Reaching back, he knew that such a moon didn't rise till around midnight, and it was now at least an hour high so it must be one o'clock or soon after. He looked at the cache again. It was undisturbed. The bear hadn't been there.

He looked around the clearing, shifting his focus to ease his eyes. He waited, eyes open, senses alert. But nothing came, and he drifted into weary half-sleep again. And thought he saw something move, knew it was an illusion. Only the moon shadows were there, moving inch by inch as the moon climbed the sky.

Then something was there, just beyond him in the moonlight. He tensed, gripped his rifle. And knew it was not the bear. It was a woman. He couldn't quite make out her face, though he forced his eyes wide open to look. He still couldn't see her features, but he knew, something deep inside him knew, who she was. She was the mother, not his own mother but the All-Mother, the mothers and the grandmothers all the way back to beginning. She was chanting, and her voice was both sad and pleading. Before he knew, he was chanting with her. But time after time he forgot the words of the chant before he came to the meaningful parts. He was singing softly, as she sang, and at last he knew he was singing the bear chant. He closed his eyes and chanted, his voice now remembering all the words, and when he had finished the chant he opened his eyes and she was gone. Only the moon was there, directly overhead. And his voice went on singing as though apart from him.

Then he saw the bear.

It came out of the shadows among the trees and it slowly crossed the opening, a few steps at a time, pausing to look and listen and nose the air. It was frosty in the moonlight. It was high in the shoulders and its face was dished, not long and straight like a cinnamon bear's face. It came slowly toward the cache, then stopped and stared at the rocks where he was hidden. It lifted its massive head and smelled the air and uttered a throaty growl and shifted its forefeet, lifting one, then the other.

He paused in his humming song and the bear's ears stiffened, alert. It rumbled the deep growl again, took two steps toward the rocks. He sang the low, humming song again, came to the meaningful part, sang it. The bear stopped, waited.

Still humming the bear chant, he carefully raised the rifle, rested it against the rocks. His eyes tried to sight it, but the light was dim. *Wait,* he told himself. *Wait for more light.* And, still humming the chant, he waited, and the bear turned away and went to the cache. It tossed leaves and dirt aside with sweeps of its powerful paws and dragged the carcass into the open. It began to eat.

He watched, and his humming slowly died away. But the beat was still in him like his own pulse. The bear paused in its eating from time to time and looked at the rocks, now accepting his silence as a part of the night. His pulse drummed the beat of the chant and time passed. First light of dawn dimmed the stars overhead. The moon began to fade. And at last he knew he could see the rifle's sights clearly. It was time to kill. He pressed his cheek to the rifle's stock, aimed low in the shoulder where the heart lay close to the ribs. He tried to squeeze the trigger, but his finger refused.

He closed his eyes, fighting with himself. *I came to kill the bear!* His throbbing pulse asked, *Why?* He answered, *I must!* And again his pulse beat, *Why?* He answered, *To be myself!* And the pulse asked, *Who . . . are . . . you?* He had no answer. The pulse kept beating the question at him. Angrily he said, *This bear has made trouble!* The question beat back, *To . . . whom?* And his own bitter answer, *To me!* Then the question, as before, *Who . . . are . . . you?* And he, having no answer he could face, said, whispering the words aloud, "This bear did not make trouble. The trouble is in me." And he lowered the rifle.

It was almost sunrise. The bear nosed the carcass, looked at the rocks, sniffed the air, lifted its lip and sniffed again. Then it turned and crossed the clearing to the trees whence it had come in the moonlight.

He watched it go, and when it was gone he asked himself if he had seen a bear at all. Then he saw the open cache, the white bones of the carcass gleaming in the first sunlight. But as he looked at the rocks and trees and sky and earth he felt like a stranger here. He waited, expecting the feeling to pass, but when he touched the rocks with his hand they were cold and unfriendly. When he moved his cramped legs the dry twigs made a harsh, rasping sound. When he got to his feet a jay screamed at him, said he did not belong here.

He rubbed life into his numb legs, left his hiding place and went down the slope to the game trail. The bushes resented him. He went to the creek and the rocks bruised his knees as he knelt to drink. The water was refreshing until he stood up again. Then it made him feel sick, weak. Weak from hunger, he told himself. He needed food. He would go back to the carcass, find scraps the bear had left. But his stomach knotted at the thought of meat that had lain in the sun all yesterday. "I will kill my own meat," he said aloud.

He sat and watched the deer run for a time but nothing came. He got to his feet, started down the mountainside, hunting, and heard the noise of his stumbling footsteps but was unable to silence them. He saw nothing to kill, found nothing to eat, not even dried berries he could suck for their scant juice. Even the twigs he plucked and chewed were bitter in his mouth.

He went down the slope and across the valley, stumbling like a drunken man, knowing only that he must return to his own camp. He came to a creek and drank and rested among the unfriendly trees. Then it was afternoon and he went on, knowing he was a stranger but knowing, too, that he must keep going.

Dusk came. Darkness deepened and the stars appeared. He tried to find a star that he could guide by, and the stars wavered in the sky. He waited for them to settle into place again, and he heard the All-Mother singing the star chant, the chant to the night. He began to sing the chant with her and after a little while the stars were clear again and steady in their places. He chose one to guide by, and he went on, chanting the night chant.

And at last he was going up the long slope of Granite Peak, climbing through the brush and among the aspens and the pines that said silently that he was a stranger there. But he was still singing the star chant, though his voice was only a hoarse whisper, and the stars stayed in their places.

It was almost morning when he came to his camp. He saw the sheltering tarp in the thin moonlight and he heard the sound of the creek. He drank, and he opened his pack and lay down and wrapped his blanket around him. He rested, dozing, only half sleeping, and when the flush of dawn lightened the sky he sat up, knowing what he must do. He put the blanket aside, stripped himself naked and went to a place where the creek made a pool among the rocks.

He stepped into the pool and the cold, black water drove fiery needles into his legs. He scooped handfuls of water and splashed it on his belly and chest, then sat down in the knee-deep pool. The cold was like knives at his testicles and knotted his whole belly, and as the current piled against his shoulders the pain sliced at his very vitals. Then the pain began to ease and he scrubbed himself with handfuls of sand from the pool's bottom. He bathed, and as the sun was about to rise he got out and rubbed life back into his legs. Then he sat on a rock facing the east and as the sun rose he chanted the song to a new day, chanting to the sun and the earth and everything between. Then, naked and unarmed, he started up the mountain.

All morning he made his way through the brush and timber, over the rocks and ledges and gravelly slopes. Noon came and he stopped to rest, and he looked up at the sun and thought how round it is and how round is the path it follows. He looked at the sky, the blue roundness of the sky, and he looked at the roundness of the aspen trunks. He closed his eyes and sang a silent chant to the roundness of all things, the great roundness of life. When he had finished he lay on his belly, close to the earth, and let the sun beat on his back. He lay there a long time, the earth and the sun holding him between them. Then he went on.

The last part was a difficult climb. It was late afternoon when he reached the top, already deep dusk in the valleys. He stood there and watched the sun sink behind a cloud on the horizon and send flaming colors that raced across the sky, gold, then pink, then purple. He watched, but he sang no song, made no chant. He had come to listen, not to talk.

When the colors had gone and the first stars appeared he

went down the mountainside till he came to a clump of wind-warped junipers with a mat of prickly needles beneath them. He crawled in and lay down, weak with fasting and fatigue. His muscles ached, his joints throbbed, and the night's chill bit at his flesh. The prickles in his bed bit into his skin like tiny coals of fire. But he slept.

Dreams came. First came unwanted dreams. He was in the corral at the agency and he was riding a huge, frosty bear. It lunged from the chute and he lashed it with a rawhide quirt and raked it with his spurs. It lunged three times, side-jumped, spun. But now it was no longer a bear but a bronc, the big roan bronc. It fell and he was trapped in the saddle. But he crawled free and stood up, and there was Red Dillon, saying "You double-cross me and I'll break your goddam neck!" He struck Red Dillon with his fist, knocked him down, and Red Dillon was not there. A horse was struggling on the ground, a big black bronc. It lifted its head, snorting bloody foam, and it said, *"A los muertos!"* Then its head fell back with a thud and a sigh and it was dead.

He wakened, so tense his muscles screamed with pain. Then he felt the cold and the fiery bite of the needles and he drew his knees up to his chest to feel his own warmth and he slept again.

He dreamed he was a boy, lost and crying his loneliness beside the cold char of the lodge. Then the ruins of the lodge were gone and he was sitting in the night, watching the flames of the barn tower toward the stars, and the stink of smoldering hay was in his nostrils. Then it was in his mouth, the taste of hospital coffee, and Mary Redmond was saying, "Put away your tomahawk and take the feathers out of your hair!" And he stared at the white ceiling, which turned to a cloud of fine white ash, then to a cloud of stars and he was awake again. Awake and staring at the starry night sky through the juniper branches.

Once more he slept, and dreamed, and he was alone,

walking over the earth in the night. He came to a mountain and he said, "I have forgotten who I am." There was no answer. He said, "I was the boy who went with Blue Elk and did what he said I must do." Again there was no answer. "I went with Red Dillon and did what he said I must do." Still there was no answer. "I killed as they taught me to kill!" he cried.

And at last the mountain's voice asked, "Why?"

He was silent a long time. Then he said, "I had to kill the past. I had to be myself. And now there is nothing left to kill except myself, for I did not kill the bear."

Then the four colors, black and blue and yellow and white, were all around him and the wind screamed and the lightning shook the earth. The colors became men and they made gestures to each other, to the four directions, then to the earth beneath and to the sky above, and they began to dance the bear dance. A deer came and joined them, a deer with a gaping wound and one loin missing. It tried to dance, but its entrails dragged about its legs, and the bear came and wept for the deer. Then everything was gone except the colors, and three of them faded, leaving only the white. And the mountain asked, "Who are you?"

He could not answer, but a voice answered for him. "He is my son." It was the voice of the All-Mother.

Then he wakened, and the white was all around him, the white light of truth and understanding. And he saw frost on all the juniper branches, shining in the light of dawn.

He lay there, at first not knowing where he was, then remembering. He sat up and crept out from among the junipers, too stiff with the cold to stand on his feet until he had rubbed life into his legs with handfuls of frosty juniper needles. He washed himself with the frosty needles, and when the sun rose he stared at it till his eyes were blinded, then sang the chant to the new day, singing softly to himself. Then he went back down the mountain.

He went back to his camp, so weak from the fasting that he had to stop often and rest. He went to his camp and opened his pack of supplies, but he did not eat. Having no corn meal, he took a handful of flour, and he went down the creek to a place where deer might come to drink. He crouched beside the water and smoothed a patch of sand with his palm, then took a stick and drew a picture of a deer. He drew the picture and spoke to it, calling it by name, and said he needed its help. He said he had killed its sister and wasted her parts because he had forgotten who he was. He said that a man's memory is a faltering thing, but that now he had purified himself and now he remembered. He scattered the flour over the picture, his offering to it, and he sang the deer chant. He said, "I will be quick and merciful, Brother Deer, and I will use your parts as I should." Then he went back to his camp.

He slept till late afternoon, still fasting. Then he put on a breechclout, took the rifle and the knife and returned to the place where he had drawn the picture in the sand. He chose a place in the brush and sat down and made himself a part of the bushes. He sang no song. He thought no thoughts. He made himself a part of the earth and the evening, telling himself he must be strong enough to see when the deer came.

Just before the light was too dim to see the rifle's sights they came, two does and a buck. They came quietly down to the water. The does drank, making little ripples in the water. The buck watched them, waiting. One doe lifted her head and water dripped from her muzzle and made little circles that spread and slowly floated away. Then the buck turned broadside and waited.

His rifle was resting on his knee, but his hands were quivering, his eyes bleared. He forced himself to steadiness, and the shot shook the earth. The rocks and the trees trembled. The does were gone in one quick rush, but the buck stood for a long moment as though unhurt. Then it took one step, faltered, went to its knees and fell with a long sigh of expended breath. Then there was silence.

He crossed the stream and his knife glinted in the thinning light. The buck's blood spilled from the slit throat and he whispered, "Earth, drink this blood that now belongs to you." He waited till the flow had stopped, then knelt and slit the skin down the buck's breast and between its legs and began to lay it back from the warm red meat. He butchered it the old way and he carried every part back to his camp. Then he broke his fast. He cooked and ate, and he slept.

## 49

He built the lodge there on the first bench of Granite Peak. But before he cut one pole for the lodge he set up a drying rack, sliced the venison into thin strips and hung it to cure in the smoke and slow heat of a smudged fire. He fleshed the hide and started the tanning with a mixture of liver and brains. He put aside sinews for sewing, saved antlers and bones from which to make awls, scrapers and other tools, boiled out and saved marrow fat. He used every usable part of the buck, as he had promised.

Then he cut poles in the pine thicket, choosing them carefully to leave no obvious gaps, and he built the lodge and banked it with brush and earth and leaves to make it winter-warm and mask its newness, make it a part of the mountain-side. When he had finished the lodge he took another deer, cured more meat for the winter; and he made rawhide from a part of that skin, for moccasin soles and snowshoe webbing, made leather from the rest of it for winter moccasins and leggings. He caught trout and smoked them. He gathered sweet acorns and piñon nuts. He found a patch of wild white peas and gathered their seeds, and he dug and dried the roots of elk thistle. He cut and trimmed ironwood and bent and shaped it to dry and season for snowshoe frames. He stowed firewood in the lodge.

Hard frost came and passed. Aspen leaves fell and lay crisp and briefly yellow in the valleys, and the dark flame of the scrub oaks faded to the brown of their bitter little acorns. The sky was clean and clear, the air was crisp. The season turned to that pause when the mountains rest between summer and winter and a man knows, if there is any understanding in him, the truth of his own being.

Now he had time for the lesser tasks. He cut the leather for winter moccasins and shaped their rawhide soles. He made bone awls and chose sinew for the sewing. And one afternoon, sitting in the sun, sewing the sole on a moccasin, he thought again of the bear. He had gone over the hunt a dozen times, remembering each detail, and he had wondered what would have happened if he had squeezed the trigger. He might have made the kill. But if his eye had blurred, if his hand had wavered the slightest trace, both he and the bear would now be dead. He had little doubt of that. If he had missed the heart with the first shot the bear, numbed to further pain, would have taken a whole magazine of bullets and kept coming, an infuriated devil. It would have caught him among the rocks and killed him even as it was dying.

He had gone over that a dozen times, what happened and what might have happened. Now, sitting in the sun with the peace of the world around him, he began examining why he was driven to the hunt in the first place and why he acted as he did. He sat back and shifted the coil of dry sinew in his mouth, softening it with his saliva for sewing. He felt it with his tongue, drew out an end and tested it with his fingers. It was still too stiff and wiry. He picked up the rawhide sole and went on making careful thread holes with the bone awl.

Searching for the whys, he reached back to beginnings. To the cub, to Blue Elk, to the school, to the quirting and the denial in the moonlight. That was where the hunt began, away back there. Not the actual bear hunt, but the hunt that led to the bear years later. That was when he began hunting down all the painful things of the past, to kill them. And one by one, over the years, he did kill them. All except the bear. All except his childhood, his own heritage. He could even list them now, Blue Elk, Benny Grayback, Neil Swanson, Rowena Ellis, Red

Dillon, Meo—he paused, considering Meo, then nodded, knowing he killed Meo too, when he burned the cabin. He could see Meo's garden patch, weedy but still with the mark of Meo's hand upon it, withering in the searing heat. No, he didn't shoot or knife or choke any of them to death. There are other ways to kill. He killed them, the memory of them, in the arena, when he became Killer Tom Black.

He killed them all, except the bear. And then he came back to the mountains, having looked death in the face himself. He came back to heal his body, to ride again, to go on trying to kill the one thing he hadn't been able to kill—the bear, his own boyhood. And he met the bear, and tried to go away again, and had to come back and hunt it down.

He straightened up to ease his shoulders and looked across the valley toward Horse Mountain, fifteen miles away but looking less than half that in the clean, clear air. He thought of the day the bear came down and killed the lamb, the way he ran after it, unarmed, and told it to go away as he had so long ago. Then he tried the sinew again and found it pliable. He drew out an end and began to sew the rawhide sole to the soft leather of the upper.

He tried to go away, after that, thinking he could forget the bear. And had to come back, knowing he couldn't forget. Thinking he could hunt it down, make an end to the matter with a bullet and leave the bear to rot and maggot away. Only to find, when the moment came, that he had done his killing, killed so many things, so many memories, that there was nothing left to kill except himself. Facing that and not knowing who he was, forgetting even his own identity, he didn't kill the bear. He went in search of himself.

He sewed to the end of the sinew and drew another strand from his mouth, remembering the penance trip up the mountain. The memory of the trip itself was vague because he had been so weak from fasting that he had done what he had to do by instinct, by willpower, knowing he must go or die in the effort. Knowing this was the answer, the ultimate hunt. Not the bear hunt, but the penance journey up the mountain. The memory was vague, but the dreams, the visions, were still clear. He accomplished, on that trip up the mountain, what he set out to accomplish, unknowing, on the bear hunt. He killed himself, the self he had been for so long. He killed Tom Black, the vengeful demon who rode horses to death. He had set out to kill a boyhood, when he turned back at Piedra Town that morning, and he had succeeded, at last, in killing a man and in finding himself.

He sighed, knowing why he had come back. And he remembered a chipmunk he had as a small boy, a pet that came when he called and sat in his hand. He had asked his mother the meaning of the stripes on the chipmunk's back. Those stripes, she said, were the paths from its eyes, with which it sees now and tomorrow, to its tail, which is always behind it and a part of yesterday. He had laughed at that and said he wished he, too, had a tail. His mother had said, "When you are a man you will have a tail, though you will never see it. You will have something always behind you."

Now he understood. Now he knew that time lays scars on a man like the chipmunk's stripes, paths that lead from where he is now back to where he came from, from the eyes of his knowing to the tail of his remembering. They are the ties that bind a man to his own being, his small part of the roundness.

He shifted the moccasin between his knees and awled more thread holes in the tough sole, then went on sewing.

It had been a long journey, he thought, the long and lonely journey a man must make when he is lost and searching for himself, particularly one who denies his own past, refuses to face his own identity. There was no question now of who he was. The All-Mother's words, in the vision, stated it beyond denial: "He is my son." He was a Ute, an Indian, a man of his own beginnings, and nothing would ever change that. He had tried to change it, following Blue Elk's way; and he had tried, following Red Dillon's way. He had tried, following the way of Tom Black. And still he had to find the way back to himself, to learn that none of their ways could erase the simple truth of the chipmunk's stripes, the ties that bind a man to the truth of his own being, his small part of the enduring roundness.

He finished the moccasin and examined it, was satisfied with his workmanship. His hands remembered, and his mind had begun to remember and accept. The moccasin, like that lodge, was a part of the acceptance. He was not a clout Indian, never would be again. But for a time he had to go back to the old ways, make his peace with his world and with himself. He had begun to feel that peace, at last. In time, he would go down to Pagosa, talk with Jim Thatcher, if he was still alive. Learn what happened to Blue Elk, try to understand why he sold his own people as he did. He would go to the reservation, eventually, to the school, and see what was happening there now, try to understand that, too. But never again would he go back to the arena. He had ridden his broncs, fought and killed his hatreds and his hurts. He was no longer Tom Black. He was Tom Black Bull, a man who knew and was proud of his own inheritance, who had come to the end of his long hunt.

He went into the lodge, put the moccasin carefully away with its mate, put the awl in its case and laid away the coil of sinew. He stirred the pot of stew and thrust a fresh stick of wood into the coals. Then he went out into the evening and up the slope a little way to a big rock where he could see Horse Mountain and Bald Mountain and the whole tumbled range of mountains. He sat there and watched the shadows darken in the valleys, and when the sun had set he whispered the chant to the evening. It was an old chant, a very old one, and he sang it not to the evening but to himself, to be sure he had not forgotten the words, to be sure he would never again forget.